*He leaned down, his face
a hairsbreadth away from hers.*

"I give you my word. You, Carissa, daughter of Mordrac the Barbarian, will die by my hand."

Carissa purposely grew a wickedly cruel smile as she brought her lips closer to his. "You, Ronan of the clan Sinclare, will never have that pleasure."

He took a step away. "Go to bed."

She had no problem obeying his order. It would put some distance between them and she would have time to determine how she would escape him.

She didn't count on him following her. Wanting to keep control of the situation, she swerved around so suddenly that he had to grab hold of her to prevent them both from tumbling down on the bed together.

She smiled. "Your body looks fit for pleasure, so why not come to bed with me?"

He shoved her away and she stumbled back, falling onto the bed.

"If you were the last woman alive I would not touch you."

By Donna Fletcher

DONNA FLETCHER

THE HIGHLANDER'S FORBIDDEN BRIDE

AVON

An Imprint of HarperCollinsPublishers

This is a work of fiction. Names, characters, places, and incidents are products of the author's imagination or are used fictitiously and are not to be construed as real. Any resemblance to actual events, locales, organizations, or persons, living or dead, is entirely coincidental.

AVON BOOKS
An Imprint of HarperCollins*Publishers*
10 East 53rd Street
New York, New York 10022-5299

Copyright © 2010 by Donna Fletcher
ISBN 978-0-06-171299-9
www.avonromance.com

First Avon Books paperback printing: January 2010

Avon Trademark Reg. U.S. Pat. Off. and in Other Countries, Marca Registrada, Hecho en U.S.A.
HarperCollins® is a registered trademark of HarperCollins Publishers.

Printed in the U.S.A.

10 9 8 7 6 5 4 3 2 1

Chapter 1

I hate her, and I'm going to make her suffer.

The thought consumed Ronan Sinclare day and night, and that hatred grew stronger with each passing day. Carissa, daughter of Mordrac the Barbarian, had robbed him of everything: his family, love, and life itself. She was the last obstacle to his returning home. Once he was done with her, he could finally go home, or could he?

Ronan paced the river's edge like a caged animal. That was how he felt—like an animal. There was nothing left of Ronan of the clan Sinclare, fourth son of Tavish and Addie Sinclare, brother to Cavan, Artair, and Lachlan.

Ronan stopped his pacing with a guttural laugh and a shake of his head. He looked down at his brown wool leggings, knee-high leather boots, and dark brown, long leather belted vest over his tan wool tunic. This was not the dress of a Highlander.

His troubled thoughts stopped him. How could he even think that he was not a Highlander? He had been born and raised in one of the most powerful clans in all of Scotland. He couldn't lose his heritage. He would return to it once this chore was done.

But the question nagged at him. Could he truly go home again? In his heart, he was always a Highlander, but now . . .

He glanced over himself with a critical eye and knew that there wasn't a shred of a Highlander there. He was now, by no means of his own doing, a mercenary, a man who would kill for a price.

That certainly wasn't the way of a Highlander. A Highlander fought for his clan and his land. His skills or integrity could not be bought. A Highlander was an honorable man, and he had been anything but that.

He stretched his hands out and took a good look at them. They bore not only the marks of battle but of his fight to survive as well. When he had first been captured by the barbarians, two of his fingers had been broken and never healed right. He had been forced to learn how to cope with the disability and how to handle his sword and bow and arrow all over again. Strangely enough, it had made him more proficient at both.

He made a fist and gave his chest a pound, a chest that was once a source of teasing from his brothers. They had reminded him time and again how scrawny he was, but no more. He had gained thirty pounds of hard muscle, not only in his chest but in his arms and legs. He also thought he had gained in height—at one time thinking himself shorter than most men, he now seemed to stand a full head above them. Though perhaps it was just his overall appearance, for his once-boyish looks were gone, replaced by those of a battle-hardened warrior. His slim nose had been broken, its perfect shape left slightly distorted. And though he was but five-and-twenty years old, age lines had dug deep around his eyes and crept around his mouth. Oddly enough, while the women seemed fearful of him, they were also drawn to him. There wasn't a village he entered where women didn't offer themselves to him though he wasn't interested.

There was only one woman he loved even though he had never seen her face. He had relished her tender and loving touch and could still feel and smell her warm, sweet breath on his cheek as she reassured him he would be all right, that she would see him get well and grow strong. She had also assuaged his worries over his brother Cavan's fate, finding out that he was also a captive but alive and well. She had given him hope when there had been none, and she had kept her word . . . she had helped him grow strong again. And it was because of Carissa, a heartless barbarian just like her father, that the woman he loved was lost to him forever.

He would not rest until Carissa felt the same pain she had inflicted upon him and Hope. He had named the slave Hope, for she had admitted in a whisper that she could not recall a given name, having been a slave as long as she could remember.

She had cleaned and mended his wounds and bathed the blood off him. She had spooned a tasty liquid into his mouth even when he protested that he wasn't hungry. She had insisted he needed to grow strong.

She had done all this, and he had no inkling of her features. He had been beaten so badly that his eyes had been swollen shut. His recovery was long, and he would have suffered even more if it hadn't been for Hope. She came to him every day, though her visits were short, Carissa arriving and, with a harsh voice, chasing her away while berating her.

However, Hope would sneak back to him at night, and they would talk. The more he learned about her, the more he fell in love with her and the more she insisted that they could never be together. He refused to believe her, but she had been right.

Carissa sold him to a band of mercenaries and, while it would have been easy for him to escape from them, or simply buy his freedom and return home, his only thought was to free Hope and take her home with him. It had proved more difficult than he had thought, and the day came when he learned that Hope was gone forever. A part of him died that day, a part he would never be able to retrieve.

The news grew worse when he discovered that Hope had died by Carissa's hand. He blamed himself for not rescuing her soon enough, and that day he swore revenge, the taste of it bitter in his mouth. He pledged never to return home until he found Carissa and avenged Hope's death.

That day was today.

He turned and walked to his old but battled-seasoned mare and swiftly mounted. She pranced and snorted, for she knew by the way he seated her that they were going into battle, and she was ready. He had discovered where Carissa was hiding, and he knew the place well, for it had once provided sanctuary for him.

A winter wind whipped around him, and he could smell snow in the air, but not even a snowstorm would stop him. By tomorrow morning, he would arrive at his destination and have his revenge.

Chapter 2

"**S**he will let us enter the village or else," Cavan commanded.

"You have met my grandmother Bethane and should know that threats, even from the laird of the clan Sinclare, mean little to her," Zia said and looked to her husband Artair, third oldest of the four Sinclare brothers.

"My wife is right," Artair agreed, walking over to her and slipping a supportive arm around her waist. "The village Black is a sanctuary for those who seek its shelter. Bethane will not let you enter if you mean anyone harm."

"She shelters an enemy," Cavan shouted, and had to rein in his stallion, which suddenly snorted and pranced impatiently.

"Your enemy, not hers," Zia said. "And you do not know for certain if Carissa is there."

"Whose side do you take?" Cavan snapped.

"The side of common sense," she said irritably.

"Zia is right," Artair said, and raised his hand to prevent his brother's protest. "We received word that Carissa *may* have sought safety at the village Black, but we cannot confirm that."

"And the only way to confirm that is to enter the village and see for ourselves," Cavan pointed out. "It was Bethane, lest you forget, who told us that when we find Carissa, we find our brother Ronan."

Zia nodded. "I am well aware of that, but you cannot go charging into the village with a contingent of warriors. My grandmother will never allow it."

"We are fifty strong. How can she stop us?" Lachlan asked, with a curious smile.

Zia sighed, and Artair shook his head at his younger brother while Lachlan's wife Alyce pointed to the treetops.

"Did you not notice the sentinels in the trees as we approached?" she asked, her finger going from one tree to another then another.

Lachlan turned a charming grin on his wife. "It is good to have a beautiful wife skilled in battle strategy. But . . ." His grin grew, and he repeated the obvious. "We have fifty seasoned warriors while they have a few men in trees."

Alyce guided her mare closer to her husband's horse and reached out to pat his face. "There are more than a mere few, dear husband, and my guess is that they are highly skilled." She turned to Zia. "Am I right?"

"You are," Zia confirmed.

This time Alyce looked to Cavan. "How do you fight what you cannot see?"

Cavan nodded. "You are right, but that does not deter me from my course." He turned to Zia. "How do we gain entrance to your village?"

"You request permission from my grandmother, though I can assure you that your warriors will not be granted entrance," Zia said. "And if Carissa is there and has requested sanctuary, my grandmother will not let you take her away."

"Perhaps she can be persuaded."

The three Sinclare brothers and the two wives turned to stare at the sudden appearance of a cloaked stranger. His hood fell over his head amply concealing his face, though his formidable stance warned he was not to be dismissed lightly.

"You have business here, stranger?" Cavan asked sharply.

"Do you?" came an equally sharp reply.

"Mind your tongue," Lachlan snapped. "You speak to the laird of the clan Sinclare."

"And that should matter to me?" he said with an irritated growl. "Now move out of my way. I have the common sense to gain entrance first and leave the particulars until later."

Though they made no effort to move, he passed by them with his mare trailing obediently behind him, and just before he reached the entrance to the village, marked by overgrown foliage, a man dropped from a tree to land with a forceful thud in front of him.

The hooded stranger whispered something to him, and the sentinel nodded and parted the bushes for him to pass and gain entrance to the village.

Cavan immediately directed his stallion to the entrance when suddenly a flurry of arrows shot out of the treetops, forcing him to halt as they hit the ground around him.

"Zia!" Cavan shouted. "Speak to your grandmother now!"

She held her hand up, so the sentinels would hold their arrows, and hurried passed Cavan, disappearing beyond the foliage.

Cavan addressed his brothers and Alyce. "That man is a mercenary."

"And for a price he will do anything," Alyce said.

"So his business here?" Lachlan asked.

"Perhaps someone placed a price on Carissa's head, and he's here to collect her," Artair offered.

"Who would be so foolish to do that?" Cavan said. "All of the Highland clans know we search for her and are in agreement. She is to be found and made to pay as her father did."

"What I wonder," Alyce said, "is how the stranger gained such easy access to the village. The sentinel seemed not to question him at all, which means—"

"He is known to them," Cavan finished, and turned to Artair. "We need entrance to the village now."

"You have it," Zia said, emerging from the dense foliage, "but not your warriors. They must remain here."

"For now it will do," Cavan said, dismounting from his stallion, as did Lachlan and Artair.

The three brothers and Alyce followed Zia through the narrow entranceway that allowed them to walk single file, their horses skittish as they followed. And the brothers didn't like what they saw as they entered the pristine village.

The stranger stood speaking with Bethane, and she was nodding and smiling as if she were talking with an old friend. When she spotted them, her smile grew and she waved. The stranger quickly leaned closer, and whatever he whispered caused her to nod.

"He has her ear," Cavan said to his brothers, as they walked alongside him. "Stay alert. Something goes on here that doesn't sit right with me."

Both men nodded.

Bethane stepped forward before they moved too close, placing a buffer between the men. "It is good to see you all again though I wish the circumstances were different."

"It is always good to see you, Bethane," Cavan acknowledged. "And I regret that a clan issue has been placed at your doorstep."

"It was inevitable," she said. "And it is better that it all comes together here on neutral ground."

"There can be only one outcome," Cavan said, taking his stance. "And your own words predicted it."

Bethane nodded, her smile never wavering. "I remember. I told you to find Carissa and you'd find your brother."

"Then you don't deny that Carissa is here?" Cavan asked.

"I don't deny it."

"Then hand her over to me," Cavan said, "for it has been far too long since I have seen my brother."

"The way you tormented him, I'm surprised you would want to see him again," the stranger said, and threw back his hood.

Cavan and his brothers stood staring at the man. It was Artair who first recognized him.

"Ronan!" Artair cried, and rushed forward to ensnare him in a brotherly hug.

Lachlan followed and did the same.

Cavan remained were he stood, as did Ronan after the hugs, slaps on the backs, and more hugs were done. Finally, the two brothers stepped forward at the same time and within seconds arms were flung around each other. Then Cavan grabbed his youngest brother by the back of his neck and rested his forehead on his.

"There is much I have to say to you, though not now. Now it is just good to have you back."

Ronan remained silent, unable to respond. He was torn between relief at being with his family once again and unease in being with them. Cavan was right, though, there was much that needed to be said, but not now. Now he had to finish the last leg of his journey home.

"Why didn't you reveal yourself to us when you first came upon us?" Artair asked.

Cavan answered. "Because the honor was due him to lay claim to Carissa first and as such have a say in her punishment."

Ronan nodded. "I want the *final* say, Cavan."

Cavan braced his hand on Ronan's shoulder. "You have it." He then turned to Bethane. "Bring us Carissa."

Her response rang through the village like a clanging bell. "No!"

Chapter 3

Carissa watched the heated exchange that followed Bethane's resounding *no*. The wooden shutters in Bethane's cottage sat ajar just enough for her to easily view the whole scene, and the close proximity allowed her to hear every word.

She had hoped that no one would learn of her taking refuge here and, for a while at least, she would have some peace. Since she had never known peace, she had been foolish to think she ever would.

"Carissa will pay for the pain she has caused the Sinclares!"

She cringed at Cavan's command, for she knew he had been relentless in his search for her and would not rest until she met the same fate as her father though she questioned if she could meet death as bravely as he had. Though Mordrac the Barbarian had been her father, she wasn't truly her father's daughter. She had not the cruelty in her that he had though she had made certain that others believed that she did. She had realized at a very young age that if she showed any empathy or sympathy, her father would make her suffer dearly for it. So out of necessity, she learned how to portray a cold, harsh exterior, not only to protect herself but also those she cared about.

She shook her head. There was no point in dwelling on the past. Her concern now was survival, and she wasn't certain how she would do that when the Sinclares intended to see her dead, especially Ronan Sinclare.

He hated her, and with good reason. She had tormented him after his capture, but he would never understand why, and she would not bother to explain. He would never believe her anyway, so there was no reason even to try.

Her fate had been sealed twenty years ago, the day she had been born daughter to Mordrac. It had taken time to accept her lot in life, but she had, and now she had the consequences to deal with—Ronan Sinclare being one of them.

There was one, however, who knew her well and would certainly come to her rescue, but it would jeopardize his life, and she couldn't do that. She couldn't put anyone else in such a dire position. She had done enough harm by coming here to the village Black. And she would need to correct her mistake, though how, she wasn't certain. She only knew that she couldn't remain here, for her presence would continue to bring strife to the village.

"I will not leave without her!"

Carissa knew without seeing who had spoken so

vehemently. Ronan hated her with the intensity of one who loves. For what truly was hatred but the complete opposite of love?

What other way did she have to judge love? She had never truly known it. Her mother had died before she could have any memories of her, and the succession of slaves who raised her did so from fear of her father. And when once she showed that she cared for a puppy . . .

She shuddered, recalling her father's cruelty, and chased away the heartbreaking memory.

She had to concentrate on her present predicament and find a solution, and as soon as possible. She did not wish to bring trouble to Bethane. The woman had been nothing but kind to her.

Carissa heard Bethane once again express her position with firm kindness.

"This is a place of sanctuary, and Carissa is welcome here for as long as she wishes to stay."

Carissa had to smile at Bethane's next remark.

"If you seek sanctuary here, you are welcome."

"We have come to visit."

From what Carissa had learned about the Sinclare brothers, that would be Artair who answered so wisely. He was by nature the most practical.

"You are welcome," Bethane said, "though I assume your visit will be brief. The snow will soon fall in earnest, and I am sure you do not wish to be stuck here. After all, your children wait eagerly for your return."

Children. Just the thought made Carissa sigh. She

so wanted children of her own. She hugged herself thinking how she would give constant hugs to her children and love them unconditionally and protect them. Lord, but she would give her life to protect them.

Artair spoke and once again with reason. "Bethane is right. Once a heavy snow begins, we won't be able to return home."

A tall woman with a long blond braid draped over her chest spoke, though she directed her response to the man beside her. Since all the other brothers were accounted for, Carissa assumed that he must be Lachlan and she his wife.

"I'd like to get home to Roark before then."

Zia was of the same mind. "I want to be able to play with Blythe in the snow."

Bethane turned to Cavan. "And what of your twin boys? I'm sure Honora would want you there before the deep winter sets in."

Family. Something she had longed for but never had. The Sinclares didn't know how lucky they were, and if they were wise, they would forget about her and return home and cherish what they had.

She shook her head slowly, doubting that would happen. The Sinclare brothers were Highland warriors and were duty-bound to protect their clan. Her father had declared war on them, and her elimination would finally settle what he had begun.

"This matter must be settled first," Cavan said with conviction.

"Cavan is right," Ronan said with just as much fervor.

Carissa shut her eyes for a moment, wishing all of this would go away, and she would be free. Free of hatred. Free of being hunted. Free to be who she truly was.

Her eyes drifted open, her wish drifting away unanswered as so many wishes before. This was her destiny, and she could not escape it. It was only a matter of time before the Sinclares captured her, and she would face the same fate as her father.

"Let us speak with Carissa, Bethane," Cavan said. "Perhaps we could come to an agreement."

Carissa quickly grabbed her deep blue, wool cloak from the peg by the door and swung it around her shoulders. That wasn't Bethane's question to answer, it was hers. With a stoic tilt of her chin, she opened the door and marched outside and straight to the Sinclares.

"And what agreement would that be Cavan Sinclare? My death at your hands?"

If looks could kill, she would have been dead many times over. Zia was the only one who offered a smile.

Ronan marched straight for her. "No! Death by my hands."

Carissa stood her ground without a shudder or a tremble, though any other would have probably quaked and begged in his formidable presence. He towered over her. But what she lacked in size, she more than made up for in her attitude.

"So the laird Sinclare feels it beneath him to deal with a woman and gives the chore to his *baby* brother?"

Carissa could almost feel the fury in Ronan's glaring green eyes. And the way he clinched his fists at his sides, she wondered if he imagined squeezing the life from her.

"You will *pay* for what you have done," Ronan said through gritted teeth.

She stretched herself up and placed her face just inches from his. "You have neither the strength nor the stomach for it, *Highlander*."

Ronan plastered his face to hers, and his warm, earthy breath fanned her face and sent gooseflesh rushing over her skin.

"I have something much more—hatred. My hatred for you knows no bounds and you will—*I promise*—die by my hands."

"Enough," Bethane ordered firmly. "There will be no violence here."

Zia stepped to her grandmother's side. "She is right. This village has always been a safe haven for those who seek it."

"And it will continue to be," Bethane said. "Carissa will be protected if she chooses to remain here."

"Then I choose to remain here as well," Ronan said.

Although his face no longer melded with hers, he stood close enough for their arms to brush. It was as if he was letting her know he would stick to her side until he got his way.

Carissa sent a different message when she slowly and with purposeful strides put distance between them.

Cavan stepped forward and looked directly at Carissa. "You know we will not give up. *Your kind* will not be able to remain here for long. It is a place of goodness and caring, and there isn't a barbarian alive who possesses those qualities. Sooner or later, this haven will become a prison to you, and you will leave. We will be waiting. Face your fate now and get it over with, for it is inevitable."

"You think highly of yourself, Highlander," Carissa said with the coldness that was all too familiar to her. "Do you think that it was you who found me?" She laughed. "I've avoided capture how long now?" She grinned. "Two years, isn't it?" She sneered, and her tone was condescending. "Truly, Highlander, you are pathetic."

Ronan took a quick step toward her, but Cavan swung his arm out, stopping him.

"Are you telling me that you intended for us to know you were here?" Cavan asked.

"Finally, a shred of intelligence."

This time Lachlan moved forward, but Cavan halted him with a firm nod.

"Why?" Artair asked.

Carissa admired Artair. He sought explanations before decisive action. "I wanted the Sinclare brothers to know that I'd bested them, that they couldn't find me, though I could have them at my beck and call." She grinned again. "Imagine. One female barbarian outwits four Highlanders."

Fury raged in every one of their eyes, and rightly so. She had gravely insulted them, and she had done so with nothing but lies. She had planned a brief stay here in the village before moving on and, hopefully, shedding her identity and finding a new life along the way. She had been insane to think that she could run from her past; her legacy never failed to follow her.

"But your plan is flawed," Artair said. "We may be here by your choice, but how do you avoid inevitable capture?"

Carissa laughed and tossed her head up, her soft blond waves bouncing before landing with a gentle caress around her lovely face. The movement was intentional, for she had learned that it never failed to grab a man's attention and muddle his thoughts, most times giving her a chance to conjure a suitable response.

To her surprise, though truly she should have realized, it failed with only one Sinclare . . . Ronan. His intense glare had remained the same while his brothers looked stunned.

She avoided a direct answer by tossing the query back at Artair. "How can you think that relevant when I managed to get all four of you here in one place?"

Artair nodded. "This is true, but given that, you would also have made provisions to avoid capture."

"Provisions that are doomed to fail," Ronan said emphatically.

"We shall see," she challenged, though knowing

it wasn't the wisest response. But they had to think her confident, or else she truly would be doomed.

"Enough," Bethane said, ending the exchange to Carissa's relief. "The air grows cold with the impending snow. A light one I would say, though soon to be followed by a heavy snowfall that will surely strand you all here. I suggest you eat a hearty supper, get a good night's sleep, and be on your way at dawn."

Cavan looked ready to protest, but Bethane stilled him with a quick raise of her hand. "That is the way of it, Cavan. I gave the respect due you when on your land; I ask the same of you."

Cavan nodded though it was obvious he wasn't happy.

Zia intervened, trying to herd everyone to Bethane's cottage. "We all need food and rest."

Cavan and Ronan were the most reluctant, while Lachlan, his wife Alyce, and Artair seemed agreeable, but then they knew that the two brothers needed time together, or perhaps they both feared Carissa's being out of their sight.

Carissa turned to walk away, but Ronan's sharp words stopped her.

"Where do you go?"

"That doesn't concern you," she answered just as sharply.

He stomped over to stand directly in front of her, though he actually towered over her. "Everything about you concerns me."

"Afraid I'll slip away from you?" she challenged.

"*I promise*—you'll never get away from me again," Ronan said.

"We'll see about that," Carissa said, and turned away, strolling off as if she had not a care in the world though her heart ached; but not a single tear pooled in her eyes.

Ronan stepped forward to follow her, but Bethane stepped around him and joined Carissa, hooking arms with her.

"Let the women be and come join your family," Cavan said. "We have missed you, and there is much for us to discuss."

Carissa waited several minutes before she dared turned to look and see Ronan enter Bethane's cottage with Cavan. Her relief was so great that her legs might have given way if not for Bethane's supporting arm.

The two women entered Zia's old cottage and, while Carissa sat at the table before the hearth, Bethane prepared a soothing brew for them both.

Carissa hugged the hot tankard in her hands, hoping it would chase away the chill that went deep down to her very bones.

"You put on a good act," Bethane said, joining her at the table and pushing a board with thick sliced dark bread toward Carissa.

Carissa smiled, though it was a sad smile, one that barely reached her slim lips. "I appreciate your concern that I eat, but my appetite has yet to return. And as far as my act is concerned? I have no choice."

"Perhaps if you trust—"

"No," Carissa said, shaking her head adamantly. "I can trust no one, not ever."

"Not true," Bethane encouraged.

Carissa sighed. "Who do you suggest I trust?"

Bethane smiled. "Your heart."

Chapter 4

Ronan sat hunched beneath evergreen branches, watching the cottage where Carissa slept. Snow fell, lightly dusting his wool cloak, and thick cloud covering kept the waning moon from shedding any light. It didn't matter. Ronan had learned to acclimate himself to any weather or circumstance, and that skill had proved a useful tool in surviving, and helped him to believe that one day he'd return home.

Now, though he was reunited with his family, he still felt he hadn't returned home. He felt a stranger among his brothers and even more uneasy with their wives, not to mention that there were nieces and nephews he had yet to meet. Then there was the death of his father during his absence. He had never gotten to see him again, and that was a painful wound that would take a long time healing. As difficult as it was for him, he could only imagine how difficult it must have been for his mother. They had been a loving, devoted couple, and he wondered if his mother could truly manage without her husband.

No, this certainly was not the family he had left; but then he wasn't the same man. And after spending only a brief time with his family, he wondered even more about his own identity.

The soft crunch of snow had him stilling his thoughts and listening more closely to the sound. It didn't take long for him to realize that the footfalls were not animal, but human. He positioned himself, knife in hand, as the steps got closer.

His knife was at the man's throat, ready to slit it if he made one move, though he dropped his hand fast enough as soon as he recognized Artair.

Artair rubbed his throat. "I am grateful you are more skillful with a knife than I last remember."

"Necessity," Ronan said, and returned to his perch beneath the evergreen branches.

Artair joined him. "You thought someone here would do you harm?"

"You never know."

"But this is a sanctuary, a place of peace."

Ronan gave a gruff laugh. "There is no place of peace."

"The people here believe so."

"They foolishly trust," Ronan said.

"Perhaps they have faith."

"Faith is an ally I have yet to trust," Ronan said.

"Do you trust me?" Artair asked.

"You are my brother."

"That goes without question, but do you trust me?"

"That goes without question as well," Ronan said.

"I can't imagine what you and Cavan have suffered," Artair admitted sadly. "I can't imagine returning home after being away from those you love for so long. But what I do know is that I am your brother and will always be here for you."

"You always were the understanding one," Ronan said, with a smile that barely reached his lips.

Artair grinned. "See, some things never change."

Oddly enough, the thought made Ronan feel better.

"Do you plan on remaining here all night?" Artair asked.

"You were the one who pointed out that Carissa had to have a plan of escape," Ronan reminded. "And I plan on being there and foiling it."

"It's cold, snowing, and with little moonlight to guide, I doubt she would foolishly attempt an escape tonight."

"You don't know Carissa as well as I do," Ronan reminded. "She is one that can never, ever be trusted. Her word means nothing and worst of all—" He had to pause, for painful memories flooded his mind. "Worst of all," he repeated firmly, "she has no heart."

Artair grasped Ronan's shoulder. "Then, my brother, we will see that she follows her father to his grave."

* * *

Carissa paced in front of the hearth unable to sleep, but then she required little sleep. She had been taught to be alert to sounds, and so she slept lightly and very little, always feeling the need to be ready at a moment's notice. And now that was more important than ever. She had to make an escape and that would not be easy with Ronan, no doubt, being her shadow.

He had to be out there right now, hiding in wait for her. She was not foolish, but then he would also know that, and that was why it would be that much harder to get away.

She stopped pacing and sunk onto a chair at the table. Bethane's words kept returning to her, but there was no way she could trust her heart, especially now, for it was so badly broken. She sometimes wondered if she truly had the strength to continue. Would it be better to meet her fate? A fate the Sinclares claimed was inevitable and perhaps justifiably so.

How could she even think that she could shed her identity and start life over as someone new? Perhaps she was foolish after all.

Carissa chased away the disturbing thoughts and forced herself to concentrate on the predicament at hand. First and foremost, she needed to escape and if that proved successful, she could take the next step. But presently, that is where her concentration was needed.

To try an escape while all the Sinclares where here would be foolish, too many eyes watching her.

Once they left, she'd have only Ronan to contend with, and that would prove better odds for her, though . . .

She raised her head, rushing her fingers through her long hair. They might be expecting that, and the others could lie in wait for her. Perhaps it would be wise of her to take her leave with everyone here. It could very well catch them off guard, and by the time they settled on a plan of action, she could be far gone.

The problem was that they were to leave in the morning, which meant she only had a few hours left if she was to plan a successful escape.

Carissa stood and went into the bedroom off the main room of the cottage and dressed quickly, donning extra layers for warmth and so she would have room to carry more important items in her bundle. She got busy, sunrise not far off. She had to be ready to take her leave. With the help of a friend, she would slip away unnoticed.

Only two inches of snow covered the ground, though the gray sky and chilled air certainly promised more. And that possibility drove the discussion among the Sinclares.

"If we leave now, we may get caught in the storm and be without shelter," Artair advised.

"And if we stay, we may get stuck here longer than we'd like," Alyce reminded. "It will only take us four days to get home."

"More if we're caught in a storm," Artair said.

"My grandmother doesn't believe the heaviest snowfall will arrive for at least two or three days," Zia informed them. "And she's usually accurate."

"With only meeting Carissa, I can't be certain, but she seems more a warrior than a woman," Alyce said. "And as such I believe she determines her options, as we do, her wisest choice being to remain here in the village for the winter and make her escape just before spring."

"I agree," Artair said. "Where would she go, what shelter and food would she have? Here she is guaranteed both, plus she would be safe."

"You'd be fools to believe that," Ronan said, looking from one to the others. "She is cunning and far more skilled than any of you realize. You told me how you attacked the barbarian stronghold and captured her father, Mordrac. Tell me, how did she manage to avoid escape?"

"If I remember correctly," Lachlan said, "she wasn't there."

Ronan shook his head. "No. She was there; her father would have made sure of that. She somehow managed to avoid capture."

Lachlan looked to Cavan. "Do you recall seeing her when we took command of the barbarian stronghold?"

Cavan narrowed his eyes, as if trying to force the memory, then shook his head, annoyed. "No."

"Make no mistake," Ronan warned. "She successfully avoided you and made her escape. And she will do so again if we do not keep a sharp eye on her." All their eyes followed his pointing finger to a cottage in the distance. "Do you know if she is still there?"

They all stared, but not one made a comment.

Cavan stepped forward, his determined strides and combined height and width causing the ground beneath him to tremble.

Ronan moved quickly to block his path, and the two brothers stood face-to-face, the younger almost matching his oldest brother's height, surprising them both. For a moment nothing was said, but pain and uncertainty were evident in their eyes.

"I have watched throughout the night," Ronan said. "She is still there."

Cavan stepped forward as Bethane approached. "You assured me—"

"And has she not remained here?" Bethane asked, and walked over to the two men.

"Carissa cannot be trusted," Ronan reiterated.

"Are you sure of that?" Bethane asked

"I witnessed it firsthand," Cavan confirmed, "as I'm sure Ronan did."

Ronan nodded. "I know well her cruelty."

"I am sorry that you both believe—"

"Believe?" Cavan snapped sharply, and pounded his chest. "She laughed while I was whipped unmercifully, then she poured a liquid on my open wounds that caused me to pass out from the pain."

Ronan raised his right hand, his middle and forefinger bent and crooked. "Thanks to her, these never healed correctly, and only because a slave cared enough to risk Carissa's wrath was I tended to at all."

"She is as evil as her father," Cavan spat.

Bethane nodded. "Her father was truly evil."

"And she will pay as he did," Cavan said.

"So you remind everyone again and again."

Cavan and Ronan swerved around to glare at Carissa.

"Bethane, may I speak with you?" she asked, and turned and walked away, dismissing the others as unimportant.

Bethane walked between the brothers, but Ronan took hold of her arm before she could go any farther. "You need not follow her command."

"Carissa did not command," Bethane said. "She asked to speak with me." She placed her hand over Ronan's. "If you would put your anger aside for a moment, perhaps you would see more clearly."

Ronan expelled a breath, releasing tightness in his chest he hadn't realized was there. And for a moment he felt at peace, until his glance landed on Carissa. She was smiling.

"I see only too clearly," Ronan said, and jerked his hand away.

Bethane made hasty steps to Carissa and walked far enough away with the younger woman so that their conversation could not be overheard.

"I must leave," Carissa whispered, while retaining a smile.

"Nonsense," Bethane said. "You are safe here and can remain as long as you like."

"As will the Sinclares."

"Ronan is the only one who will remain. The others will take their leave shortly."

A perfect time for her to escape.

Bethane took her hand. "Stay here. I believe if you and Ronan could talk—"

Carissa laughed and shook her head. "His hatred for me is too great. I must leave."

Bethane smiled softly. "Then let me help you." She continued before Carissa could protest. "A heavy snowfall will arrive soon, and you will need shelter. There is a cottage deep in the woods where I sometimes tend those who prefer not to come to the village. It is well stocked with provisions, and no one knows where it is. You should be safe there for now."

"You have created a safe haven here, and I don't wish to jeopardize that."

"Trust me when I tell you that you won't," Bethane insisted. "Go to the cottage, and all will be well."

If it were possible for her to cry, Carissa would have, but to protect herself she had not shed a tear since she was very young. She had rarely known kindness, so when it was shown her, it touched her heart though none believed she had one.

"The only problem I foresee is how you can escape without detection," Bethane said.

Carissa smiled. "I only need a moment to disappear."

Chapter 5

Ronan kept his eye on Carissa, who ambled around the village as he helped his brothers ready for departure. Since Zia had attended his wounds once, he knew her, but not well, though what he did know had him concluding that she was a good match for Artair. However, he found Alyce a strange choice for Lachlan. It certainly wasn't her features that he found odd, for she was a beauty. It was that Lachlan was a charmer where Alyce seemed a warrior woman and a capable one at that. Earlier, when they had discussed options, she had offered sound advice and made an accurate assumption on Carissa's nature.

One thing the two women did have in common was that you could see in their eyes how much they loved their husbands, and his heart ached even more for the woman he had loved and Carissa had murdered.

He glared at Carissa kicking at a puppy that playfully nipped at the hem of her skirt. She was a mean woman, even to animals.

"You do know that it will be difficult to restrain

mother from coming here," Cavan said. "Only the weather will be able to deter her, and even then I don't believe it will stop her."

While Ronan addressed his brother, he kept sight of Carissa from the corner of his eye as she pulled her hood up over her head, the sharp wind having grown colder. "I have missed her. Tell her to stay put, I will be home soon."

"She never doubted you would return home."

"She always had more confidence in me than I did," Ronan said. "How has she fared since Father . . ." He couldn't say aloud that his father was dead. It sounded much too final, and the pain of his loss continued to be a heavy burden.

"It's been a struggle for her," Cavan said, "though lately she's been much better. I suppose having three daughters-in-law and four grandchildren has helped."

Ronan could only nod, for he still couldn't believe how much his family had changed and gained since his absence, whereas while he might have changed, he had lost far more than he had gained.

"I still feel our departure places a sole burden on you that should be shared by us all," Cavan said. "You have suffered enough and have been away from home far too long. You should be returning home with us."

"I'm not ready to come home yet, and you of all people should understand why."

"I do understand." Cavan nodded. "My wife Honora would as well, for she was the one who had to deal with me when I returned home, though truth be told, she was the one who helped me heal."

"I honestly don't know . . ." Ronan paused and turned to look at Carissa still fighting off the puppy. "I don't know if I can ever heal."

Cavan rested a firm hand on his brother's shoulder. "Time is the only potion that will heal your wounds."

Ronan wanted to believe that, but it was difficult. His pain and hatred were too great right now to think he would ever heal, feel whole again, let alone love again.

"I will see you soon," Cavan said confidently.

Ronan hoped that would be so and was soon receiving hugs from his brothers that brought back happier memories, and well-wishes from his sisters-in-law.

"When the worst of winter passes, we will return for you and Carissa," Cavan said after mounting his horse. "I am anxious for you to meet my twin sons. One is named for you."

Ronan was struck speechless and could do nothing but stare after his family as they rode slowly away. He could not believe the honor his brother had bestowed on him, and it struck him like a fist to his gut just how much Cavan and he had been through.

The reminder had him spinning around, for he had foolishly taken his eye off Carissa and he worried . . .

While she ignored the puppy, he delightfully

pranced around her as she made her way to her cottage. The pup didn't even seem perturbed when she shut the door in his face. He simply plopped down by the door as if he intended to wait for her, but a young lass came along and scooped him up, and he went without protest.

Ronan turned to see his family gone out of sight, and in a way he felt relieved. He didn't need the distraction of their presence. He needed to focus all his attention on Carissa. He was certain she would attempt an escape, and once she stepped away from the sanctuary of the village, he intended to capture her and return her home. Where he would, only too gladly, see that she paid for her crimes. A light snow began to fall, and he decided to make Carissa aware that he was now her shadow.

He walked over to her cottage, tapped on the door, though he didn't expect her to open it and said, "Make no mistake. Where you go, I go." He sat on the narrow bench beneath the window, the shutters tightly closed and waited.

Ronan winced as he stretched awake, his neck a bit painful from the odd angle of his head when he had fallen asleep. With barely any sleep last night, he should have known he would doze off, but he supposed he had dozed feeling safer that he sat right outside her door.

Then he realized what had woken him, and shaking his cloak, now covered with more than a dusting of snow, he stood and scooped up the puppy, who had returned to scratch at the cottage door.

"Why bother when she's not interested," he asked the little pup, and got a lick on the nose.

"Damn," he said, suddenly realizing his foolish mistake, and plopped the pup on the ground. Then, without knocking, he opened the door and rushed in.

The pup scurried past him and into the outstretched arms of the woman who bent down to scoop him up.

"Where is she?" he asked the woman who was basically around the same size as Carissa.

"I do not know," she said pleasantly.

Ronan turned and stormed out of the cottage. There was only one person who would know the truth. He headed with angry strides to Bethane's cottage.

The door opened before he touched the handle.

"I was just coming to see if you would care to join me for the noon meal," Bethane said with her usual glowing smile.

"Where is she?" he demanded, wanting answers not pleasantries.

"Come in out of the cold. You need some warmth and nourishment." She stepped aside for him to enter.

Her words held wisdom, since he realized he had slept far longer than he had thought, and his empty stomach was reacting to the delicious scents drifting from her cottage. Reluctantly, he entered.

"Eat, and we will talk," Bethane offered as she slipped his cloak off his shoulders and draped it over the back of the rocking chair near the hearth.

Ronan didn't argue. One thing he had learned during his capture was that when food was offered, you should eat, for you never knew when next you would.

Ronan broke off a chunk of dark bread while Bethane ladled a good portion of meat-and-barley stew into a bowl, then placed it in front of him. She filled a bowl for herself from the cauldron in the hearth and joined him at the table.

"You tricked me," he said, pouring himself a tankard of hot cider from the pitcher on the table.

"I did nothing."

Ronan ate another spoonful before responding. "You helped her."

"Everyone helps each other here. I thought you realized that."

"If they knew her as I do, they would shun her," he said angrily.

"Most came here because they have been shunned."

"You defend her?" Ronan asked, anger still edging his voice.

"I defend all who seek help and healing."

"Healing?" he asked incredulously. "Carissa inflicts pain and feels none herself. She is cold and heartless and deserves not an ounce of sympathy. And if she thinks she can escape me, she's wrong. I *will* find her."

"I have no doubt you will."

Ronan shook his head. "Then why bother to help her?"

"I cannot, nor would I, stop people from traveling their own paths. I did not stop you when last you were here."

"I had to leave," he insisted.

"You were not yet healed."

"I had no choice."

"I believe Carissa felt the same," Bethane said.

"You cannot compare us," he argued. "I left to save a life. She left to save her own. And the longer I debate this with you, the greater distance she puts from me."

"Then you will be leaving?"

"After I gather the provisions I will need," he said.

"Take whatever you need, but be aware that a severe winter storm approaches, and you will need shelter."

"I would hope to find Carissa before then, but if not . . . there is that cottage the mercenary brought me to when first you tended me."

Bethane nodded with a smile. "And it remains stocked with provisions, but what if Carissa isn't traveling in that direction."

"She would not return from where she came, there is no help for her there; therefore, she would seek a new route to take, and that path would more than likely cross with that cottage."

"You are welcome to make use of it."

Ronan shook his head. "Why do you help both of us?"

She laughed softly. "At my age you see the wisdom of it."

"Then either you see deeper than most, or your eyesight isn't what it once was."

Bethane laughed and patted his hand. "I'm sure you will let me know which it is."

"You do realize that once I capture Carissa, I won't be bringing her back here."

"I assumed as much," she said with a gentle nod. "You will take her straight to your home?"

"Yes, and it is there she will meet her fate."

"I daresay you will meet yours as well."

"In a way, I suppose I will, for my journey will finally be done."

"No, my son," Bethane said. "It will just be starting."

Chapter 6

Carissa made it to the cottage by nightfall. She was grateful for the continued snowfall, her tracks concealed as soon as she made them. She had gone out of her way to misdirect anyone following her, purposely breaking tips of tree branches and leaving snags of her wool cloak stuck to bushes. If she were lucky, no one would find her, and she could at least wait out the impending storm in peace and solitude.

The cottage was as Bethane had promised, stocked with a multitude of provisions, including firewood stacked high right outside the front door. She found the root cellar that Bethane had advised would see her through the winter if necessary, and the older woman had been right. There were several covered crocks and barrels containing food staples, including dried apples and plums and oats and barley, not to mention dried meats. Cider and ale were also in abundance, as were candles.

She gathered what she would presently need and climbed the ladder, securing the latch, then spreading the rushes back over the top. It took a couple of hours to get settled, bringing in enough wood not only to start a fire in the hearth but to keep it going throughout the night. She also shed her extra clothing once the fire's heat warmed the one room, placing the few garments she had in the chest beside the bed.

The quarters were sufficient, though certainly not for more than two people, and even then the single bed would be a tight squeeze. The fireplace divided the space, the bed braced against one wall, a small table and two chairs against the other, with a rocking chair in the middle facing the hearth. Six candlesticks lined the mantel, and Carissa stuck a candle in each one, though she lit only one to place on the table. The roaring fire cast sufficient light in the room, so there was no sense wasting the candles.

She yawned and rubbed the back of her neck. She was tired, not having slept the night before. That, combined with her long walk, at times over hilly terrain, had taken its toll. She also was hungry. She had not wanted to waste time to stop to eat, so instead she had sparingly munched on some of the bread and cheese Bethane had provided.

Now, her choice was food or sleep. She needed both, and not having the strength or desire to fix a hot meal, she chose once again to munch on bread and cheese after slipping into her warm wool nightshift.

She nestled in the rocking chair, tucking her bare feet beneath her. She had moved the chair close enough to be wrapped in the fire's warmth, and for the first time in a very long time, she felt safe.

No one knew she was here, and with a winter storm approaching, there was a good chance that she could spend a month or more, if she was lucky. She prayed for such a reprieve, if only for a short time. She had grown weary of running and hiding. She'd been doing it much too long and desperately wanted it to end.

Naturally, she wished that Carissa could just disappear, but she was finding that it wouldn't be as easy as she had hoped. Her father's evil legacy followed her everywhere.

Her eyes began to close, and she rested her head against the back of the rocker, the gentle sway and comforting heat lulling her into a light slumber. She didn't fight it as she usually did, since there was no worry of anyone disturbing her sleep tonight, though still she should take precautions.

She forced her eyes open and forced herself out of the rocking chair. She unearthed her dagger from her folded clothes and placed it beneath the pillow. A smaller knife she tucked under and near the edge of the straw mattress.

It had been a ritual of hers, ingrained in her since she was young and one she wished she could abandon. She then added a good-sized log to the already roaring fire, knowing that once she crawled into bed, she would fall into a deep slumber, and she did not wish to wake to a cold room.

With a cupped hand around the candle's flame, she carried the candlestick to the bed, placing it on top of the chest. After she was finally settled beneath the wool blankets and gave a final glance around the room, satisfied all was well, she blew out the flame.

She was grateful that the hearth cast enough light to keep the room from total darkness. She didn't care for the dark though she had learned to survive it. She would sleep better knowing some light would greet her whenever she woke.

With a yawn and a stretch, she snuggled contentedly beneath the blanket and was asleep in seconds.

She felt the warm, earthy breath on her face. It wasn't a heavy breath as if someone had run or walked a great distance, but a calm, steady, almost confident breath. And a weight settled over her as if she had been covered with a dense blanket.

And darkness, so much darkness that she wanted to scream, but she couldn't. Good lord, she couldn't speak. Her mouth was clamped shut, and no amount of struggle would release it. The weight shifted over her slow and easy, and she tensed as heat seeped into her body, alarming her senses as it spread. It was no heavy blanket that covered her. It was a man. A man's body lay over the length of her.

No! No! It couldn't be. She was dreaming. It was nothing more than a dream, and she had to get out of the dream. She had to get out of the darkness, had to fight to wake up. She would be all right once she woke. She would be safe.

Wake up, Carissa, for God's sake, wake up!

Her eyes flew open and fear gripped her heart.

"I've got you."

Carissa stared into startling green eyes, and her heart beat wildly.

"Did you truly think that you could escape me?" Ronan asked.

Carissa wasn't surprised at the arrogance in his smile. What warrior wouldn't feel such arrogant pride when having bested his prey? But that self-indulgent satisfaction could also be a vulnerable spot that she could use against him. He was so sure that he had captured her, and yet she had weapons close at hand, weapons she intended to use first chance she got.

The thought that there was still a possibility to escape this man calmed her pounding heart and relaxed her wide-eyed stare, but not for long. She suddenly realized that no blanket separated them, and that he was completely naked. His big, muscled body covered all of her, every inch. Through her wool nightshift, she could feel the cords of muscles that ran down his chest to his stomach, and his thick muscled legs made her slim ones appear puny in comparison.

But it was the thick bulge of him settled between her legs that had her heart once again pounding in her chest. Not that she worried he would force himself on her. He hated her too much for that, and, besides, she'd found the Highlanders to be honorable men, unlike the barbarians, who needed no reason to take a woman.

No, her worries rested more on how big this man was in every sense of the word, in the overall size of him, in his determination and in his convictions. A man of such tremendous strength and honor proved a difficult opponent to beat.

And beneath all that was the deep, dark secret she harbored that made every bit of this all the more difficult, but then she was who she was, and that would never change.

"I know what you're thinking," he said.

Carissa couldn't answer with his hand over her mouth.

"How can I reach my weapons?"

Her heart nearly stopped beating, while he smiled, and his green eyes filled with mirth.

"I found them," he said with a hint of amusement.

She kept her eyes on his, intending not to show any fear, though it raced through her like an uncontrolled fire.

"There's a question *you will* answer."

She knew the question, and though it truly had no simple answer, that would be all she could give him. She nodded.

He moved his hand off her mouth, though his face remained close to hers.

"Why did you kill the slave who tended me?"

With her throat dry, she choked on her answer. "I had no choice."

He jumped up and pointed an accusing finger at her. "That is no answer."

She sat up slowly, knowing quick moves would only cause a quick reaction. "It is the only answer I have for you."

Ronan shook his head. "No, there is more, and you *refuse* to tell me."

She wished he would don at least his leggings, for his disregard of his nakedness made him appear even more of a formidable foe. But if she should suggest that he cover himself, he would surely view it as a sign of weakness. She had to pretend that his sculpted body awash with muscles disturbed her not in the least.

"I will have an answer from you even if it is before you take your last breath."

"How did you find me?" she asked, knowing her best defense was to ignore his threats though privately take them seriously.

He walked over to the hearth and grabbed his leggings. She thought he would get dressed, but he simply ran his hands over them and returned them to the back of the rocking chair, where his other garments were obviously set to dry.

"Let's say you led me on quite a chase," he said.

"Not a long enough one," she said, wishing she could reach out and pull the blanket across her, but that would indicate vulnerability, and she would dare not let him see that.

She stood and hastily braided her hair as she walked across the room.

He quickly blocked her path, his shadow looming large over her petite size.

It was hard for her not to admire the warrior he was; forged and branded in battle, he had earned it all, and that she had to respect. Though it went deeper than that, so much deeper.

She called on the cold nature she'd developed to serve her as it always had and had earned her the reputation of being heartless.

She tossed her chin up and slammed her hands on her hips. "Don't tell me you're foolish enough to believe that I would make an escape in my night-shift in the dead of night, and in the snow?"

"I wouldn't put anything past you."

"I'm not stupid, I'm parched." She stepped around him and emptied part of the water bucket she had filled earlier from the rain barrel outside into a small cauldron and set it to bubble in the hearth.

She was glad for the distraction, glad for a moment to gather her thoughts and assess her situation. And it was a difficult one. Ronan Sinclare had her in his clutches, and he would do whatever was necessary to see that she remained his captive.

As she prepared the leaves, she asked without thinking, "Would you like some?" As soon as her uncharacteristically thoughtful offer had spilled from her lips, she wished she could retract it. But his caustic response set her at ease.

"It could be poison."

"No poison, just a gentle brew." She filled a tankard and steeped the leaves, and when it was ready, she blew softly to chase the rising steam from the top and carefully sipped the hot drink.

He walked over to her and snatched the tankard from her grasp. Some of the hot liquid sloshed over the side onto his hand, but he didn't even flinch. He took the tankard and walked over to sit in the rocking chair.

She fixed herself another, then took a chair from the table and placed it near the hearth, though not near him. She sat and enjoyed the pleasant taste, realizing that the drink was stilling her inner shivers.

He turned his head and stared at her for several moments, the firelight making his green eyes glow like fiery emeralds.

"You don't fear me, do you?" he asked.

"Not the least."

"You should."

She almost shuddered with fear, his voice was so calm and empty. She couldn't help but recall how kindly he had spoken to the slave. She had never had a man speak kindly to her, and it had been at those moments that she had envied the slave he had grown to love.

She gathered her courage, and said, "Fear is a foe I conquered many years ago."

"I am a foe you will never conquer."

"Is that a challenge, Ronan?"

"It's a promise," he said.

"Then I needn't worry, for you aren't good at keeping promises."

She knew her words would pierce his heart like a dagger dug deep, for he knew full well the promise she referred to, and the consequences the slave suffered because he had failed to keep it. Surprisingly, his only reaction was the clenching of his jaw . . . until he stood and walked over to her.

He leaned down, his face a hairbreadth away from hers. "Then I give you *my word*. You, Carissa, daughter of Mordrac the Barbarian, will die by my hand."

Carissa purposely grew a wickedly cruel smile as she brought her lips closer to his. "You, Ronan of the clan Sinclare, will never have that pleasure."

He took a step away and commanded sternly. "Go to bed."

She had no problem obeying his order. It would put some distance between them, and though she doubted that she would sleep, she would have time to determine how she would escape him.

She didn't count on him following her, and she worried that his intention was to join her in bed. Wanting to keep control of the situation, she made a quick decision and swerved around so suddenly that he had to grab hold of her to prevent them both from tumbling down on the bed together.

With the situation to her advantage, she smiled, and said, "Your body looks fit for pleasure, so why not come to bed with me?"

He shoved her away, and she stumbled back, falling onto the bed.

"If you were the last woman alive, I would not touch you."

The malice in his voice made her want to cringe, but instead she shrugged indifferently. "A pity. I would have enjoyed the size of you between my legs tonight."

Disgust wrinkled his face and filled her to near choking, though she laughed. She couldn't let him know the truth. God forbid he learned the truth; the consequences were unimaginable.

"Get in bed and lie close to the wall," he ordered. "I don't want your body touching mine."

Relieved, she immediately obeyed his dictate and scrunched herself as close to the wall as possible.

He got in bed after her and slipped beneath the blanket. Even though he kept to the edge, their bodies remained dangerously close. Any movement, and they would touch.

This was a moment where many women might find tears stinging their eyes, but Carissa hadn't cried since she was six years old. Her father had taught her not to cry, and she had learned the lesson well.

No, tears wouldn't do any good here. She would devise a plan of escape and return to the only life she knew. She had been foolish to think she could escape who she was, but she had hoped. Hoping, however, had never gotten her anywhere. She didn't know why she ever thought it would.

Fate had decided her life many years ago, and she had no choice but to live it that way. And she had to keep her heart stone cold; she couldn't be as foolish as to ever let herself hope again.

And she could *never, ever* let Ronan of the clan Sinclare know how very much she loved him.

Chapter 7

Ronan woke with a start, Hope's desperate cries for help pounding in his head like an endless, resonating bell. The dream haunted him almost every night. No matter how hard he tried, he couldn't save her. He was always too late.

He wondered if she cried out to him from the grave, if, when her murder was finally avenged, she would know peace. Then perhaps so would he. He turned slowly in the bed to rest an angry glare on the woman who had caused him so much heartache and grief.

She slept on her back, her arms tight to her sides, her fisted hands rigid on her chest and pressed against one another. She appeared ready to defend herself even in sleep, though one look at her lovely face would have you thinking differently.

Even in sleep, she was simply radiant, her features angelic rather than one spawned of the devil. But then Lucifer was thought to be the handsomest of angels, which made his offspring just as tempting. It was hard for a man to look on Carissa and not want her, she was that desirable. Her hair was the color of rich honey and soft as the finest spun wool, and long lashes of deeper honey framed eyes the color of the bluest summer sky. Full rosy lips and highly structured cheekbones with a hint of a blush rounded out her gorgeous features. And then there was her body, which he had come to know briefly from when he lay across her naked, her thin wool nightshift the only barrier between them. She might be petite, yet she had been sculpted by a master artist. Her perfectly balanced curves and mounds were surely meant to drive a man mad with desire. And you would think one so incomparably beautiful would be one of God's creations: good, unselfish, and loving.

Not so.

Her body suddenly jerked and her breath caught and for several moments he waited for her to take a breath. He released his own held breath, relieved when she sighed heavily. He wished her death to be at his hands, not something as simple as taking her last breath while in a peaceful slumber. She needed to pay for her crimes, for her sins, and he would see that she did.

Her beauty and tempting body would not prevent him from carrying out justice. He sprang from the bed and hurried into his dry clothes, briefly wondering if he would ever feel worthy of wearing the Sinclare plaid once again. With more important matters to consider, he brushed the never-ending question from his mind though he knew it would linger and continue to torment him.

They would need to get a good start against the

approaching storm. The farther he had traveled from the village Black, the worse the weather had grown. The snowfall had turned heavy, and the wind whipped wildly, sending shivers down clear to the bone. Twice he had to stop, once due to poor visibility and the other time due to an unexpected icy rain that had soaked him enough that he worried he'd freeze to death. Gratefully, he had been only a short distance from the cottage. And it had been easy to slip the latch with his dagger and gain entrance.

Lucky for him, the journey had been just as hard on Carissa, and she lay in a deep slumber, unaware of his arrival. It had given him time to shed his wet garments and warm himself in front of the hearth to stop his shivers. Then, with his blood heated and his determination renewed, he had been able to subdue her by surprise.

Now, however, he needed to get them both out of there before the storm became such that they would be trapped in the cottage for weeks, if not months. And that wasn't a prospect he liked to envision.

He also was well aware that he could not return her to the village Black. If she stepped one foot in the village, she would once again be protected, and he was tired of delays. He wanted Carissa on Sinclare land, where he knew her fate would be sealed, but he worried that the weather would not permit it.

When he was fully dressed, he went to the door. As soon as he opened it, it was ripped from his hand by the fierce wind with such force that it almost knocked him down. He had to struggle to remain on his feet as he grabbed hold of the door and forced it closed and locked against the raging snowstorm.

It took a moment to catch his breath, then he quickly hurried to the hearth to chase the intense chill and dry his garments before the dampness soaked through. He held his chilled hands out in front of the flames, though he doubted the heat would chase the cold dread that descended over him.

"Looks like you'll be sharing *my bed* a lot longer than you ever thought possible," Carissa said, sitting up with a smile and a slow stretch.

He wished he could strangle her right there and then, but that would make him like her, and he wasn't anything like her. No matter how he had lived these past two years, he had not become a barbarian . . . at least he prayed he hadn't.

"While that is not an appealing thought," he said, keeping his focus on rubbing the warmth back into his hands, "what is appealing about our forced cohabitation is that it will provide more than enough time for me to get answers from you."

"If you prefer talking to sex, that's up to you."

"Have you no morals?" he asked with a vehement snarl.

She sighed dramatically. "I forget I talk with a Highlander, honorable through and through." She gave a shrewd laugh. "But I have heard stories that Highlander's truly enjoy—"

"Enough!" he shouted. "I will not degrade myself by resting between the legs of my enemy, or for that matter going where far too many men have been."

Carissa popped out of bed. "Too bad. You're missing the enjoyment of your life." And with that said, she yanked off her nightshift.

Ronan stood speechless, staring while she took her time dressing. Damn but she was gorgeous. She had the most curvaceous body he had ever seen. And where he thought she'd have hard muscles from her noted and often used skill with a sword, her arms bore no trace of it. Rather, her arms appeared soft, her skin silky. Her slim legs were toned but not hardened, and her stomach not completely flat but with just enough of a curve to match the rest of her. No sculptor could ever do her body justice. She was perfection. The thought was like a shot of icy water in his face, and he quickly turned his head away.

"Enjoyed the view?" She laughed, having finished dressing in a dark blue wool skirt and blouse and busy twisting her hair up to pin to the back of her head with an intricately carved bone comb.

While her clothing was plain, down to her leather boots, she looked exceptional, as did her hair, a few strands breaking loose to add a carefree wickedness to her appearance.

She was fast with her quips, and, unfortunately, he wasn't. It took him a moment or two to evoke a wise response, which is why at times he preferred silence to be his answer. Silence oftentimes said more than words.

"Too shy to admit it?" she taunted. "Well, I'm not. You are a splendid male specimen. It's a shame you only let me look but not touch."

He cringed with gritted teeth as he rounded on her. "Do you forget how much I hate you?"

"No, you have made that abundantly clear. But you don't need to love or even like someone to couple with him," she said.

"I do," he claimed adamantly.

"Have it your way," she said with a shrug, and pushed the rushes aside with her foot.

"What are you doing?" he demanded.

"I'm going down into the root cellar to gather food staples so I can cook the morning meal since I'm starving."

"You know how to cook?" he asked, surprised, recalling that she had slaves who had done everything for her.

"I can manage a simple meal," she said, "but then you don't have to eat my cooking if you do not want to."

His grumbling stomach answered for him, and she laughed as she yanked up the door in the floor. She turned and reached past him for a candle on the mantel, her soft wool sleeve whispering across his face, and he caught his breath.

"Like my scent?" she asked softly, candle in hand.

He quickly regained his senses. "What fool likes the smell of death?"

After a lazy, sultry laugh, she said, "That isn't death you smell, that's my scent, and obviously you like it."

He dug his fingers into the edge of the mantel, angry with himself and swearing beneath his breath that he should be trapped here with an evil woman who would seduce her enemy to gain her freedom. He had to keep his wits about him and keep Carissa at a distance.

Carissa sagged against one of the posts in the small cellar. She should be used to maintaining a farce; after all, she had done so since she'd been young, but she was so tired of being someone she wasn't. However, she had played her part far too long and far too successfully to think anyone would believe otherwise of her. She was so good at her ruse that she often forgot who she truly was.

And to have to play this game with Ronan tore at her heart, especially after hearing him claim that he preferred love to sex with a stranger. He hadn't even hesitated or gone into a long explanation. He stated it simply and forcefully, letting her know he would have it no other way.

How she wished he could love her with such intensity. She laughed to herself, the quiet rumble rippling down her throat. How did she ever allow herself to fall in love with him? As soon as the first stirring had occurred, she should have distanced herself from him, but she hadn't. This was all her own fault, and now she was left with the consequences.

Enemies didn't forgive, and they certainly didn't fall in love. She was amazed she had been able to fall in love at all, having been taught that love was for fools. Her father had warned her repeatedly that love destroyed. It caused empires to fall and brought nothing but madness to great leaders. He had insisted that she avoid it completely, and when the time was right, he would arrange a lucrative marriage for her. That was, after all, a daughter's duty to her father.

However, she discovered that love couldn't be ruled, and it certainly couldn't be ignored. But she also learned it could cause more pain than she ever imagined possible.

How she would ever be able to survive time alone with Ronan and in such close quarters wasn't a prospect she liked to imagine, unless of course it was under different circumstances. But with that not being the case, here she was, doing what she had to do, playing the coldhearted, self-centered daughter of Mordrac, in order to survive.

As she collected the food staples, she repeatedly reminded herself not to stray from her role. Ronan had immediately questioned her cooking skills and rightly so, since that was the chore of slaves. But it was a slave who taught her the benefit of cooking. The old woman, Ula, had told her it was an art that could bring peace, pleasure, and control to her life. Carissa had thought her crazy, but Ula was far from mad; she was perceptive, wise, and grateful to Carissa for saving her.

What else could she have done? If Carissa had

not claimed the slave for her own use, her father's cruelty would surely have seen the old woman dead in no time. So she had insisted she required the slave's help, and her father relented.

It was at night when she and Ula were alone that the old woman began to teach her how to bake bread and buns, apple buns being her favorite, and mix herbs to make tasty stews and meats. And she looked forward to every moment spent with the woman.

Unfortunately, Carissa knew she was endangering Ula's life by learning how to cook. Her father would be furious that his daughter was doing the work of a slave. And besides, Ula missed her village and her family, though she assumed all was lost after the barbarians attacked.

Carissa made discreet inquires and found that Ula's son, daughter-in-law, and two grandchildren had survived and had made it safely to another village. Carissa made arrangements for the woman's escape and reunited her with her family.

Ula shed tears when they bid each other goodbye, and as she hugged Carissa tightly, she told her that someday Carissa would shed tears once again, but they would be tears of joy, for goodness comes to those who are good.

Carissa wanted to believe that, but it was difficult. Even more so when her father realized the slave was gone. He demanded to know what had happened to her and Carissa related a tale she knew would please her father and cause no more questions.

She had told him that the old woman had died and, as the ground was frozen from the winter snow, Carissa had had the body tossed into the woods for the animals to feast on. As she expected, the story delighted him. So much so that he gifted her with precious jewels.

The question now was, did she dare take the chance and let her cooking skill be known? Or did she play ignorant and suffer through tasteless meals?

She had been confined for so long, that she ached to break free and truly live, which if Ronan had his way, wouldn't be for long.

A rumble of laughter spilled from her. What a fool she was for loving a man who wanted her dead. But then, he didn't know who she truly was, and she didn't know if it would matter if he did. What a laughable state of affairs.

"What are you laughing at?" Ronan yelled down to her.

"The thought that I should want to bed the man who wishes me dead," she called up to him, and that was the truth. She would love to know his touch, taste his kisses, and dare to be intimate with him, if only for a short time. But the crux of it was that she too would prefer being loved to bedding a stranger.

"Hurry," he urged. "The cold is drifting up here."

She hurriedly finished gathering the items she needed and climbed the ladder. Surprisingly, he leaned down to help her, taking several items out of her hand, then taking hold of her arm and assisting her out of the cellar.

His hand was warm, his grip strong, though not hurtful. And when he was sure she was safe on her feet, he gently released her. It was a simple helping hand that meant so much more to her, for no one had ever helped her in such a manner.

He placed the items he had taken from her on the table and went to sit in the rocking chair, his brow knitted tight.

"Say what's on your mind," she challenged, while starting to mix ingredients for apple buns.

"My thoughts are my own."

"We share tight quarters, nothing will be our own," she said.

"My thoughts remain my own, no matter how tight the quarters," he insisted.

"Then don't wear them so blatantly on your face for me to see."

"Ignore them," he ordered.

"How can I ignore a sour expression?"

"Don't look at me."

"I like looking at you," she said, staring directly at him. "You are a handsome man."

Ronan glared at her, his mouth set tight.

"This is where you return the compliment," she said with a chuckle.

"You're an ugly, coldhearted—"

"Watch what comes out of your mouth, Highlander," Carissa warned, "or I'll make certain I cut out your tongue before I leave you for dead."

Ronan jumped up, sending the empty rocking chair rocking as he approached her. "Is that what you did to Hope? You warned her enough times that she spoke too much. Did you cut out her tongue?"

He stopped mere inches in front of her, his green eyes glaring with anger.

"Answer me," he demanded.

"No, I took mercy on the poor fool and killed her swiftly."

Chapter 8

Ronan reacted without thinking, his hands went straight to Carissa's neck, though they fell away quickly enough when he caught a whiff of an all-too-familiar scent. He stumbled, bumping the table as he shook his head.

Apples. Hope had forever smelled of apples.

Her fruity scent had always followed her. It was how he knew when she had entered the stable pen where he had been held. It had always been a welcome relief from the constant stench.

He glanced down and saw the dried apples in the bowl. Her scent brought back a rush of memories that pained his heart even more. And he wondered if somehow she had reached out in death and reminded him of a promise she had asked of him.

Late at night, when all slept and the world seemed at peace, Hope would sneak into the stables and visit with him. She would bring him food to help him grow strong, though Mordrac had ordered the captors to be given but one meal a day. They would whisper, so as not to be heard by anyone.

One night Hope had asked him to promise her something that he had had a difficult time doing, but she had pleaded with him and he, out of love, relented. She had asked that he not hold anger or hatred in his heart if fate should keep them from being together. After he promised, he did, however, teasingly tell her that he would hunt down fate and demand an explanation.

She had laughed and snuggled beside him, and the scent of apples had filled his nostrils just as it did now.

"Apples," he whispered, and looked to see that Carissa was staring at him, and what he saw puzzled him. Fear was evident in her wide eyes and pale face, and never had he known her to fear anything.

She seemed to regain her composure after a quick shake of her head, color flooding back into her cheeks, her blue eyes intent. "I'm making apple buns."

He noticed that her hands trembled slightly as she scooped up dried apples to chop into smaller pieces. She had been upset as much as he had, but then, the possibility of being choked to death would do that to anyone.

"Do you know what you're doing?" he snapped, more annoyed with himself for losing his temper and reacting as he had. He wanted her punished, but it would be a fair and fitting one.

"I'll manage."

His stomach grumbled.

"It sounds like you'll eat no matter the taste," she said.

"I've eaten slop to survive before; I can do it again," he said, knowing she understood that it was she herself who had served it to him.

"Then it will be like old times, won't it?"

"Not quite," he reminded. "This time you're my prisoner."

Ronan finally sat at the table having waited almost an hour for the food to be done. He didn't care what it tasted like. He was starving, not having eaten since early yesterday morning.

Carissa sat, leaving him to serve himself. He didn't waste a minute. He spooned a good portion of creamy porridge into his bowl and helped himself to the largest apple bun drizzled with a honey-colored liquid. He poured himself cider that she had heated in the hearth and reminded himself that no matter the taste, he had to eat it. His strength depended on it.

He took a mouthful of porridge, prepared to swallow in one gulp, until he realized how flavorful it tasted. And then he savored it and was anxious to eat more. After several spoonfuls, he tried the apple bun. It tasted so delicious that he devoured it in seconds. He continued to fill himself until the only food left was one last, small apple bun.

"Finish it if you'd like," Carissa said.

Ronan grabbed it and with two bites it was gone.

He sat back in the chair with a contented smile. "That was good."

"I appreciate the compliment," Carissa said.

And he could see that she actually did. Her cheeks were rosy, her smile delightful, and her eyes bright.

But he had to ask the obvious. "How does someone who has slaves doing everything for her learn to cook?"

"I thought it best I be prepared in case circumstances should arise where I needed to tend to my own meals, and obviously it was a wise choice."

"Can you stitch as well?"

"I am adept with a needle," she admitted.

"I have a shirt that needs mending," he said with a grin.

"I stitch flesh better than cloth," she said bluntly.

"Isn't tending the wounded another chore for one of your slaves?"

"Not when your father trusts no other hands to tend him."

"Your hands could not be tending him that long that he had no other to help. How many years are you? Eighteen at the most, and you needed time to learn, so that leaves you tending your father for—"

"I am twenty years, and I have mended my father's wounds since I've been seven."

Ronan leaned forward in the chair. "How is that possible? You could never be proficient with a needle at seven."

"If a needle was thrust in your hands when you were five years old, and your father commanded you to learn, you could."

"Your father did that to you?" he asked, as if such a thing were incomprehensible.

"It was my duty."

"You were five, your fingers tiny. And stitching cloth is different from stitching flesh," he said.

"I didn't learn to stitch on cloth."

Ronan stared at her. "Are you saying that your father had you learning on wounded warriors?"

"No, he wouldn't be that cruel to his men," she said. "He had me practice every day on dead warriors."

"What?" he asked, and shook his head, not believing what he had just heard. "You were only five."

"As my father constantly told me, I was not too young to learn. And it taught me another valuable lesson besides learning how to stitch."

"This I must know," he said, "for I cannot imagine what a child of five can learn from stitching dead warriors."

Carissa raised her chin. "It taught me not to be afraid of death, for no one can hurt you anymore after you die."

She was letting him know that her death would only bring her peace. If she thought of death as an end to her suffering, then he certainly wasn't punishing her, he was freeing her, and that truly disturbed him.

However, it also disturbed him to learn what Mordrac had done to his five-year-old daughter. The image of her—so very young—stitching dead men was horrifying, and he couldn't help but wonder what else the evil man had made his daughter endure.

Carissa stood and reached for her cloak, hanging on the peg by the door.

Ronan also stood. "Where do you think you're going?"

"Out to collect some snow to clean the plates, then get rainwater from the barrel to start a stock for a hearty soup for later."

"I'll do it," he said.

"Don't trust me?" she asked with the hint of a smile.

"You'd have to be a fool to attempt an escape in this weather and with only a wool cloak to protect you." He walked over to her and captured her chin with his fingers. "And if anything, Carissa, I know you're no fool."

He draped his fur-lined cloak over his shoulders, grabbed the bucket near the door, and, taking a tight hold on the door, he opened it and stepped outside, closing it firmly behind him.

Carissa almost sunk to the floor, her legs trembled so badly. He was learning too much about her, and she feared his piecing things together and discovering the truth. What then? Would he hate her even more? Or could he love her?

They were enemies, she reminded herself, and

hadn't her father warned her time and time again that once an enemy, always an enemy. Could she ever truly trust Ronan?

The door opened, and he hurried in, setting the full bucket on the floor. "Give me what you want filled from the rain barrel."

Carissa grabbed the larger cauldron near the hearth and gave it to him. He once again disappeared out the door. She sunk down on the chair at the table. How was she ever going to survive her time here with him? She feared revealing too much of herself. She had to remember who she was. Hadn't her father told her that often enough?

Never forget that you are Carissa, daughter of Mordrac the Barbarian.

And didn't Ronan remind her the same often enough?

The door opened again, and Carissa stood, quickly gathering the bowls. She didn't want him to find her sitting there in thought.

"Can you hang it on the hook in the hearth?" she asked him.

He did, then hung his cloak on the peg beside hers.

"The weather worsens," he said, sitting down in the rocker and holding his hands out to warm them. "The snow grows heavy, and the skies look to promise more. If it keeps up, we will be stuck here for some time."

She didn't need to hear her worst fear confirmed though she hadn't expected any different.

"Is there enough food in the root cellar for us?" he asked.

"More than sufficient," she assured him. "There is even dried meat."

"Good, for it would not be easy to hunt in this weather."

"The sky shows no promise of change?" she asked, seeking a shred of hope.

Ronan shook his head. "The sky is barely visible, the snow falls so heavily, and it feels like the storm brews as if it has yet to reach its peak."

Carissa nodded, knowing that it wasn't the only storm out there brewing. The one inside the cottage had yet to gain momentum, and when it peaked, she feared the results.

Chapter 9

You would think that there would be nothing to do but wait out the storm, but there was a matter of survival to consider. Which was why Ronan braved the harsh weather several times during the day to gather as much of the firewood as possible to stack inside the cottage. It needed time to dry in order to burn properly.

Carissa had suggested that they collect certain food staples from the root cellar to keep in the cottage so that they didn't have to continually open the root cellar and lose the much-needed heat.

She also found two extra blankets in the chest beside the bed. Ronan watched as she took a chair from the table, placed its back to the hearth, and draped one blanket over it. She turned the blanket several times, exposing all sides to the heat. She'd test it with her hand now and again, and when it seemed to please her touch, she moved it to the bed and placed the second blanket over the back of the chair.

He wondered over her domestic actions. He never imagined her capable of anything useful.

To him she was the spoiled and selfish daughter of a barbarian, who demanded and got whatever she wanted, and that included killing people at her whim.

He had a difficult time seeing her as a capable woman, especially one who could cook more than a decent meal and see to keeping a bed warm with little to help her accomplish the task. Least of all, he had not expected her to provide him with a tankard of hot cider every time he had come in out of the cold.

He had to remember who she was and ask himself why she acted so contrary to her nature. The answer was obvious. She was a cunning creature who would do anything to survive, even change her demeanor. He had to be very careful around her. He couldn't allow her to deceive him. He had to remember always who she was . . . the person who had killed the woman he loved.

Night had fallen hours ago, and for supper they had enjoyed the hearty soup that had simmered in the cauldron all day. Carissa had baked two loaves of dark bread, saving one loaf for tomorrow. She had also made some type of apple spread to go with it, and Ronan had savored every delicious bite, not leaving a drop of soup or crumb.

Still, no matter how much he enjoyed her cooking, he had to remember she was a deceitful woman and remain on guard.

She sat in the rocking chair after taking a flat pan from the hearth, placing it in the middle of the bed, and pulling the covers over it. A small crock sat in her lap, and she scooped some salve from it and rubbed it over her hands.

The scent drifted over to him . . . lavender.

He grew annoyed by the peaceful family scene they shared and stood to rest a hand on the mantel, and to question the woman hiding inside Carissa.

"How did you escape when my brother Cavan attacked your father's stronghold?"

"I always paid attention to my father's advice, not that I always agreed," she said. "He had been abundantly clear about making certain always to have a means of escape wherever one was." She shook her head and moved the crock from her lap to the floor. "He should have taken his own advice, but then he was so certain all would go his way."

"And you weren't?"

"Not in the least," she admitted. "You don't declare war on a powerful clan like yours without forethought and a strong strategic plan. My father didn't have enough of either."

"Did you express your concerns to him?"

She laughed. "I cherish my tongue, so I kept my opinions to myself."

He was about to suggest that her father would not harm her in such a brutal way when he was suddenly assaulted with images of her at five years stitching dead warriors and realized that her father was capable of that and more.

"You didn't believe that your father could conquer my clan?"

"Your clan's reputation precedes itself, and your friends"—she smiled—"are too many to ignore. A point my father failed to realize. While his troops may have outnumbered your clansmen, they did not outnumber your allies."

"So you escaped, leaving your father to deal with his foolish actions."

"It was the wisest choice," she said. "There was nothing I could do to save him. Fate already had its hand heavy on his shoulder."

"But not on yours?"

"Not if I could help it."

"How did you avoid my brother's warriors?" he asked.

"When I was young, I would escape into the woods and pretend I was fleeing a horrible monster. Most times I could only hide from him, but one day I discovered a way out, and I revisited it often. In case one day I would need it."

"And that day came," he confirmed.

"And I was ready."

"You shed no tear leaving your father behind, knowing he most certainly would face death when captured?"

"Another lesson I have to thank my father for. I don't cry. He taught me not to shed a single tear. It is a wasted action, serving no productive purpose."

"When was the last time you cried?" he asked curious.

She shook her head slowly. "I don't recall."

Ronan didn't believe her. He had a feeling she remembered full well when last she cried. She just didn't want to tell him. He had time. He'd find out; though why he wanted to know, he couldn't say.

But he did, and he also wanted to know *why* she had cried.

"Tell me more of what your father taught you," he said.

"I'm too tired," she claimed. "I want to go to bed."

He stepped away from the hearth. "A good night's sleep will do us both good."

She stood, slowly unfastening her blouse. "Then you'll join me in bed?"

His memory of her naked was still strong in his mind, and he knew it was not a wise idea to go to bed with her.

"We can keep each other warm," she said, and slipped off her blouse.

Her breasts swelled beneath the shift, her nipples growing hard beneath the white linen. And while he would rot in hell before he touched her, he couldn't say she didn't tempt him.

"You have the bed warming," he reminded. "You don't need me."

She smiled that damn wicked smile of hers that could probably cause a priest to sin.

"Ahh, but there's nothing quite like warm bodies pressed against each other to heat you right down to the soul," she said.

"I didn't think you had a soul." He could see that his remark had stung her, and oddly enough, he felt a pang of regret for his hurtful comment though he couldn't understand why. After what she had done, she deserved no sympathy from him.

"Go to bed," he ordered, and sat in the rocker, turning it so that his back was to her. He had no desire to look upon her naked body, and he wanted her well aware of that.

He heard the creak of the bed as she climbed into it, but he refused to turn around and look at her. He had no doubt she would continue to attempt to seduce him, hoping to win her freedom. And he intended to make certain that would not happen.

He leaned his head back against the rocker and closed his eyes, thinking how Carissa would never taste freedom again, and the thought brought him a modicum of joy though only for a moment. He recalled with great clarity what she said death had taught her.

No one can hurt you anymore.

As he dozed off, he couldn't help but wonder if perhaps the best punishment for Carissa was something other than death.

Carissa snuggled beneath the three blankets and, while she wanted to keep her distance in the bed, in case Ronan decided to join her, there was a chill that drifted off the wall if she got too close.

She was relieved he hadn't come to bed yet. She feared if he lay beside her, he would detect the rapid beat of her heart and the tremble that rippled through her body. His remark had affected her more than she cared to admit. She had been accused of many things, but never had anyone dared suggest that she had no soul. She had bravely and under great duress maintained and protected the integrity of her soul. It was the one part of her she never shared until . . .

She fell in love.

Stop. Stop. Stop, she silently scolded in her head and continued to berate herself. *For a short time love brought you joy, then it was gone. Why linger on it?*

Ula the old slave had told her to embrace joy when it came her way and not to be sad when it left, for it would return and then take its leave once more and that was the way of joy, forever coming and going.

She just wished that joy had remained a bit longer.

A strange sound interrupted her thoughts, and she lay still, listening. It took her a moment to realize that it came from Ronan. He must have fallen asleep in the rocking chair, for he was snoring lightly.

She smiled and stretched out in the bed. It was all hers tonight, and pleased that she didn't need to worry about keeping to her side, she drifted off into a peaceful slumber.

Ronan woke and rubbed his aching neck. He silently cursed himself for falling asleep in the chair and for not having added more logs to the fire before dozing off. It had dwindled enough for the room to have chilled, and he quickly added more kindling and logs, stoking it until once again the fire roared in the hearth.

He walked over to the bed, shedding all but his leggings as he went. He wasn't surprised to see Carissa curled in a ball on her side beneath the blankets. He shivered from a sudden chill and realized that cold drifted in through the wall. The bed would have to be moved, though not tonight.

He slipped beneath the blankets before his body lost its warmth, the chilled bedding giving him a shiver, and when he finally stilled, he realized that Carissa's body trembled. He reached out and rested his hand lightly on her arm and almost cringed, she felt so cold.

He moved closer, but not enough for their bodies to touch, though hopefully enough for his body heat to reach her. He couldn't help but stare at her. In sleep she looked so vulnerable, especially curled up as she was.

Her trembling continued, and he grew chilled instead of her growing warm. If they were ever to get warm, they would need to embrace, lock themselves around each other, and share their heat. As reluctant as he was at the thought, the idea that they both should suffer the cold when it wasn't necessary seemed ridiculous.

Her trembling increased, shaking the bed, and he didn't hesitate. He wrapped himself around her, the front of him melded to the back of her, his arms secure around her, his hand resting over her fisted ones and his legs snuggled over her curled ones.

In mere minutes her trembling began to subside and, soon after, her body began to heat. Before

Ronan knew it, his eyes were closing, and he was fast asleep.

Carissa was so warm and comfortable that she didn't want to wake up. She preferred to stay as she was in this wonderfully snug cocoon. She was safe here, protected. She had never felt this protected. There was strength to this cocoon that she could not quite understand. She only knew that it was there and that she could count on it. And she didn't care if it was just remnants of a dream, she would linger and take joy in it.

She cuddled closer, snuggling her face against the hard, though pleasant, surface. She rested her cheek there and before long she detected a sound, a steady rhythmic sound that was quite soothing. Somehow it made her feel all the more safe.

Her ears picked up another noise, a whistle of sorts, and she recalled the storm and realized it was the winter wind whistling a sharp tune. It was then she remembered where she was and it struck her that it was no cocoon she was wrapped in . . . it was the Highlander's arms.

Panic almost gripped her, but she quickly chased it away. For a brief time, she had a chance to lie in his arms and pretend that she belonged there. She relished the steady beat of his heart, the warmth of his flesh, the safety of his arms wrapped snugly around her. At that moment she felt as if they belonged together, that somehow fate had found a way, against all odds, to make it so.

She tried not to move, fearing she would wake

him and her dream would vanish as quickly as a whiff of smoke in the air. A moment, she wanted a moment more, though she would have preferred much longer.

His body suddenly stiffened, and she knew her cherished moment was over. He had awakened and realized that he embraced his enemy.

Chapter 10

Ronan was livid. He had woken to find that it was all a dream. It had all seemed so very real, the scent of apples, her soft body, the silkiness of her hair. But it wasn't Hope he held in his arms, it was Carissa.

Lord, but he hated her even more at that moment, and himself, for he felt that he betrayed Hope by holding the evil woman in his arms. What had he been thinking last night when he climbed into bed? Why had he even cared that she was cold? She had never cared about him when he was her father's prisoner. He should have just let her shiver all night.

But then that would make him no better than her.

She stretched full against him, pressing her chest to his and nuzzling her face in the crook of his neck. With his eyes shut and the faint scent of apple drifting off her, he could think of nothing but Hope.

Hope, who had been so kind, so loving, so innocent.

Her lips brushed his, and for a moment, a sheer moment, he wished . . .

"Damn," he cried, shoving her away and scrambling out of bed. He retrieved his clothes from where he had shed them last night and quickly dressed, grateful he had left his leggings on. He grabbed his cloak from the peg and, with haste, hurried out the door.

The sharp wind slapped him in the face, and he smiled, needing the pointed greeting to bring him back to his senses. He had to remind himself that it wasn't Carissa who had stirred his passion but his own dream of Hope. And the devious woman that she was probably realized that and took full advantage of it.

He walked to the woodpile, remaining close to the cottage as he knew that it was easy to get lost in such a storm. He retrieved a few logs, hoping Carissa would take the time in his absence to get dressed. He had no desire to see her naked again.

While he wouldn't mind losing himself in a woman, it wouldn't be Carissa he would give that pleasure to. And lose himself was all he would do, for he couldn't, nor would he give any more of himself. Besides, there was nothing left for him to give.

He had lost much during his captivity, but he had lost even more when he had lost Hope. He had lost his ability to love.

With his hands near stiff, he hurried his steps and reluctantly entered the cottage. He busied himself arranging the wood and discarding his cloak before he would even look Carissa's way.

She smiled at him as she threaded the ties of her blouse closed. "I'll have you between my legs yet, Highlander."

"Not likely."

She walked over to him, her smile spreading and her steps lazy, and ran her hand slowly down his shirt. "You are a challenge."

He grabbed hold of her hand before it slipped beneath his shirt. "That you will lose."

She laughed, a throaty laugh that had him tensing. She sounded sinister and sensual all at once, and damn if it didn't prickle his skin in more ways than one.

"We'll see, Highlander, we'll see."

Ronan never found conversation lagging with Carissa. If he wasn't asking her questions she was asking him. Whether she was cooking or they were sitting by the fire, they talked.

"Tell me, did you enjoy your time with the mercenaries?" she asked, joining him in front of the fire after the morning meal.

He ignored her question, and instead asked, "Why did you sell me to the mercenaries?"

"What makes you think I sold you? You were my father's prisoner."

He silently cursed himself though what did it matter now? Hope was gone. What difference did it make if Carissa learned the truth? "Your slave informed me that it was you who convinced Mordrac to sell me to the mercenaries."

"I knew she was feeding you information," Carissa said angrily. "And she could not hide her feelings for you. I believe the poor fool even thought that you would rescue her." She shook her head and laughed. "How ridiculous of her to think that one man could rescue her from a horde of barbarians, let alone my father."

"I would have rescued her," Ronan said.

"Don't be a fool," she chided. "There was no way possible for you to have rescued her."

"I would have," he insisted adamantly. "There was no way that I intended to leave her there. I was coming for her and nothing—not even Mordrac himself—would have stopped me."

She stared at him, her blue eyes wide. "You loved her that much?"

"I did. I still do. I'll never stop loving her."

"You did not know her long enough to love her," she said.

"I knew from when she first spoke to me," he said remembering. "Her voice was soft and gentle and her touch kind. It didn't take long to realize how special she was, or for my feelings to stir for her. She was easy to love. There was no pretense about her. She was who she was . . . a kind soul. And she tempted her own fate, sneaking me extra food and blankets and visiting with me late at night when all was quiet."

"I knew it," Carissa snarled.

"Is that why you had me sold?"

"You should be grateful to me," Carissa snapped. "You two could have never been."

"Yes, we could. All you had to do was to let her go," he said with a touch of sadness.

Carissa stared at him, and he thought for a brief second he saw regret, but then her blue eyes turned icy cold.

"She was a slave."

"Not anymore," he said. "She's free."

"Yes," she agreed with a nod. "Death does that."

They both sat silent, staring into the flames, lost in their own memories.

Ronan finally broke the silence. "We need to move the bed."

"Why?"

"The draft from the wall is too much."

She smiled. "You worry I will catch a chill."

"And die before I can kill you myself."

"Do you truly intend to kill me yourself?" she asked.

He ignored her question. "Help me move the bed."

She shrugged. "To where?"

"In front of the hearth."

"That would be wonderfully cozy."

Again he ignored her and walked over to the bed. She followed him.

He looked her up and down. "I doubt you have the strength to help me."

"I have more strength than you know."

"Then prove it," he challenged.

And she did. Together they managed to position the bed lengthwise in front of the hearth, a perfect distance from the flames, so as not to be too warm or too cold.

While she folded the blankets at the foot of the bed, allowing the heat to warm the bedding, he moved the chest to the end of the bed.

"We will need to be vigilant in tending the fire," he said. "We don't want any sparks to jump from the hearth to the bed."

She plopped down on the bed with a grin. "You're right. We best make sure no sparks ignite the bed."

He shook his head. "You don't even tempt me."

"Pity," she said with a pout.

He sat in the rocker, which remained by the hearth.

"Will you grant me a last wish before I die?"

"That depends on the wish," he said.

She laughed and threw herself full length on the bed. "I want one night of making love with you, Highlander."

"That's one wish that will never be granted."

That night they both kept their distance from each other in bed, not that Carissa could sleep, nor, due to limited space, could she toss or turn, though she felt the need. She was restless, with fitful thoughts.

Would Ronan really have fought her father for the slave? Not that he could have gotten past her father's men, but still, the thought that he would have even considered it made her wonder. Love certainly had helped conquer his fears.

She recalled how frightened he had been when he was first captured, though she couldn't blame him. Not able to see, wounded and worrying not only over his fate, but over his brother's as well, gave him much to fear. But through that fear he had somehow found love, or had it found him?

Who would expect love to be found in a stable pen between a Highlander and a slave? An unlikely couple in an unlikely place, and yet they had found something rare in the harshest of conditions.

And she had no choice but to destroy it.

He would never understand why. At times she wondered herself. Had she made the right choice, but then hadn't love made the choice for her? Just as much as he had wanted to rescue and protect Hope, she had wanted to protect him, and still did.

She carefully turned on her side so as not to disturb Ronan. He slept soundly, and all she wanted to do was look upon him. The firelight danced across his face, and she admired his features. There was a rugged handsomeness about him that she loved.

It had startled and touched her heart to discover that he had felt the same as she when they had first met. Just as he had known she was special, she had known the same of him. He was unlike any man she had met. He showed his fear, and yet he was brave. He was kind to her and ever so gentle, and she had never known either.

And there had been something about the way he touched her that had stilled her heart and stirred her soul. She had never known the desire for a man until Ronan, and she had never tasted love until Ronan.

With him, she allowed her true nature to surface without fear. As he had mentioned, no pretense, he knew her and loved her for who she truly was.

The problem was that she had played her part well, so very well that no one would believe she was anyone other than Carissa.

Certainly, Ronan would never believe that the kindhearted slave he loved was actually the cold-hearted Carissa.

If she could have cried at that moment, she would have, but no tears came. What was done was done, and she couldn't undo it. Even though she wanted with all her heart to shake him awake and tell him she was Hope, the woman he loved.

She almost laughed aloud. How foolish it sounded to her own ears. He would think her desperate or crazy, but never would he believe her. In saving him, she had lost him, and it broke her heart.

How was she ever going to get through this sequestered time with him? The more she heard of his love for Hope, the more her heart ached. And the more she slept beside him without being able to reach out and touch him, the more she ached. The more she spent each waking and sleeping moment with him, the more she knew that, when they separated, the ache would turn unbearable.

She had no doubt that she would escape him. She had a friend, one person other than Ronan who knew her true nature, but then he had spent his childhood with her. He had seen why she had become callous, and he had kept her secret, and she, in turn, had seen him safe just as she had with Ronan.

He would help her, she had no doubt, and she would return to what she knew. But for now she would deal with Ronan. She would pretend as she had always done. She would play the heartless Carissa while all the time her heart was breaking.

Chapter 11

Days passed in similar fashion while the snow continued to fall, though not as heavily. And the steady accumulation made certain they wouldn't be going anywhere anytime soon. You would think that they would grow tired of each other's company since they were far from friends, but they never seemed to lack for conversation, or a good debate. And more often than not, and to Ronan's dismay, Carissa could be found wrapped in his arms in the morning.

Lately, Carissa had begun to ask him about his childhood, and he had to admit he enjoyed revisiting it.

"So being the youngest of four brothers, they picked on you?" Carissa asked, as they sat in front of the hearth after supper.

"They tried"—he smiled—"but I outwitted them most of the time."

"You played them against each other," she said with a laugh.

Ronan chuckled. "They were so gullible. It was easy, except for Cavan. He allowed me to have my fun, but he was well aware of what I was up to."

"You admire him."

"And I respect him." He frowned. "He nearly gave his life for me and lived through a year of hell because of me."

"Not because of you," she corrected, *"for you."*

His frown deepened. "What do you mean?"

"My father thought him a fool for turning back to try to save you when it was obvious the battle was lost and you captured. And yet Cavan rode into certain capture or possibly death to try to save you."

"My fault," he said, with an angry pound to his chest. "I called out to him like a coward."

"You cried out to a brother who had never failed you, and so you believed was your only hope. And he, as a loving brother, returned *for you*, not because of you, not because you called out, but *for you* . . . his youngest brother, who he could not, or would not, leave behind."

"He should have left me."

"Would you have left him?" she asked.

"Never," Ronan said without thinking.

"See," Carissa boasted, "you both think the same and therefore would react the same. You and Cavan are more similar than either of you realize, and far different from your other brothers."

The realization made Ronan wonder if Cavan carried as much guilt around with him as he himself did? He had dreaded, but also ached to reunite with his family. All this time he believed he had failed Cavan. When he had come upon his brothers at the entrance to the village Black, joy and terror had gripped him.

What did he say to Cavan? How would Cavan react to his return? And again he believed he had taken the coward's way out. He had simply walked past them without letting them know who he was. And what had Cavan done when Artair asked the logical question of why he hadn't announced himself immediately? Not only had Cavan made a plausible excuse for him, he had let him know that he was leaving Carissa's fate in Ronan's hands.

Cavan had even let him know that they would talk later, and Ronan wished his brother was here right now, for there was much that had to be said between them.

"You would think that since you and Cavan are so much alike, that Artair and Lachlan would be similar." Carissa shook her head. "But they seem nothing alike."

That brought a grin to Ronan's face. "That's for certain. Artair relies on his pragmatic nature, while Lachlan on his charm." He laughed. "And Cavan always knew exactly how to handle each of them."

"Just like you."

"That's because I watched my big brother and learned."

"As Cavan does with people," she said. "He watches, studies them. You can see it in the way his dark eyes survey everything around him. By the way, I noticed that your three brothers have brown eyes while you have green."

"I get the distinguishing color from my mother," he said.

"If her eyes are anything like yours, they must be beautiful."

"My mother is beautiful, but she taught me that true beauty comes from a loving nature. And I discovered how true her words were."

"Are you telling me I'm not beautiful?" she asked with a sharp tongue.

"If beauty were judged solely on features, you would certainly be claimed a beauty. But if you believe as I do, that beauty comes from a good, decent soul, then I'm afraid it would be hard to look upon you."

Carissa simply shrugged. "It's what I expected to hear from you though talking about surface beauty, I'd have to say that your brother Artair is the handsomest of the lot of you Sinclare men."

"So say all the women, though Lachlan would disagree," Ronan said. "But what of you? Not one sibling to torment or tease or rescue you?"

"I always believed that, with my father's salacious appetite, he had to have sired many bastards, though he laid claim to none. I was the only legitimate child born of his loins, though . . ."

Ronan watched as if a mask slipped off her face, her eyes softening and her tongue along with it.

"There was a young boy . . . we grew close like siblings."

"What happened to him?

The mask returned so swiftly that Ronan wondered if he had seen the change in her at all.

"He was sent away."

"Why?"

She shrugged again. "He was no longer of any use to my father."

Ronan noticed that Carissa often shrugged as if indifferent to the matter, but for a moment he thought he had caught a glint of hurt in her eyes when she spoke of the young boy. Could it be possible that she wasn't as coldhearted as he believed?

"You must have missed him?"

"I got over it fast enough," she said.

Her dismissive response convinced Ronan that her heart was as cold as ever.

Conversation dwindled after that, Ronan lost in his thoughts and Carissa in hers. He wished the storm would abate so that they could depart. It was difficult sharing close quarters with his enemy, especially finding her in his arms each morning when he woke.

He had thought with the bed in front of the hearth there would be sufficient heat to keep them apart. But not so, they seemed to drift together, heat or no heat, and that troubled him. He tried logic as Artair would do, telling himself that the bed was narrow and therefore it would seem only reasonable that they would sleep close. But it wasn't closely they slept. They slept wrapped in each other's arms, almost as if they feared being parted.

Every morning he woke and found his arms wrapped tightly around her and her snuggled close against him, he grew more annoyed. And his agitation continued to grow when he felt a punch to his gut as if warning him not to let her go.

He was going mad, completely insane with the thought that he would have any desire at all for a woman who had caused him so much suffering.

Tonight, he told himself, tonight he would keep his distance from her, no matter what it took.

Carissa hugged the edge of the bed, facing the hearth and watching the steady yet awkward dance of the flames. It was one of those moments she knew that tears could normally fall, but not a drop slipped from her eyes.

She had trained herself too well not to shed a tear, though she often wished that old Ula's words would come true. That one day she would cry tears of joy. She would love not only to cry, but to feel joy without the sense of impending doom.

But why hope? It had never done her any good. Actually, anytime she had hoped, it seemed she suffered the consequences.

Her father had warned her time and again never to trust, especially anyone who claimed himself a friend. But her heart had thought differently, and she had dared to make friends with a slave boy when she was young. Dykar became like a brother to her and she a sister to him. They had made certain no one knew of their friendship, for her father would certainly have punished her, and in all likelihood he would have killed Dykar. They played in the woods, sturdy branches being trusty swords and imaginary games helping them to learn to track and plot against an enemy.

While they had been stolen times, they had also been memorable and had made her life that more bearable . . . until Dykar, like any brother, started to become more protective of her.

He hadn't been able to stomach the way her father treated her, especially when Mordrac raised his hand to her. Carissa knew it was only a matter of time before Dykar couldn't stand it any longer, and to Carissa's horror it happened. Six years ago, when she was fourteen and Dykar had just turned eighteen, he had spoken up in Carissa's defense.

Her father had grown furious and ordered Dykar to be whipped at sunrise and left on the post to die. Carissa could never have allowed that to happen to the young man she loved like a brother. So she helped him escape. Dykar had begged her to come with him, but she had refused and for good reason.

Mordrac would have searched heaven and hell to retrieve his daughter, and find her he would have, and then have brutally killed the man with whom she had dared to run off. However, if she remained and convinced her father that Dykar wasn't worth the trouble, and she was glad he was gone, then Dykar had a good chance of surviving.

He reluctantly departed, and while her heart broke, she shed not a tear. She could not let her father see how much Dykar's absence hurt her. And so she returned to being Mordrac's daughter, steeling her heart and losing all hope . . . until Ronan.

She almost laughed. He thought Carissa beautiful and ugly at the same time. Her father would have been proud of her, for he wanted everyone to see her beauty yet fear her as they did him, since he certainly had no soul.

Carissa believed that she must have gotten her kindness from her mother. She often wondered if her mother had simply died because she could not live with Mordrac's cruelty and in death finally found peace. At least she could take comfort in knowing that when she met death, she would be reunited with her mother in the afterlife.

She had thought her father's death a fitting punishment, and she felt no sorrow when she had learned of it. She had believed it inevitable. He couldn't have inflicted that much suffering on so many and think he wouldn't reap the consequences.

From what she had learned, Cavan hadn't wasted a moment in condemning Mordrac to death for his crimes, and that made her admire the Highlander even more. But it was the fact that he had carried out his own edict that made her respect him. Cavan had no other man soil his hands on the task, but rather he had, in front of all to see, ended Mordrac's terrifying reign.

Oddly enough, she believed her father probably also admired and respected Cavan for that, for he had not died at the hands of a mere warrior but at the hands of a leader of men.

Fear suddenly gripped her, and she turned to face the man she loved and the man who intended to take her life.

Try as she might, she couldn't stop a shred of

hope from surfacing. Maybe, just maybe, the heavens would finally smile down on her, and Ronan would see her for who she truly was, the woman he loved. And they would live happily ever after.

She almost laughed again. How many times did she need to be hurt and disappointed before she accepted that there was no hope for her, and least of all for them?

She almost reached out and touched his lips, the lips that had kissed her and left her wanting more. She recalled their first kiss with a smile. He hadn't been able to see her, but that hadn't stopped his hands from exploring her face with a tender touch.

One night when she had sneaked to see him, he had whispered while brushing his fingers across her lips, how kissable they felt.

"I want to kiss you," he had said.

"I want you to kiss me," she had responded, and recalled the eager thudding of her heart.

And he had. His lips replaced his fingers, and he gently captured her lips with his, and he feasted on her and she on him, the exquisite sensation spreading throughout her entire body and making her shiver down to her soul.

She hadn't wanted him to stop, and he hadn't wanted to. stop. If a sound hadn't frightened them apart, she had often wondered how far the kiss would have taken them.

Other times and other kisses and added touches had brought them close to making love, but it was never to be, and she wished, how she wished, they could be lovers for one night, just one night.

Lord, can't you give me one night?

A foolish wish that would never be answered, just like all the other foolish wishes.

Carissa turned over and once again faced the hearth. She had to keep her distance from him and keep her mind on an escape. It could never be between them and if her father had taught her anything, he had taught her to survive.

And survive she would, even while losing the man she loved.

Chapter 12

Ronan woke alone in bed, pleased that he didn't find Carissa in his arms. Then realizing she wasn't in bed, he bolted up to look around the single room. She was nowhere. He jumped out of bed and dressed quickly.

He didn't know if he was the fool for thinking she wouldn't attempt an escape, or she was the fool for even thinking she could survive such horrid weather. He mumbled several oaths as he pulled on his boots and just as he was about to grab his cloak and rush out the door, it opened.

He took firm hold of it, the wind trying to force entrance as Carissa stumbled in with a large cauldron of snow. After shutting the door, he grabbed the cauldron from her, setting it in the hearth.

"It's brutal out there," she said, her teeth chattering as she unsuccessfully tried to untie her cloak.

Ronan was appalled to see how red and cramped her hands were and he quickly offered his assistance and undid her ties. He hung her cloak on the peg by the door, then returned to take her hands gently in his.

They felt like ice, and she cringed when he touched them.

"You should not have gone out there," he scolded, and hurried her to sit in the rocking chair in front of the hearth. He then continued to gently rub warmth back into her hands.

"I wish to wash myself from head to toe," she said, her teeth still chattering.

His tone continued to scold, though not sharply. "You should have waited for me to wake."

She smiled. "Since you snored heavily, I didn't expect you to wake anytime soon."

"I snore?" he asked, surprised, while concentrating on her fingers. They were long and slim for one so petite, and though the cold had taken a harsh bite, her flesh warmed to his touch and slowly grew silky soft.

"Not all the time," she said.

Gently and methodically, he worked on the stiff joints, massaging heat back into each individual finger. Speech lapsed between them while he continued to rub and stroke her delicate flesh.

It heated further with every stroke, and the more soft and pliable her flesh became, the more he wanted to continue to touch her. He even extended his massage up along her arm, slipping his fingers under the sleeve of her blouse and kneading the supple flesh to further chase the chill.

He moved his body in closer, and as his fingers moved past her breast, he slowed, allowing the sides of them to brush dangerously close. Though her soft wool blouse prevented him from feeling her plush breasts, just the thought of them hardened his loins.

He turned his head, not realizing how close their faces were, and was startled by the surging passion in her blue eyes, and the plumpness of her moist lips. And for a moment, a sheer moment of utter madness, he was tempted to kiss her.

The sudden realization was like a sharp slap in the face and he sprang off his haunches to stand a distance away from her, saying, "Let the flames do the rest."

"The flames will only heat me more," she said with a sultry passion that had his loins growing tauter with desire.

He silently told himself that the problem was simply that he had gone too long without a woman. He needed to release his pent-up passion and be done with it. But he'd be damned if he was going to release it between the legs of the woman responsible for Hope's death.

"I could satisfy you."

Her whispery voice conjured up images of her rising naked over him and riding him until he burst with pleasure.

He shook away the tempting pictures and gathered his wits. "I have no doubt you could since you obviously inherited your father's salacious appetite."

"Then why not taste?" she offered.

"I believe it would be too *bitter* to my liking."

She laughed. "Or perhaps the taste would be so *intoxicating* you could not get enough of it."

"I knew such an intoxicating taste once, and I relished it." He shook his head. "And never will I know it again, for I will never love anyone as I love Hope."

They both turned silent for a time until Carissa finally stood.

"While the snow melts and heats the water, I'll prepare the morning meal, then I intend to wash myself from head to toe, so if you prefer not to see me naked, I suggest you find something to keep you distracted."

Ronan moved out of her way, brushing quickly past her to take refuge in the rocking chair. She was challenging him, and it galled him to wonder if it was one challenge he'd have a hard time winning.

Breakfast was a silent affair and over much too soon for Ronan's liking. There truly wasn't anything that would keep him distracted. He couldn't go and collect extra logs from the stack outside without causing a chill while she washed. He was left with one option, and he took it.

As Carissa readied a spot close to the hearth, Ronan took the rocking chair and turned it around and sat with his back to her, waiting for a stinging comment from her.

"A wise move, Highlander," she said with a hint of a laugh. "But don't expect the same of me. I'll take great pleasure in watching you."

Damn, if she hadn't backed him into another corner. He couldn't very well go without washing.

Just hearing the cloth scrub against her flesh had him itching to take a cloth to his own skin. And he fought to keep that thought in mind, trying to avoid any image of her nakedness from invading his senses.

He'd find a way to wash up without her sitting there staring at him.

She was petite like Hope.

Where had that thought come from? But now that it had popped into his head, he couldn't get rid of it. Carissa was as petite as Hope. Thinking on it, he realized that their fingers were similar, long and slim. But their voices were not at all alike. Hope's was soft, more like a whisper, where Carissa's was bold and her tone direct.

He shut his eyes, the darkness bringing back memories of his time with Hope. He had never looked upon her, his eyes swollen shut and healing slow. But he felt as if he'd know her when he saw her, though he never had the chance. Now, thinking on it, he recalled how soft and wavy Hope's hair was, and long. He had loved running his fingers through the thick, silky strands, the waves bouncing down along his arm and making his flesh tingle.

And then there were her lips, plump to the touch and taste, much like Carissa's. The thought startled his eyes open. He didn't like the comparisons he was making. The two women were not at all alike.

But there were similarities, and why had he only just noticed them?

Them. That was the key, there was more than one.

He shook his head. But there were also differences. One difference was their voices, another was . . .

He thought . . . this was nonsense. Complete nonsense.

Carissa and Hope were two different people. Hope was kind and caring. Carissa was coldhearted and selfish. But both were masks that could easily be worn.

Was he mad? Thinking the two women could be one?

Impossible!

His mind was playing tricks on him. Being stuck here with Carissa was causing crazy thoughts. He missed Hope, ached for her, and in his pain, his mind played tricks on him. Hope had been real, and she had loved him as he loved her. He would have never fallen in love with his enemy. Carissa would never have been able to hide her harsh nature. He would have known.

He closed his eyes again and rested his head back, recalling the stolen moments he had spent with Hope. He most loved the nights she would come to him and lie beside him, their fingers entwined—long, slim fingers.

"Damn," he mumbled and sprang out of the rocker, almost upsetting it as he turned and, too late, realized his mistake.

She was stark naked, the firelight dancing off her damp skin. Wisps of her long, blond hair escaped the comb that tried to hold the chaotic waves, falling along her slim neck and framing her face. Her face was flushed from the heat of the fire, or perhaps more from the passion he saw spark in her eyes. That she was exquisite was undeniable, that he was tempted to take her was undeniable, that he would . . . *never*.

He marched right past her, his hands fisted tightly at his sides to keep him from reaching out and snatching her into his arms. He clamped his mouth shut, for fear he would be too tempted to taste her nipples, which taunted him with their round, hard peaks. And he kept his eyes averted from the curvaceous lines that he was certain promised paradise on earth, or more likely endless damnation.

Instead, he swiped his cloak from the peg, and said. "You had best get dressed. It's going to get mighty cold in here as I bring in stacks of firewood."

He shut the door hard behind him and stood a moment, grateful for the sharp wind that bit at his face. He needed his ardor cooled, and he wouldn't stop refurbishing the woodpile in the cottage until he was doused like a cold campfire.

Carissa hurried into a clean linen shift and donned a dark green, wool skirt and blouse. She dug out knitted black stockings from her bundle of clothes and pulled them on. She was sitting on a chair by the fire combing her hair when he entered.

He didn't glance her way. He took the chopped wood over to the spot where the bed had once been and stacked the wood on top of the pile that was already there. Then he turned and marched out the door, again not casting a glance in her direction.

Her hands trembled slightly as she arranged her hair up on her head, forcing one comb to hold all the thick waves in place. She didn't bother with the few that escaped, fearing if he returned, he would see her hands trembling.

Staying true to Carissa's audacious nature, she had purposely goaded him about watching her wash though she hoped he wouldn't, and she certainly hadn't wanted him to.

She truly wished to keep him at a distance, especially after he had so gently tended her iced fingers. He had touched her with such tenderness and came so near to kissing her that she realized he could be dangerously close to discovering the truth.

He might not have seen Hope with clear vision, but with his every touch he had become familiar with her, and those loving touches could not easily be forgotten. And then what would happen if he discovered Hope was none other than Carissa?

She shook her head, not wanting to think of the consequences. He would certainly believe she had tricked him. He would never accept that she was more like Hope than Carissa. He had too much hate invested in Carissa to think otherwise.

The door swung open again, and Ronan kicked it shut so hard behind him that it trembled. She remained sitting on the chair by the hearth. Now was not the time for chatter. She much preferred silent observation.

He stacked the wood with more force than necessary, and this time as he strode past her, he didn't take his eyes off her. He glared at her as if he were looking through her. However, Carissa would never shrink away in fear.

No, she'd boldly speak her mind, so she tossed her chin up, and said, "It looks like you regret not accepting my offer."

His nostrils flared, and he looked ready to pounce on her, though certainly not with passion. Instead, he stormed out of the cottage. The door once again trembled as he slammed it shut, and she shuddered.

She had been foolish. She had hungered for his gentle touch and surrendered to it. He and Hope had laced fingers so often, that there was a chance he would recall her familiar touch. And yet she had dismissed it without a thought.

If she wanted to survive this ordeal and eventually escape, she would have to be more diligent. And she would need to make certain that Carissa remained dominant. She couldn't allow Ronan even a brief moment of doubt.

He was back in no time, again stacking the wood with more force than needed.

"Angry with yourself," she shot at him as he hurried past her.

"No," he nearly shouted. "With you."

She laughed. "Because I tempt you?"

"Who are you?" he demanded as he approached her.

She bolted off the chair. "You know very well who I am."

He tore off his cloak and flung it on the bed, then ran a rough hand through his hair as if he wanted to tear it out. He turned his head away, and Carissa knew that he was trying to temper his anger.

What disturbed her even more was that his present reaction was a good indication of how he would feel if he learned the truth about her. He would not be happy to discover Hope alive. He would think Carissa an even-more-deceitful woman. He would never believe the truth.

He turned to glare at her, his anger abated, though his eyes still heated. "You are a deceitful and selfish woman, who I will never trust."

"You mean who you *fear*," she corrected smugly.

He moved closer to loom menacingly over her. "I never feared you, hated, yes, but never did I fear you."

She didn't shrink away from his attempted intimidation. With a prideful stretch and her shoulders squared and calling on all the courage she possessed, she looked him straight in the eyes. "And you have good reason to, for it was a pleasure squeezing the last breath of life out of the woman you loved."

Chapter 13

Ronan was dangerously close to doing to her precisely what she had done to Hope, but he controlled himself. Perhaps it was because that shred of doubt that had suddenly risen to torment him lingered in the back of his mind. And he had to settle it before he did anything else.

"In time, Carissa, you will pay for all you've done to me and my family."

"I'll worry about that when"—she laughed—"or rather if it ever comes about."

"Still confident you'll escape me?" he asked, his own confidence and calm restored.

"I know I will," she answered, and walked past him to turn the rocking chair around and sit.

He remained standing, feeling he had gained the upper hand somehow and suddenly wanting to discover more about this woman, who he realized was more of an enigma to him than he had suspected.

"Even if you managed such a remarkable feat," he said, "where would you go? I don't imagine you have many friends left in the area."

"You think I would admit to any resources?"

"I truly can't imagine you having any," he said. "Your father was the last of a dying breed of vicious conquerors who had no true homeland and wanted nothing more than destruction and power. He made only enemies, no friends, and since you are his daughter, you suffer from the same foolishness."

"I can assure you that I'm not as foolish as my father."

"And yet here you sit," he said with a wave of his hand toward her, "captured."

"We're both captives," she corrected.

"Of a storm that continues to brew," he finished.

She smiled. "Inside as well as outside."

He leaned toward her. "With nothing but time on our hands, let's discuss how you acquired the slave I called Hope."

Warning bells sounded in Carissa's head. Why did he suddenly wish personal information about Hope? He had asked once or twice about where she had originally come from, but she had managed to redirect the query to him and his family, which, of course, wouldn't bode well for her now. If he discovered the truth, he would think she had been trying to garner information about the Sinclares.

"Can't remember?" he asked accusingly when her answer took too long in coming.

"We had many slaves. I'm trying to recall when and where it was we acquired her." She grinned for fear of being discovered. "But shouldn't you know that? After all, you two were in love and should know everything about each other."

"I'm realizing that sometimes we don't truly know a person as well as we thought."

His response would have knocked Carissa off her feet if she hadn't been sitting down. Something obviously had stirred a memory that sent him doubting. Damn her for being such a fool.

"Are you saying that you didn't truly know Hope?"

"I'm saying that I want to know what *you* know about Hope."

"What would I know about slaves?" she said, trying not to sound too defensive. "They were brought to the compound after raids, and my father decided their fate."

"What fate did he decree for Hope?"

"To serve my needs."

"So Hope was *your* slave," he confirmed.

"All slaves were property of my father." Carissa bit her tongue, for she knew as Hope she had told him that very same thing.

"But she answered to you."

"That's right. Hope did my bidding."

"And out of the generosity of your heart, you had her tend the captives that were wounded?"

She laughed. "My father cared little for the wounded warriors he captured. They died or he sold them to mercenaries for a sizeable purse. You, however, were special, and I was ordered to see that you survived. So I had my slave tend you."

"How long had Hope been your slave?"

"If I recall correctly, since she was young," Carissa said cautiously.

Ronan nodded as if agreeing. "Hope had told me she had been a slave for as long as she could remember."

"That was probably because there was nothing else for her to remember."

"She never told me her age," he said.

"It was never recorded or celebrated," she said. "I'd say she was around eighteen or nineteen."

"What did she look like?"

How did she describe herself? No, not Carissa, but Hope. What did Hope look like? She thought a moment then said, "She was gentle, soft-spoken, kind—"

"I mean her features, not her nature."

"Her nature was her features," she said, knowing that was all she could say to describe Hope.

His silence and scrunched brow reflected possible confusion or perhaps doubt. And either was better for her, for she imagined he much preferred to believe Hope real rather than think Carissa had played him for a fool.

She rested her head back on the rocker and turned to gaze at the flames, grateful for the continued silence. She didn't want to talk about Hope any longer. She would much rather *be* Hope.

When had she begun to hide her true nature? Had she been four? Five? She couldn't recall for sure. She only knew that her compassion infuriated her father, and so she hid it away and only took it out when he wasn't around. If she accidentally allowed it to show, others suffered, so she learned to wear a mask at all times.

Her father's constant lesson had been that hate endures and love doesn't. Therefore, hate served a better purpose than love. Her father had never once told her that he loved her. The only one who ever showed her any kind of love, which she cherished, had been Dykar.

When she first found herself falling in love with Ronan, she'd been surprised and fearful. Nothing good would come of it, only more sorrow and disappointment for her. But it had been so very easy to fall in love with him. He had been vulnerable and frightened, and yet in spite of it all, he possessed courage. And he was unselfish, a trait she had only seen in a few people. He was not only concerned for his own welfare but asked often about his brother and worried about her.

It had been so very odd to have someone care about her, worry over her, want to protect her, and to feel that his every touch had simply been remarkable. To be touched so lovingly had been even more remarkable. Never had she been touched like that in her life, and she craved for more, so much more from him, only him. That was why it had been difficult to pull away from him when he had taken her hands in his.

But her foolish mistake had cost her, and now she needed to be on guard more than ever. To her disappointment, her father had been right about something: Hate endures.

* * *

Ronan sat in the rocking chair, watching Carissa sleep. He hadn't been able to bring himself to get in bed with her. He didn't like what he was thinking, the possibility infuriated him. If Carissa had pretended to be the slave Hope, she had made a complete fool out of him.

And why hadn't he ever considered it before?

Being unable to see had been traumatic and more fearful than he had ever imagined possible. He hadn't known where he was, hadn't known if he was alone or if someone stood silent guard over him, hadn't known how severe his wounds, hadn't been able to help himself at all. Hope had been God sent. She had been kind and had immediately eased his fears and concerns with thoughtful words and a gentle touch. As ridiculous the thought, he had felt safe with her. Not that she could have protected him, but her calm, reassuring presence had brought him at least a modicum of relief. And to think it possible that all along it might very well have been Carissa playing him for a fool, made him want to make her suffer even more.

He shook his head as it rested in his cupped hands. The things he had confided in her about himself and his family. He raised his head and shook it again. Could it truly be so? Or was this forced confinement driving him crazy with thoughts that were simply ridiculous?

Her nature was her features.

Carissa had been right about that, and that was

the one thought that kept him wondering. Could a woman with such a cold, uncaring heart portray a woman completely opposite in nature?

He had never once thought Hope anyone other than who she was, a good-hearted woman who he had easily fallen in love with. Why did he allow himself to doubt that now?

Hope had been just that to him . . . hope. Her encouraging nature had made it easier for him to believe that everything would be all right. He would survive, and he would eventually be free. Without her constant encouragement and care, he doubted he would have survived his confinement. So to question it now, to think it had all been a lie, a ruse, a trap not only infuriated him but left him feeling empty.

If Carissa proved to be Hope, then the woman he loved had never existed. Everything they had shared had never existed, and that ripped at his heart as sharply as the mighty talons of a falcon.

He sat back, sending the rocker into a soothing rhythm that began to lull him to sleep. He didn't fight it; it let his eyes drift shut. In sleep, he would escape his doubts and never-ending thoughts . . . or would he?

He smelled the familiar scent of apples before he felt her touch. Gentle, so very gentle. She bathed his swollen eyes.

"You will see again, I promise."

He reached out, eager to touch her face, and she took hold of his hand and placed it against her cool cheek. His fingers were quick to search out her lips. He loved the feel of them and even more so after they kissed, for they would be plump with passion.

"Kiss me," he said.

And she obliged.

Their kiss started out gentle, but it wasn't long before it turned hungry with desire. And it wasn't long before his loins hardened to an ache he longed to ease.

A sudden noise tore them apart.

"It's nothing," she assured him.

"Then kiss me again," he said, "for I miss your lips."

She laughed soft and easy before obliging him, and when it ended, she said, "I love you. I will always love you."

He took hold of her hand and laced her long slim fingers with his. "Nothing in this world will make me stop loving you. My heart forever belongs to you."

"Nothing?" she asked. "Nothing at all will stop you from loving me?"

"Nothing," he reiterated. "A strong, unwavering love connects you and me. We are one and always will be."

"Promise?"

"I give you my word."

"I will hold you to it, Highlander."

Ronan's eyes sprang open and he bolted straight up in the rocker.

Carissa was the only one who called him Highlander, and he looked to where she slept in the bed. Had it been his worries that produced the dream, or had he been shown the truth?

No answer came to him, but he would have one. No matter what it took he would find out the truth.

Chapter 14

The storm ended abruptly, just stopped as if someone had turned off a spigot. The gray clouds remained, but they didn't portend more snow, merely dreary winter days.

Carissa sat sharing the morning meal with Ronan. He had informed her of the change in the weather.

"I'm going to scout the area and see if it's feasible for us to leave here soon," he said, finishing the last of his porridge.

She nodded, knowing there was no point in disagreeing with him. And knowing she couldn't prevent him from forcing her to go with him. She had thought to make her own escape but knew that wasn't a wise choice, and she had realized just this morning that Bethane would no doubt send word to Dykar of her departure from the safety of the village Black.

Over the years, Dykar and Bethane had become friends, and he would often bring his wounded warriors to her. Once he discovered that she had left and was on her own, he would look for her and, no doubt, Bethane had told him exactly where she could be found. With the weather clear, she knew Dykar would be coming for her. Her only course of action was to try to remain at the cottage until he arrived.

"While I scout, I'll also see about hunting fresh game for tonight," he said.

"I could make a fine stew if you're lucky in your hunt."

He shook his head. "It still amazes me that you are an exceptional cook."

She smiled. It pleased her to hear him acknowledge it. She never had the opportunity to prepare meals for anyone. This forced confinement had provided her the chance, and she was grateful for having the opportunity to do something she actually enjoyed. Miraculously, she seemed to have all the ingredients she needed to prepare decent meals, and she had Bethane to thank for that. Evidently, she had made certain the cottage had been stacked with necessary provisions. The older woman probably had envisioned such a scenario as her own, a person stranded by a winter storm and needing shelter, and so she had prepared the cottage. Carissa often wished she had Bethane's awareness.

"You will miss my cooking?" she finally asked.

"No need for me to," he said. "You'll be held at the Sinclare keep, and while awaiting your fate, your hands will prove useful in the kitchen."

Her smile widened. "I look forward to it."

Her easy compliance seemed to annoy him, for

he bristled and hurried to snatch his cloak off the peg. "I'll be close by."

"Afraid I'll attempt an escape?"

He flung his cloak around his shoulders as he turned to face her. "You wouldn't get very far. I'd find you in no time."

"That confident are you?"

"That determined to see you pay," he said, and was out the door.

Having heard the threat from him all too often, she barely paid heed to it. She knew her situation was precarious and needed no reminders. But ironically, this is where her father's teachings helped. He had taught her no matter what the circumstance, never panic. Keep a clear head and never doubt yourself, and always keep a forward momentum, never, ever look back.

Her heart disagreed. It continued to hope. It wanted to prove her father wrong about love. Her heart wanted to show that love not only endured, but conquered hate. Her father certainly would have laughed at her, told she was foolish. Furthermore, he would have punished her for believing such nonsense.

But her father wasn't here. She was free of his tyrannical rule, free to believe as she chose, free to hope.

The thought lightened her burden, and she busied herself clearing the table. She was going to make bread. The whole process provided her with a peaceful calm she cherished. Ula had taught her that baking was an important skill and one born of love. It should be done with pride, for you are providing those you love with sustenance necessary to life. The thought that one day she would be able to do that for a family of her own had always lingered in her mind. And this brief time spent with Ronan had given her a glimpse into that, at least when they shared a meal. He never failed to enjoy any of the meals she prepared, and conversation always remained light when they ate. It allowed her to imagine and, in a sense, that gave her hope.

Carissa got started, and the hours ticked away. It was near noon that she began to worry. Ronan should have returned hours ago. Something was wrong, she could feel it. If he had gotten hurt, he could be lying somewhere in the snow in need of help.

She didn't waste time with indecision. She grabbed her cloak from the peg and was out the door. The only thing she regretted was not having a weapon with her. Ronan had confiscated the only two she had, and though there was the knife she used for cooking, it wasn't an adequate weapon.

She wasn't worried for herself. She had been trained to survive the wilderness with nothing more than her wits. She would do fine. It was Ronan who concerned her, and so she carefully followed his tracks, worried that something dreadful had happened to him. After all, he had reminded her time and again that nothing would stop him from making sure she paid for her crimes. Yet he hadn't returned, which could mean only one thing.

He couldn't. Something had to have happened to him.

With observant eyes and cautious steps, she followed his tracks, fearful of what she would find.

The cold seeped into Ronan's body, and he shivered as he struggled out of his stupor. He silently criticized himself for not being more careful as he tried to roll off his back and onto his side. The sharp pain that sliced through his head quickly quelled his effort.

It was difficult to ascertain how long he had been lying on the ground with so much cloud covering overhead. At least with the sun and where it sat in the sky, he'd have a good indication of the time of day, but the clouds masked time, and so he had no idea how long after his fall he had lain unconscious. He also knew it was imperative that he not continue to lie there. He had to get himself moving.

His vision began to clear, though not in his right eye. When he examined the area with his hand, he realized that he had suffered an abrasion just above his right eye and some of the blood had pooled there.

He flinched as a pain shot through his wound, but what followed was far worse. Snow began to fall, and he cursed his own stupidity. He should have been more careful where he walked. He had been so eager to chase down the only animal, a wild deer, he had seen in the hour he had been surveying the results of the storm that he had slipped and hit his head on a snow-covered rock.

"Get up," he scolded himself, then wondered if Carissa would come in search of him. But why would she? It would be to her advantage if he didn't return. That thought spurred him on and gave him enough impetus to roll on his side, though the effort cost him, the severe pain almost rendering him unconscious once again.

The snow had already coated him with a light blanket, and he continued to shiver. He had to get on his feet. He had to get moving. His life depended on it.

He struggled through the hazy dizziness the pain produced as he finally made it to his feet. He felt as if he weighed more than he could carry, and his vision turned blurry once again. He stumbled along, uncertain of the direction in which he traveled or what direction he should travel. Did he move farther away or closer to the cottage?

He couldn't determine; he only knew he needed to keep moving.

"Ronan."

He thought he heard someone shout his name, so he stood still and listened but heard nothing. He dragged his feet while the pain continued to hammer at his head.

"Ronan."

He was sure he heard it that time. Someone was calling out to him. He stilled and listened.

"Ronan! Ronan!"

He knew that voice, was familiar with the concern that echoed in his name. But it couldn't be, Hope was dead. How could she be here searching for him?

"Ronan!"

It was her. He was sure of it. He had heard that fearful anxiety in her voice before. It was just before they parted, and as she had lain wrapped in his arms, he had promised that he would return for her and set her free.

"Hope!" he shouted. "I'm here. I've come back."

His frantic response caused his head to spin, nausea to rise, and his legs to grow weak. He fought to remain standing, but he could feel himself losing the battle. And just before he collapsed, he felt arms wrap around his middle, a head push upward from beneath his arm, and a petite body struggle to support the brunt of his weight.

"Hope." He sighed, trying to clear his vision enough to catch sight of her.

"I'm here," she said, "don't worry. You'll be all right. I'll get you home."

"I've come back for you," he said, trying hard not to weigh too heavily on her.

"I never doubted you would," she said.

"I love you," he said, and winced from another sharp pain.

"And I love you, but you mustn't talk. You must save your strength."

"Promise me you won't leave me." He winced again, the pain shooting through his head.

"Stop talking."

"Promise me," he said with a moan.

"I promise," she said anxiously. "I promise I will never ever leave you."

He smiled then cringed. "The pain—"

"Keep silent," she ordered. "We will be home soon."

He obeyed, though he wondered. Had that been Carissa who had ordered him silent?

Carissa prayed to the heavens that she would be able to get them back to the cottage safely. The snow grew heavier with each step they took. If not for the markers she had left along the way, it would have been impossible to find their way back.

Her heart soared with relief when she spied the cottage up ahead. A few more feet, and she would have collapsed under his sagging weight.

She staggered getting him to the bed and stripped off his cloak before he fell into bed. She hurried to close the door and hung his cloak up to dry. She kept her cloak on, grabbed the smaller cauldron, and hurried outside to collect fresh snow. She set it in the hearth to heat, then discarded her outer garments.

Carissa rushed over to Ronan and fear gripped her. He was unresponsive. She tried to revive him, but to no avail. The only thing she could do was to clean his wound, keep him warm, and hope that he was in a healing sleep.

Bethane had once explained to her that the body was more aware of what we required than we were, and so, when necessary, it took charge. If sleep was necessary to healing, then the person would sleep and wake when the body deemed itself ready.

She hoped and prayed Ronan was in such a state.

Closer examination of the wound revealed that it wasn't as bad as she'd first suspected, though it did require a few stitches. She was relieved that he wouldn't be awake for the painful stitching, given the good-sized lump beneath the abrasion.

As his shivers hadn't entirely ceased, she hurriedly removed his boots. His feet were cold as ice. She tucked all the blankets securely around him. Then she placed the flat pan in the hearth to heat so that she could use it to help warm his feet.

She rushed around, gathering everything she needed and, though she was busy, she couldn't keep her mind off the fact that he had believed it was Hope who had come to his rescue. She was no fool. She knew his delirium had been caused by his wound. But to hear him call out to Hope and once again to hear him say he loved her brought joy to her heart and soul.

However, she needed to remain cautious. She didn't know when he woke if he would recall the episode. And if he did? The truth would suffice, he had merely been delirious.

For now, though, she would remain Hope and tend him as she had once before, with gentle hands and all her love.

Before she started, she wrapped the warmed pan in her wool shawl and tucked it beneath his feet. His shivers stopped almost instantly. She then spent the next twenty minutes tending his wound. The stitches went fast since she was so prolific at setting them. The suturing complete, she managed to clean all the blood off him and away from his eye.

When he woke, he would have no trouble seeing her.

After she was done, she set a broth to brew in the hearth so that if he woke hungry, she'd have something to feed him. When she was finally finished, she moved the rocking chair next to the bed and took his hand in hers.

She smiled, the warmth of his hand spreading through her own, and fell asleep, content.

Chapter 15

"**H**ope?"

"I'm here."

Ronan squeezed the hand in his, relieved to feel it there. "I'm cold, and my head hurts so badly that I can't bear to open my eyes."

"Keep your eyes shut. It's late, and you need to continue to rest. I'll put more wood in the hearth and—"

"—Then you'll crawl in bed with me and keep me warm."

"If that is what you want."

"More than anything I want that," he assured her with a gentle squeeze of her hand.

He wanted so badly to look at her, but every time he tried to open his eyes, the pain would force them closed. At least he had Hope. She was there with him, and soon she'd be in his arms, but this time he wanted more.

"Hope," he said, and held out his hand. When she took it, he locked his fingers firmly with hers. "I want your loving body heating mine. Undress and help me to do the same."

He was glad she didn't hesitate and with great effort, her tender assistance, and more pain than he cared to experience, he undressed. It didn't take her long to shed her clothes and join him beneath the blankets.

She cuddled against his side, her hard nipples poking his chest as her hand splayed across it. Her leg dug between his two, to nestle comfortably close to his groin, and she gave a quick kiss to his chest before resting her head there.

His arm wrapped around her protectively. She was warm and ever so soft, and he wasn't surprised that his body reacted to her nakedness. But he didn't have the stamina to pursue his desire. He would have to be satisfied with simply holding her.

They lay embraced, Ronan stroking Hope's arm and drifting closer and closer to her breast until finally his fingers skimmed across it to toy with her hardened nipple.

"I love the feel of you," he whispered.

"And I love your touch."

"I wish I could make love to you tonight, but I can barely move without it paining me."

She slipped ever so slowly over him until her naked body covered his, and she whispered against his lips, "Then let me make love to you."

"I don't have the strength—"

"You need none," she cajoled between kisses. "You need only to let me give you pleasure."

He tried to protest, wanting this time with her to be special, but he couldn't speak; he could only feel. And he felt every touch and kiss, his own hands seeking her intimate flesh, frustrated when it seemed beyond his reach.

Damn, why did it have to be this way? He had waited so long, so very long to be with Hope, and now his pain was too great to allow him the pleasure.

Still, she wrung groans and moans from him, or was that from the pain? He and she intermingled, and he wasn't sure where one ended and the other began. He only knew that he was lost in a haze of pleasure.

Her lips seemed to sear every part of him, top to bottom, side to side, and all areas in between. She explored every inch of him, and he relished the pleasure. This was how he had imagined it. This was how it had been meant to be between him and Hope.

This was her loving him.

He was on the precipice of tumbling off, falling into the abyss of pleasure, when suddenly light blinded him, pain tore through his head, and his eyes sprang open.

He wasn't sure where he was. It took him a moment to remember what had happened to him. Then, when he finally had his senses about him and realized he was in bed at the cottage, he realized someone slept beside him naked.

He shut his eyes against the inevitable, but knew he had to look, and when finally he did, he grew furious.

There beside him, pressed intimately against him, was his archenemy Carissa, stark naked.

He would have bolted from the bed if the pain in his head hadn't stopped him when he tried to move. He did, however, push her away.

She woke startled, and he was surprised when she anxiously pulled the blanket over her nakedness. Then, as if she realized where she was, she grinned and let the blanket fall away from her breasts.

With an exaggerated stretch, she said, "What a night."

Ronan wanted to choke her, or was it he who deserved the punishment? Had he truly made love—no—had sex with his enemy? Good lord, what had he done?

Carissa twisted her blond hair up and reached across Ronan to snatch her comb off the seat of the rocking chair and secure her long locks in place. Then she turned, and with a wicked grin and a lick of her lips, said, "Feeling better?"

"What did you do?" he demanded, realizing that if he didn't move too fast, he'd suffer no pain.

"Nothing you didn't want me to."

"You're an evil woman."

"You didn't think so last night," she said with a self-satisfied smirk.

Ronan couldn't believe that he would mistake Carissa for Hope. It just wasn't possible. But then that would mean . . .

Before he turned glaring eyes on her, she slipped out of bed and dressed.

"Don't torture yourself, Highlander. You weren't up to performing."

"Give me my clothes," he demanded, truly relieved.

She tossed him his garments once she was finished, then moved the rocking chair to where it usually sat by the hearth.

He was slow to dress but not to question her. "It was you who found me?"

"Who else would it be?"

Yes, who else, he thought. Certainly not a dead woman.

"You were delirious."

Was I? He wondered if his mind had played tricks on him, or had Carissa been playing tricks all along?

"You thought me Hope," she said, walking to the table to slice bread for breakfast.

"And you responded as Hope."

She shrugged. "As I said, you were delirious."

"You sounded like Hope."

"Did I?" she shrugged again. "Or was it what you wanted to hear?"

He moved slowly from the bed to the rocker, the pain slight. "You're petite and slim like Hope."

She jabbed the tip of the knife into the wooden tabletop, and it stuck there as she glared at him. "Say what you mean, Highlander."

"There are too many similarities between you and Hope. And when I think of it, I also wonder how a slave could sneak away from her master every night without being caught."

"So you're suggesting that I'm Hope, the dead slave you still love?"

"It seems more and more obvious," he admitted.

"Why would I bother to pass myself off as a slave?"

"To gain my confidence and information about the Sinclares."

"That sounds as ridiculous as my claiming that I am truly more like Hope than Carissa, that somehow I felt safe enough with you to be my true self, a kind and thoughtful woman."

He gave a robust laugh and instantly regretted it. The sharp pain struck like lightning, at the side of his head, then down along his neck. He gasped as he said, "That's a tall tale if I ever heard one. Mordrac's daughter kindhearted and thoughtful. Please spare me the absurdity."

"Your tale may not be tall, but it is ridiculous," she said. "It makes not an ounce of sense for me to have posed as a slave and pretended to love you."

He cringed, though it wasn't from the pain in his head. It was from the pain in his heart. Had Carissa truly played him for a fool? Had he laid bare his love to his enemy?

"And why would I sell you to the mercenaries?"

"To keep me imprisoned," he said, as if just realizing it himself. "You knew I wouldn't go anywhere until I rescued Hope."

"And what would be the point of keeping you imprisoned?"

"I would make good fodder for barter."

She shook her head. "If that were my intentions, I would have used you to save my father's life. But

I was wise enough to realize that my father's fate was inevitable."

"Just like yours."

"Spare me your repetitive threats," she said. "They are as meaningless to me as what you now suggest."

"Why? Because I've caught you at your little game?"

She sauntered over to him, her slim hand resting provocatively along her hip. "If it is a game, what makes you think that I don't have you right where I want you?"

He jumped up; the intense pain slamming his eyes shut, and he grabbed hold of the mantel to stop from collapsing.

"Sit."

Her anxious order sounded just as Hope had when she worried over him, and it made him angrier to realize that more than likely the woman he loved had never existed.

"Sit," she urged again, and took hold of his arm, tugging him down.

Her hand never left his arm after he sat, and her warmth poured into him just as Hope's had always done. He had teased her about it once, and she responded by telling him that it was her love for him that radiated the warmth.

He glanced down at the hand resting on his tan shirt. Even the linen couldn't stop him from feeling her heat, or was it her love? Damn, but he didn't want to believe that Hope had never existed.

He wanted her to have been a real warm, loving woman. He wanted everything he had shared with her to have been real; most of all, he wanted their love to have been real. He could endure loving a woman who had died, but not loving a woman who had never lived.

She removed her hand from his arm, and a bleak emptiness descended over him. Could it be true? Could Hope have never existed? Had he been merely chasing a dream?

He grabbed his head with his hand, not knowing if the pain came from his wound or his troubled thoughts.

"I'll fix you something to eat," she said.

Her voice was sharp like Carissa's, or was he merely trying to find reason not to believe what he suspected?

"I'm not hungry," he said, and moved from the chair, climbing into bed slowly.

"Rest," she said, pulling the blankets over him. "I'll set a fresh broth to brewing for when you wake."

Now she sounded like Hope, considerate, and his head began to spin as he prayed for the blessedness of sleep.

Carissa collapsed in one of the chairs at the table. All hope was gone, but what had she expected, Ronan to embrace her and be grateful that Hope was alive? Hope wasn't alive in any sense. He reacted as she had suspected he would. He had rejected her. Not for a moment had he believed, or even considered, that she could be more like Hope than Carissa.

If he hated her before, this would make him hate her even more.

So had her father been right? Hate endures while love doesn't last.

Ronan believed the worst of her. To hear him say that she had sold him to the mercenaries to imprison him couldn't have been further from the truth. She had sold him to free him. She had assumed he would contact his family, pay the money the mercenaries had paid for him, and return home, intending eventually to rescue Hope. Instead, he had remained with the mercenaries and begun plans to rescue Hope.

When she had realized he wouldn't give up, she had no other choice but to make him believe Hope had died. That was why it had been so easy to answer him when he had asked why she had killed Hope.

It really had been necessary.

Foolishly, she had not given thought to Ronan possibly wanting revenge. She thought he would be so heartbroken that he would return home to his family to grieve.

She had to admit that part of her cherished knowing he had loved Hope so strongly that he abandoned reuniting with his family for her. And even when he learned of her death, it had not driven him home but only made him more determined to revenge Hope.

Carissa shook her head silently admonishing

herself. It had been foolish of her from the start to play such a dangerous game. But it had been done without malice and with such innocence. He had been needy; but then so had she.

She had, however, made it worse.

His sorrowful groan had her off the chair and to his side in seconds. He looked in the throes of a nightmare, his face scrunched in agony and his mouth tightly gripped. It broke her heart to know she was the cause of his suffering.

She stroked his face with gentle fingers, running them lightly across his forehead, then drifting down to circle his cheek and in a waving motion across his chin and along his jaw from ear to ear. She repeated the route until his face relaxed, and he slept contentedly. She had done the same to him before, when he had thought her Hope, and he had loved it. He had told her that she possessed magic hands.

She had told him that her magic only worked on him.

With a teasing boldness, he had informed her that soon they would work magic together. But they had never had the chance, and now he suffered even more because of her.

She couldn't stand to see him hurt anymore.

This had to end.

And she was the only one who could end it.

Chapter 16

In four days, Ronan felt better. He had rested and eaten well and spoken little to Carissa. And he wasn't surprised that she had kept her distance from him. He had caught her in her lies, revealed her ruse, and sealed her fate.

He could try to convince himself that he was wrong, that Hope truly had existed, but the more thought he gave it, the more it was obvious that Carissa had played him for a fool, and like a fool, he had fallen right into her trap.

She and her father must have had a good laugh over him, the young, blind Highlander who was stupid enough to trust while in enemy hands. He had shared stories of his childhood with her, and in turn she had learned about his brothers, about his family, about his own hopes and dreams.

Whatever had made him confide in the slave?

She was a complete stranger to him, but she had also been the only one who had shown him any help or kindness. Being blind had been challenging in itself, but being wounded as well made it that much more difficult. She was a ray of hope in an otherwise hopeless situation.

Oddly, though, he felt safe with her, and that was what he didn't understand. How could he have so badly misjudged his own gut instinct? He had always prided himself on being a good judge of a person's nature. And though he had no visual to go by with the slave, it had been her caring way and her consistent encouragement that had his gut believing she was a good, honest person.

His musing was interrupted when he noticed Carissa reach for her cloak on the peg. He waited and watched as she turned and grabbed hold of the small cauldron.

"Don't be long," he ordered.

It surprised him that she didn't respond but simply walked out the door.

That the last couple of days had been a strain on them both was obvious. The truth had to be told, this matter settled. He needed to know for certain. He needed his pride to heal, and his heart.

She returned, and after shedding her cloak and setting the cauldron in the hearth, she sat on the chair to stare at the flames. He had expected her to retire to the table to chop or mix, or do whatever it was she did when preparing a meal.

"Say what you have to say to me and be done with it," she said solemnly.

"I want the truth," he said.

She laughed and shook her head. "You wouldn't believe me."

"The truth speaks louder than lies."

"Truly?" she asked.

He nodded. "If you speak the truth, I will hear it.".

She folded her hands across her chest and with a firm tilt of her chin she said, "Good, then I will tell you the truth."

He sat forward eager to listen.

"I am not what you think, and when I met you, I felt safe to be who I truly—"

"Stop," he shouted, annoyed, and rose to brace his hand on the mantel. "I hear no truth in your words."

She jumped up, and although her height by no means matched his, her annoyance did. "Then you are deaf."

"I hear well enough, and what I hear is you thinking you can make a fool of me yet again." He shook his head. "That will not happen."

"Of course not," she argued. "Once a fool always a fool."

"Now I hear the truth."

"You know nothing of the truth," she said, her voice growing loud. "You wouldn't know the truth if it stared you in the face."

"Now that I'm not blind, I can see your lies clearly."

"You saw better when you were blind," she said, giving a frustrated groan and turning away from him.

"How you must have laughed at me," he said with a mixture of anger and sorrow.

She swiveled around, her long blond hair

bouncing wildly to fall in riotous waves around her face. "Hope would never laugh at you."

"Stop!" he yelled again. "There is no Hope. There never has been."

She held her head high. "You're right; there's never been any hope."

"Finally, you speak the truth."

She turned away from him again; though this time she went to the table and began preparations for a stew.

"We're not finished discussing this," he said.

"I am."

"I want to know more," he insisted.

"There's no more to tell." She continued cutting wild onions and potatoes. "Besides, it changes nothing. My fate had already been sealed just by being Mordrac's daughter."

"This makes your fate all the more justifiable."

She laughed. "So you tell me that I am to die because I lied?"

He glared at her. "You've done much more."

"What have I done?" she demanded.

Her query set hard over him. What did she actually do? She had not accompanied her father into battle, and she had raised no sword against the Sinclares. Were her crimes, as she said, being the daughter of Mordrac and lying about Hope?

He didn't care for what such a conclusion meant. She couldn't very well be put to death for minor matters, and his brother Cavan would agree. She should be punished, though was it his pride that called for justice?

"We will let the Sinclare laird decide your fate," he said, knowing it was the only reasonable decision to make though he didn't feel like being reasonable.

"I saw only hate for me in your brother's eyes," she said.

"Perhaps, but Cavan will judge fairly. You have my word."

"Why should I trust you?" she asked.

"What choice do you have?"

She nodded slowly. "And if Cavan judges me innocent, I will be free to leave, free of the Sinclares?"

"Yes, you'll be free."

"Then I will go willingly with you," she said. "The snow has stopped over a full day now, and the skies are clearing. If this continues, we should be able to leave in a few days. So you had best rest."

He answered by going to the bed and stretching out. He had grieved once when he had learned of Hope's death, but he refused to grieve over a love that was never real. He much preferred anger. It churned in his gut, and he knew that, by the time it reached his heart, he would again hate Carissa as much as he had loved Hope.

When Carissa heard a light snore coming from the bed, she quietly slipped her cloak on and sneaked out the door. She made her way through the snow, the air feeling more chilled than it had that morning.

Dykar had made his arrival known to her yesterday when she had gone outside to retrieve ice from the water barrel. She had heard him approach, though most people probably would not have detected his light step. She, however, could always tell when he was about. It was almost as if she sensed him, and she had turned with a flourish to greet him.

He had come to rescue her and grown annoyed and frustrated when she refused to leave until Ronan was well. He had made it clear he believed the Highlander didn't need her concern or care. He certainly wouldn't give it back to her.

Dykar was not going to be happy when he learned of the recent turn of events, but knowing him as well as she did, she assumed he would understand.

It wasn't long before she came upon a makeshift lean-to with a campfire roaring in front of it. She signaled to the two men to remain where they sat, and when she was close, she hunched down and warmed her outstretched hands by the fire.

"Are you ready to leave?"

Carissa smiled at Dykar. "Ever so patient."

"You know me well," he said, and stood.

He was an inch or so taller than Ronan, with long auburn hair and dark eyes that almost matched his hair. He was broad and heavy with muscles, and his stern expression made him appear more formidable, when actually he truly was a thoughtful and good-natured man.

Though the man who remained seated was more strikingly handsome than most men, Septimus was an enigma to Carissa. He appeared too handsome, too knowledgeable, and too aristocratic to have joined the mercenaries.

But he had, and she still wondered why.

"You are like a brother," she said, staring up at Dykar. "And a sister would know her brother."

"And a brother knows his sister just as well," he said, and rubbed his chin before letting his frustration lose. "Damn it, Rissa, you're not leaving with us, are you?"

That brought Septimus to his feet. "That's not a wise idea."

"Let me explain," she said, standing though feeling small in front of the two men. Strange that she didn't feel that way with Ronan, though he was similar in size.

"Will it matter?" Dykar asked, annoyed.

"I think it will," she said, and continued, "Ronan has learned the truth about Hope."

Both men shook their heads.

Dykar turned to Septimus. "We need to get her out of here."

"I think not," she said sternly. "I have a chance to clear myself and be free of the Sinclares."

Both men looked at her with raised brows.

She recounted her discussion with Ronan.

"What if Cavan decides to imprison you?" Dykar asked.

"I have done nothing to justify imprisonment other than being Mordrac's daughter."

"Some would believe that crime enough," Septimus suggested.

"A chance I must take to be free."

"I don't like this," Dykar said.

"I didn't expect you would, though I knew you would understand it."

Dykar nodded. "I know how badly you yearn to be free."

"Then you know I must try."

"We will keep close eyes on you," Dykar said like a stern parent. "If things don't go as you hoped—"

"I'm not counting on hope," she said sadly. "I'm counting on Cavan's seeing the truth of the situation, being fair, and releasing me."

"But will he see it that way?" Septimus asked.

"There's only one way to find out," she said. "And now you both must go. The air has chilled since morning. If you leave now, you could possibly reach the village Black just after nightfall and have warm shelter and hot food."

While Septimus started extinguishing the campfire, Dykar took her arm and walked a distance away with her.

"You take a dangerous chance entering enemy territory," Dykar said. "It could be a trap."

"A chance I'm willing to take. Just think how wonderful it would be to not have to look over my shoulder to see if the Sinclares chase me."

"They aren't the only ones who cry for your blood."

"But if the Sinclares free me, the others will surely think it's not worth coming after me."

"As you say, it's a chance you must take. Though I don't favor it, I do understand," Dykar said, taking her hand. "You helped me to be free, and I would never want to live any other way. Besides, there's no stopping you, but you will at least listen to some reason."

"I'm all ears."

"Hagen stays for a time at a croft on Sinclare land. He fancies Addie, the late laird's widow."

"Does she fancy him?" Carissa asked with a smile.

"She seems to, though I think them both foolish and too old for such nonsense. Her sons would never allow such a match." Dykar shook his head. "Enough of that; if things should not go as you hoped, then you must alert Hagen so that we can get you out of there before it's too late. We have a large contingent of warriors, but not enough to combat the Sinclare clan and the friendly clans they would surely call upon for help."

"I know," she said with a nod. "I will keep in touch with Hagen and let you know of an escape plan I will ready in case things go wrong."

She shivered.

"You're cold. You must go back to the cottage."

"I'm more worn-out than anything. A good night's sleep should see me fit," she said, and gave him a hug, then turned to Septimus. "Take care of him for me."

"I always do," he said. "And you take care of yourself."

"I always have, and I always will," she said, and after a quick kiss on Dykar's cheek, she took her leave.

She was gone longer than she intended and prayed that Ronan had remained asleep. She quietly opened the door and cringed when it creaked. She peeked in before entering and when she heard him snoring louder than before, she sighed softly with relief.

She shivered as she hung her cloak on the peg and went to sit by the hearth to get warm. She took off her wet boots and realized her stockings were wet, so she stripped them off and placed them near the fire to dry.

She held out her feet to the fire to get warm, but she shivered again and decided to tuck them beneath her instead. A double yawn attacked her. She felt sluggish and so tired, not only in body but of mind. She told herself to be angry with him. How could he so easily disregard his love for Hope? How could he think all that she had said to him was nothing but lies? How could he not have faith in their love?

The answer was relatively simple though she didn't care to think of it. Ronan's hatred for Carissa ran deeper than his love for Hope. Otherwise, he just might be able to see the truth.

She glanced over at him, sleeping soundly and safely. It was strange that he didn't realize that there was a part of him that trusted Carissa, or else he wouldn't have been able to sleep so peacefully in her presence just as she did in his.

She believed that somewhere deep inside of him, his love for Hope survived. Given time, would he realize it, or was she once again clinging to an impossible hope?

She silently chastised herself for her foolishness and settled her attention on the flames. The stew would be finished soon, Ronan would wake, and they would eat supper. She should rest instead of dwelling on her troubles.

She rubbed at the ache in her head and thought her brow too warm, but then she sat close to the flames. What did she expect?

She was soon asleep.

Chapter 17

Ronan woke with a slow stretch and was relieved that no pain throbbed in his head. He assumed that the stitches would be removed soon enough. The sleep had served him well, and he was starving. And recalling his conversation with Carissa, there now was a good chance they'd be leaving the cottage soon. He'd finally be going home, and this matter would be brought to justice.

He didn't need to look far to find her. She was asleep in the rocking chair, her head lolled to the side, her feet tucked under her and her hands limp in her lap. Her cheeks were flushed, and she appeared fast asleep.

He stared at her, unable to stop himself from wondering. Could Hope possibly reside within her? Was there a chance that the woman he loved actually lived? The idea sent a spark of yearning shooting through him. Then, as if emerging from a dream, he realized the foolishness of his thought. Carissa was who she was. There never had been a Hope, there never would be.

He sat up, swinging his long legs off the bed and

accidentally hit the rung of her chair, sending it rocking.

She jumped, startled, and glared at him, her eyes like wide, round saucers. "Are you all right?"

"Better than I was," he admitted, "and hungry."

She rubbed the back of her neck as she slowly stood and found her footing. "The stew should be ready."

Ronan watched her as she moved across the room, her hand reaching out as if she required support. Then she stopped, turned to face him, and he watched as all color drained from her face.

Her hand went out to him, and she barely got his name out before her body slowly slumped.

He shot off the bed and caught her in his arms before she hit the floor. He lifted her. She weighed hardly anything, less than a sack of grain. He sat on the edge of the bed cradling her. Her face was as white as the freshly fallen snow, and he could feel the heat drifting off her body. He hesitated to touch her brow, fearful of what he would find.

Sure enough, her body was raging with fever.

She struggled to say his name. "Ronan."

"You're burning with fever," he said, unable to ignore how very much she sounded like Hope, but he reminded himself yet again that there was no Hope.

"You must"—she paused for a breath—"cool me down"—Another pause.

"How?" he asked anxiously.

"The snow."

"Are you crazy?"

"You must," she said, her voice growing weaker. "Or would you prefer I die?"

"No," he said stubbornly. He would not allow that to happen and realized he didn't want her to die. The thought startled him, and he grumbled.

"Just get me outside, I'll do—"

"Quiet," he said, annoyed that she assumed he wouldn't take care of her. She had rescued him, which made him beholden to her. Even if he weren't, he couldn't just sit by and not help her.

He stood and again was amazed by how small and vulnerable she felt in his arms, how he felt the overwhelming need to protect her. He almost laughed. Carissa needing protection? That made no sense. But then nothing of late made sense to him. All that he had believed had disappeared in an instant, and he wasn't sure now what to believe or whom to trust.

She snuggled her face against his chest, and, feeling as if he had been branded by a hot iron, he feared her fever had worsened in the brief time since they had been talking.

He didn't bother to retrieve his cloak, but simply yanked opened the door, walked out, and deposited her in a bank of snow that almost covered her.

She shivered. "My face."

He scooped up a handful and gently rubbed the icy snow over her feverish brow and cheeks. He grew concerned when her lips began to tremble.

"Enough," he said, and was ready to scoop her up.

"Not yet," she argued.

He saw that she dug her hands and her bare feet into the snow. As helpless as she was, she still managed to attempt to do for herself. She was stubborn, or was she courageous? One described Carissa, the other Hope, but they were one woman.

"No more," she said shivering.

He lifted her up and held her close as he hurried into the cottage and shoved the door shut with his foot. It was only then he realized that his own feet were bare and damn cold.

He ignored the icy sting and rushed her to the bed. He didn't need to be told to undress her, but she continued instructing him.

"Take my clothes off."

"This one time I will oblige you."

A smile tugged at the corners of her mouth. "I always loved your humorous nature."

Her remark surprised him, and he warned himself to ignore it. It meant nothing; after all, her ruse had merely been a game. He concentrated on getting her out of her clothes, which didn't take long.

She shivered the whole time he undressed her, her flesh cool in spots and warm in others. If he had been disrobing her for a far different reason, he would have taken his time and been more attentive to every inch of her tempting body. Damn she was tempting. And damn him for even thinking it.

He finished quickly and lifted her in one swoop, gently depositing her on the bed and tucking the blankets around her.

"What now?" he asked.

"Warm your feet before *you* come down with a fever."

He couldn't believe she had noticed that he was barefoot or that she was concerned for his welfare when she was the one ill.

"I'll see to it, but first what else can I do for you?"

"I need you to prepare a special brew"— Her eyes began to close, and she shook her head to keep alert. "I'll explain how to do it, and if I grow hot again, rub my face and neck with snow."

"You sound as if you are leaving instructions for me while you go somewhere," he said with concern.

"I will sleep, and you may not be able to wake me."

He could see that her eyes had already grown heavy, and no doubt she would be asleep soon. He had to know all he could before she slumbered.

"What do I do?"

"What I told you."

He was astonished how hard she fought to remain awake even though her body seemed of a different mind.

Through pauses and shakes of her head, she instructed him how to prepare the brew and to make certain he gave it to her, even if he just dribbled some in her mouth.

"I'll take care of you," he assured her.

"Care for Hope," she whispered, her eyes closing. "You love her."

Ronan sat on the edge of the bed, in no hurry

to leave her. He simply stared at her. Was there even the remote possibility that she could possess a thoughtful nature like Hope's rather than a hellion nature like Carissa's?

He shook his head as he stood and walked over to the table to mix the brew and set it to simmer as she had instructed. It wasn't until he sat in the rocker warming his icy feet that he allowed his thoughts to return to Hope.

He grumbled, "There is no Hope."

He recalled what his mother had told him when he was young and feeling hopeless over what now he would consider a trivial matter, but to a young lad had been a life-or-death situation.

His mother had told him that hope resided in the heart, and you only needed to trust and believe for its magic to work.

Did he dare trust and believe?

He shook his head. Carissa was a mean-spirited woman. How could he ever trust or believe she was anything other than what she was? But if he was to find out the truth, at least a truth that fully satisfied him about Hope, wouldn't he have to do just that? Trust and believe?

He certainly would have the chance to discover more by taking Carissa home with him. But she would only remain there until Cavan passed judgment on her. Cavan wasn't one to take long in making a decision, especially an important one. Would that give Ronan sufficient time?

He turned to look at Carissa. Her cheeks weren't burning red any longer, though she remained pale. And he couldn't understand how suddenly she appeared so vulnerable to him. He had never imagined Carissa weak. She was the epitome of strength, mean-spirited as can be, but nonetheless she was brave. She seemed to let nothing stand in her way.

Yet suddenly she needed protecting, much as he had when Hope had come into his life. And oddly enough, he felt the need to protect her. Was it simply inherent in a man to want to protect a woman? Or did he feel the need to keep her safe for a far different reason?

He grew tired of all the conjecture, all the questions, all the doubts.

He stood and stirred the simmering brew. He spotted the cauldron of stew and moved it off the flames. It smelled delicious, and no doubt would taste the same. Carissa had a remarkable way with food, and there hadn't been anything that she had cooked that he hadn't enjoyed.

He went to the table to grab a plate when he noticed that a puddle of water sat beneath Carissa's cloak. He walked over and was surprised to find the hem, not damp, but wet to his touch.

It took him a moment to realize that she had gone out while he had been sleeping. And it wasn't a brief excursion; the puddle was evidence of that, as was the fact that her cloak had yet to dry.

Where had she gone?

Why had she been gone so long?

He walked back to the bed and stared down at her.

"What are you hiding from me?" he asked.

She moaned and twisted fitfully, as if uncomfortable with his query.

He hunched down beside the bed. "Who are you truly?"

She moaned softly, and what spilled in a whisper from her lips shocked him.

"Ronan, help me."

He almost lost his footing and fell backward. That was Hope's voice and it stung at his heart.

"Please, don't leave me."

Her hands had reached out from beneath the blanket as if searching for his, and he didn't hesitate, he grabbed hold of them.

"Stay," she pleaded.

"I'm not going anywhere," he reassured her, though he wasn't sure that she could hear him. Nonetheless, he had to tell her just in case she could hear him.

She twisted fitfully once again in her sleep, then suddenly sprang up in bed and grabbed tightly to Ronan's arm.

"Don't let him kill him. Please, he is so tiny, don't let him kill him."

"I won't."

"Promise me," she pleaded frantically. "Protect him. Promise me."

"I give you my word. No harm will come to him."

Her head fell to his shoulder and rested in the crook of his neck. He realized that her fever had spiked. He tried to lay her back in the bed, but she refused to relinquish her hold on him, so he sat there holding and reassuring her.

When he was finally able to tuck her comfortably in bed, he saw that her cheeks once again flamed red. He pulled on his boots and grabbed the empty bucket as he passed the table and headed outside.

He scooped up snow and noticed that gray clouds had grown heavy overhead. He dreaded more snow, especially now, with Carissa needing care. If the weather remained clear, he could at least get her to Bethane.

He hurried inside and sat on the bed beside her. He rubbed small handfuls of snow across her brow and over her cheeks. He did the same to her neck until he was satisfied that she had sufficiently cooled down, He even rubbed a little snow along her hot arms.

The blankets remained off her until he noticed her shiver; only then did he cover her with the lightest blanket. Satisfied she rested comfortably; he took the bucket outside, added more snow to it, and left it just outside the door for future use.

Before heading back inside, he took a moment to survey the area. He couldn't help but wonder if they weren't alone. Had Carissa gone to speak with someone? And if so, who?

He went inside and finally helped himself to a bowl of stew and a thick slice of bread. He sat in the rocker so that he could keep an eye on Carissa while he ate.

As he enjoyed the flavorful stew, he recalled

Carissa's plea about protecting a tiny . . . who or what?

He wondered if it had been the fever that made her speak nonsense, or had she recalled a painful memory. Whom had she been trying to protect?

There were far too many unanswered questions concerning Carissa as far as he was concerned. It seemed the more he discovered about her, the more there was to discover.

In all the time he had searched for Carissa, he had only wanted one thing . . . revenge. He wanted to make her pay and dearly for the suffering she had put him through. Now he wondered if she was truly responsible for his suffering?

He looked over at her in the bed. She slept peacefully and he couldn't help but wonder yet again who she truly was.

Chapter 18

Ronan tended Carissa all through the night, her fever rising and falling in intervals. She never truly woke though she stirred and spoke incoherently. When the sun dawned and her fever still remained strong, he grew more concerned.

Fearing he wasn't doing enough for her, he decided the best thing for him to do was get her to Bethane. If he left early and kept a good pace, they would reach the village Black by nightfall.

"Ronan?"

He hurried to her side, her voice full of fear.

"I'm here," he said, sitting beside her and taking her hand, which was much too hot.

"How long have I slept?"

"It's almost dawn."

She shook her head. "The fever remains."

"I've done all I can," he said, feeling helpless.

"Some fevers simply won't let go," she said, as if resigned to her fate.

However, he thought differently. "I'm taking you to Bethane."

She sighed as she shook her head. "I'll never make it."

"I'll fashion a sleigh of wood to pull you along on. If we leave shortly after dawn, I can have you there before nightfall."

She shook her head.

He leaned close and whispered, "Ye of little faith."

She smiled. "I always had faith in you."

Her response shook him to his soul. How could she have faith in a man who had wanted her dead? More and more he wondered who this woman was. "Good, then hold on to it. We leave here today."

He fed her a few tablespoons of the concocted brew and set to work. He made certain not to feed the fire in the hearth, wanting it cold before they took their leave. With the single-room cottage soon to lose heat, he dressed Carissa in her linen shift, wool skirt, and blouse, left her stockings off until later, and tucked blankets around her.

It took more time than he liked to form a sleigh from branches and pine, but when he finished, he was pleased with the sturdy piece. He packed the wooden bucket with a few food items and set it aside.

He then went to collect Carissa. He threw the blanket off her and gently took hold of her foot, noticing how small it was. He had always thought of Carissa as a formidable woman, and he supposed one would then believe her tall, but not so. Carissa was petite, much like Hope.

He shook his head. This was no time to let his mind wander. He grabbed hold of her stockings, ready to slip them on to keep her warm during the journey, but her feet were already warm.

"No," she protested, waking from a light slumber. "I'm too hot. No more clothes."

"It's cold out."

"The blankets and my cloak will do."

He acquiesced to her concern and wrapped her cloak around her after he sat her up in bed, and as he lifted her, she placed a hot hand to his cool cheek. It felt as if she branded him, but then maybe she already had.

"Thank you."

"It's the right thing to do," he grumbled, annoyed that once again he heard Hope in her voice.

"No," she said softly, "it's love."

He sat her in the rocking chair and shoved the narrow bed away from the hearth against the wall. Though he would douse the embers left in the hearth, he wanted to make certain there was no chance of a single one remaining and jumping to ignite the bed.

Almost like embers of their love jumping forth and igniting his heart.

Was he dousing the embers of love in his heart? He grumbled beneath his breath at the crazy thought. He had to stop this. There was no love, never had been.

He rushed around like a madman, wanting to be on their way. And in no time they were. He took the stuffed bedding and placed it on the sleigh. He cocooned Carissa not only in her cloak, but two blankets; the third he placed over her, tucking it around her after he had placed her on the sleigh. He pulled her hood up, making sure to tuck her hair away from her face.

When he was finally done, he hunched down beside her, surprised to see that she had fallen asleep. He felt her brow, and it was hot, though not raging. But if the fever followed the course it had been on, it would spiral soon enough.

He stood, took hold of the rope of knotted pine that served as the reins, dropping it around his chest and stepped forward, pulling the sleigh behind him.

"I won't tell you."

"Where is he?"

"Ask me all you want, Father, but I will not tell you."

"You dare defy me?"

"I love him, and I will not let you kill him."

"What did I tell you about love?"

"I don't believe you."

His large hand stung and her head snapped back from the blow.

Her knees trembled, but she stood defiant. "I won't tell you."

She winced, pain shooting up her arm from his sudden grip.

"You will tell me or suffer the consequences."

"I will die before I tell you. I love him, and I will protect him."

She cringed as he crushed her slim arm with his powerful hand.

"You will learn the foolishness of love."

Her head shot back from another stinging blow, then she felt the heat. She screeched as the flames greedily licked her flesh. "I love him. I love him. I love him."

"Do something," Ronan said frantically. "She's in pain."

"I am doing all I can," Bethane assured him. "Dreams and memories cause her pain. Also that grip you have on her arm may be too tight."

Ronan immediately let go, though he remained by Carissa's side on the bed. "She appears to have grown worse since we arrived yesterday evening."

"Some fevers like to trick, sinking low before spiraling out of control, while some remain constant, locking onto a person and draining her of all strength."

"Will she survive?" he asked curtly, though he didn't mean to, but he was worried.

Bethane placed a comforting hand on his shoulder. "Do you want her to?"

"Yes," he answered without hesitation. "I want her to live."

"Why?" she asked walking around the bed to stand opposite him.

"That's a foolish question," he snapped.

"No, a logical one. When you left here almost two months ago, you wanted Carissa dead. What has changed?"

He looked down at Carissa in a fitful toss, her cheeks burning red. "Everything."

Bethane nodded. "You should get some rest. You have barely slept since you arrived."

"She may not recall us leaving the cottage and will look for me when she wakes."

"She will feel safe once she realizes where she is," Bethane assured him.

He was going to continue arguing but thought better of it. He already sounded foolish to his own ears. What must Bethane think of him? But then she had asked him what had changed.

Everything.

His answer reverberated in his head, and he stood.

"There's a bed in my cottage. Go rest."

He hesitated.

"If she asks for you, I will come get you."

He gave a sharp nod and left the cottage, walking the few steps from the door to Bethane's place, and dropped on the bed, exhausted. Only a short time ago he'd wanted to strangle Carissa with his bare hands and now . . . he wasn't even sure who she was.

He sighed with exasperation and slammed his eyes shut as if he could force sleep to claim him. He didn't want to think, but he had no choice. Thoughts rushed at him, and no amount of dodging prevented them from hitting.

Could he have been the one Carissa had saved from her father?

Had she risked her life for him?

He fell asleep with no answer forthcoming.

Carissa was hot, and something weighted her down. She struggled to get free, pushing past the darkness to a spot where she saw a shred of light.

"Hope."

Was that Ronan calling out to her? She tried to answer, but she couldn't find her voice. She continued to struggle. She had to get this weight off her, had to get out of this heat and out of the darkness.

"Hope."

She stopped suddenly and listened.

"Hope."

She didn't move. It wasn't Ronan calling out to her. It was her father, and he wasn't calling out her name.

He laughed then, that evil laugh that always shivered her to her soul.

"There is no hope."

He was wrong. There was hope. She was Hope. He couldn't take that from her.

"There has never been hope."

"No!" The scream ripped past her dry throat and shot out of her mouth.

"Hope doesn't exist."

She fought the darkness, the weight, and her father's cruel words.

He was wrong. Hope existed and love would prove it.

"Ronan," she screamed.

* * *

Ronan battled the darkness. He had to find his way out, but first he had to find her. He had to save her. He tore through the dark with his hands, calling out to her. He thought he heard her and stilled, but there was no sound, nothing. He continued clawing the dark.

"Ronan."

He heard his name clearly.

"I'm here."

"You promised."

"I'm here. I'm here." He clawed viciously at the dark, but seemed to get nowhere.

"Too late."

"Hope."

He sprang up in bed.

"Ronan!"

He was off the bed and out the door before she called out again. He burst into the cottage and saw Bethane struggling to hold Carissa down.

"I'm here," he shouted, and she quieted instantly.

Bethane stepped away when he reached the bed. He sat beside Carissa and took hold of her one hand and brought it to his lips. Her skin was warm, and he kissed her palm, then placed it against his cool cheek.

"I'm here," he repeated.

She sighed, her sleep finally peaceful. "Don't leave me."

"Never," he said.

When after a few minutes she said no more, he looked to Bethane. She was closing the door he had left open when he rushed in.

"She'll be all right?" he asked anxiously.

"If the fever continues to go down, she'll be fine."

"What if it climbs again?"

Bethane did not hide her concern. "She's weak from fighting the fever. If the fever jumps again, I don't know if she'll survive."

"She's a fighter."

"It would seem so," Bethane agreed.

"Is there anything else we can do?"

"I would say that you are already doing it," she said with a smile and a nod.

He realized how odd it must seem, him sitting there holding his enemy's hand to his cheek. He barely understood it himself. He had gone from having a deep-rooted hatred for Carissa to possibly loving her.

The incredible thought had him placing her hand on her chest and him getting up and walking away from her.

"You're confused," Bethane said.

"I—I don't know what happened," he said, bewildered, and glanced over at Carissa. "I don't know who she is." He ran a rough hand over his face and shook his head. "I don't even know who I am anymore."

Chapter 19

Carissa felt a weight on her as she woke. She struggled to open her eyes as if emerging from a fitful sleep that had claimed her much too long. She tried to move her arms, but was only able to get one free, and as her surroundings finally came into focus, she was stunned to see why.

Her arm was stuck under Ronan's head as it lay on her stomach, his hands at her waist. With a tentative stretch of her free hand, she reached out and gently laid her hand on his head.

She smiled at the feel of his soft dark hair, and as she stirred the strands, the scent of fresh pine drifted off to tickle her nostrils. She carefully cleared his face of loose strands so that she could look upon him.

To her he was the handsomest man alive; though his features were more rugged than sculpted, there was something about him that caught the eye and made the heart jump. She felt that she had been lucky to get to know him first as a man, then as a warrior, for she found the man more courageous and kind than any warrior could be.

She never regretted pretending to be a slave when she had tended him, for if she hadn't, she would have never gotten to know him. And he would have never gotten to know her.

She missed the time she spent with him as Hope. It hadn't taken long for them to trust each other or to fall in love. It was as if they were meant to be, as if they had known each other long before meeting.

There was a comfort with Ronan she had never known and a safety she had always longed for but had never found. He was to Hope a hero, a man who would never fail her.

She traced a finger along and around one of his eyes, recalling how swollen both had been when she first had seen him. Her father had wanted to use him as a pawn against his brother, but she had somehow managed to convince him that it would be far better to have Ronan's vision cleared so that both brothers could see each other during torture.

Her father thought that a splendid idea and ordered her to see to his care. That had been the only reason she had been permitted so much time with the prisoner. She had hoped to heal him, then somehow see him freed. She had never intended to fall in love with him.

But she had . . . and it had changed everything.

Ronan stirred, and she pulled her hand away, not wanting to be caught touching him. He moved slowly at first, then, as if realizing where he was, his head shot up and his wide eyes went straight to hers.

"Good morning," she said with a croak to her dry throat.

He sat up, and the weight lifted off her, though to her way of thinking she had lost a shield of protection.

His hand went to rest at her brow, then on her cheek and with a smile he proclaimed, "The fever is gone."

"Thanks to you."

He shook his head. "No, thanks to Bethane."

"That's right. We're not in the cottage anymore," she said with a sadness that overwhelmed her. She would no longer be alone with him, no longer share a bed.

Silence settled over them as if neither knew what to say. Bethane broke the awkward moment when she entered the room.

Ronan hastily stood and stepped away from Carissa as if embarrassed that he had been caught in such an intimate pose with her.

Carissa felt rejected, and her sharp tongue took over. "No need for you to care for me anymore. Bethane will tend me."

"Fine," Ronan snapped, annoyed, and stormed out the door.

Bethane smiled. "He cared for and worried over you."

Carissa struggled to sit up. "He did?"

Bethane nodded, helping her up. "And you cried out for him."

"I did?"

"Yes, and he was there for you, refusing to leave your side. And I cannot believe that he walked all day pulling you on that makeshift sleigh to get you here."

"I remember him putting me on the sleigh, but I recall nothing after that," she admitted, to her chagrin.

Bethane sat on the bed beside her and rested a comforting hand on her arm. "He left here wanting you dead and returned wanting you to live."

"How do you know that?" she asked anxiously.

"I asked him, and he told me that he wanted you to live. What happened while you both were gone?"

Carissa thought a moment, then whispered, "Everything."

It wasn't until that evening that Ronan returned to Carissa and only out of necessity. Bethane was called to a cottage to deliver a babe and she asked him to see that Carissa got supper.

She was sitting up in bed when he walked in with a covered tray.

"I've brought you supper," he said a bit abruptly.

"Thank you, I'm starving." She pushed the blankets off and swung her legs off the bed.

"What are you doing?" he scolded, placing the tray on the table and hurrying over to her.

"I want to eat at the table. I'm tired of being in bed."

"You're not strong enough yet."

"I am so," she said, and stubbornly stood. Her legs trembled as she took a step, her eyes turned wide, and her face turned pale as she began to collapse.

Ronan had her in his arms in no time, and she had her arms around his neck just as quickly. Their faces were so close they almost touched and Ronan instinctively rested his cheek on hers.

Her flesh was cool and soft, and he shut his eyes and thought how it felt with Hope. And for a moment he allowed himself to believe that he held the woman he loved.

Finally, he moved his head away, but as he did, his lips lightly brushed over hers. The intimate contact shocked them both, and they turned their faces away.

He returned her to bed.

"I prefer to sit—"

"You stay in the bed until you gain back your strength," he finished.

She opened her mouth to disagree.

"Don't bother to argue," he informed her, tucking the blanket around her. "You'll stay put for at least tonight."

He put the wood tray on her lap and slipped off the cloth that covered it and placed it across her chest.

She smiled and happily dug into the soup, which was thick with meat and vegetables.

He pulled a chair close to the bed and straddled it, resting his arms along the top. He wanted to talk with her, but didn't wish to interrupt the meal she was obviously enjoying. He intended to wait until she finished, but she had a different idea.

"Ask me what you want?" she said between spoonfuls.

"What defense do you propose to present to my brother?"

"The truth."

"Define the truth."

"I harmed no one," she said.

"That could be debated."

"But it cannot be denied, and as you told me, your brother is a fair man."

"You expect to be freed?" he asked.

"I expect the truth to set me free."

He stood, pushing the chair aside. "Then speak the truth about Hope."

"She once lived, but does no more. That is all there is to Hope."

"Why did you conceive her?"

"The same reason why I let her go . . . necessity," she said. "Just as you should have let her go."

She held out the tray to him, the soup only half-finished.

"You should eat more," he said.

"I'm no longer hungry."

He took the tray and set it on the table.

"Do you think we could ever be friends?"

Her question shocked him as did his answer. "You are an enemy of the Sinclares."

She nodded. "I understand."

Odd, since he understood nothing. He was more

confused than ever, and she had been the one to confuse him.

She slipped down under the covers. "I'm tired. I wish to sleep."

"I'll stay until you fall asleep," he offered, though the truth was he didn't want to leave her.

Carissa's curt tongue surfaced. "I prefer to be alone."

He walked over to her. "Alone can be a lonely place."

"It is the only safe place when there is no one to trust," she said, and turned her back to him as she slipped farther beneath the blanket.

Ronan was glad for Bethane's company several hours later. He had been alone with his thoughts much too long, and nothing, absolutely nothing, made sense to him.

"Everyone rests peacefully," Bethane said upon entering the cottage.

Not quite everyone, he thought, but said nothing.

"Now it is my turn," she said.

He rose from the rocker, offering it to her.

"Stay," she said, "at least until I prepare a hot cider for myself. Would you like one?"

He nodded, thought to return to the rocker, but didn't, though it caught his attention. It was similar to the rocking chair in the cottage, almost identical. He turned to glance at Bethane.

"You have a question?" she asked, handing

him a tankard before she took hers and sat in the rocker.

He had a thought, but dare he express it?

"So is it my eyesight or wisdom?" she asked. "I've been waiting for you to let me know."

He stared at her for a moment, then he recalled their talk. Before he went chasing after Carissa, he had asked Bethane why she helped them both.

"It isn't your eyesight," he said, "though I may question it being wisdom."

"Wisdom is not easy to accept simply because it reveals the truth. Is the truth too difficult for you to accept?"

He shook his head. "When I find out the truth, I'll let you know."

"Don't forget to open your heart along with your eyes," she warned. "Now, I must get some sleep. I'm exhausted. Would you mind sleeping in the healing cottage? Carissa needs tending until her strength returns."

Ronan downed the last of the cider and placed the tankard on the table as he passed it on the way to the door. He turned around. "There is no need to offer Carissa sanctuary, she is willingly returning home with me."

"I thought as much."

Puzzled, he asked, "Why?"

"Carissa is far too skilled ever to be captured. If she wanted to be free of you, she would be."

Chapter 20

Bethane's words haunted Ronan for the next couple of days. And was one of the reasons he didn't mind remaining at the village Black for a while. It gave him more time to do as Bethane suggested and open his eyes, though his heart was a different matter. However, he did wish to see Carissa as clearly as possible.

Another reason they would not take their leave was that he wanted Carissa fully healed and feeling strong once again before they embarked on the journey to his home.

In the meantime, with Carissa improving, there was no reason for her to remain in the healing cottage, and Bethane suggested she occupy her granddaughter Zia's cottage for the duration. And Ronan could make use of the small nook with a single bed that was part of the sleeping quarters but separated by a curtain.

Neither objected, and he wondered if she felt as he did. He could find any number of reasons to remain near her, but the simple truth was he did not want to be separated from her just yet.

Everything had changed, and he had to define that change if he was ever going to find peace when it came to Hope.

He walked toward the cottage, snow crunching beneath his boots, an icy wind stinging his face and his arms wrapped around a covered basket. He struggled to open the door when he reached it and finally managed to get it open, though the wind whipped it out of his hand.

He was giving it a forceful shove closed with his shoulder when Carissa stepped forward to help him. He shook his head. "It's too cold near the door."

She remained where she was in front of the hearth.

"What do you have in the basket?" she asked.

"All of what you need to make apple buns." He smiled and yanked the cloth off the top.

Her joyous smile stunned him. She looked as happy as a young lass who had just received the most wonderful gift. However, he was more stunned when she rushed around the table, threw her arms around him, and kissed his cheek.

His arm instinctively circled her waist, and he held her against him for a moment until they realized the awkwardness of the situation. But instead of pulling away, he moved his mouth to hers.

He needed to taste her, fully taste her, and see for himself if there was any remnant of Hope. And she didn't deny him. She closed her eyes and waited.

He did the same, wanting no distractions just the taste of her. When he pressed his lips to hers it was as familiar as returning home. The thought startled him, and he abruptly stepped away from her.

She stumbled back and quickly braced her hand against the table, while her other hand grabbed at her stomach.

"Are you all right?" Ronan asked.

"I don't know," she answered.

The woman who answered him was far from the brashly confident Carissa. Her voice trembled with an uncertainty that left her vulnerable. There wasn't a time he could recall when Carissa was ever defenseless. If she had no weapon, her tongue served as a good replacement. Even when he had surprised her at the cottage, she didn't appear helpless. She had challenged him at every turn. And that's what made it so difficult to believe that a kindhearted soul could actually reside in Carissa.

It could all be a ruse for her to obtain her freedom.

She seemed to gain control and immediately got busy emptying the basket and preparing to bake. Like him, he assumed she didn't want to discuss the kiss that had tasted all too familiar.

"The apple buns are my favorite," he said, sitting at the table, hoping to dig through the lies to discover the truth.

"Mine too."

He suddenly realized that her smile was different. It was bright as if she was truly happy, rather than her usual wicked grin. Or was it because he was seeing her with open eyes?

He watched her hands move skillfully and expertly, and it made him wonder how she had learned to cook so well. It was only one of many questions he intended to ask of her.

"How did you acquire your cooking skills?"

She hesitated to answer.

"I would truly like to know," he said with a smile, reaching across the table to grab a piece of dried apple.

She stared at him for a moment, and he felt his heart catch; he couldn't believe that he saw deep sorrow in her eyes. He didn't believe Carissa would ever feel the slightest sorrow. She had no heart, but Hope did.

He attempted to encourage an answer out of her. "I'm grateful to whoever taught you, for I've enjoyed every meal you have cooked."

Her smile brightened along with her eyes. "Ula taught me."

"Is Ula your mother?"

"No, my mother died when I was young. Ula was a slave."

"*Was* a slave?"

Carissa nodded. "She escaped."

"How?" he asked, curious, since Mordrac's stronghold wasn't a place from which to escape easily.

She shrugged. "I don't know."

"Was Ula an old woman?"

"She spoke of her grandchildren to me. She loved them dearly and missed them terribly."

"It's amazing that an old woman could do

what few if any have done. Escape your father's stronghold."

"Your brother did it," she reminded.

"And I've often wondered how."

"He is a resourceful and determined man."

"Was Ula the same?" he asked.

She stopped what she was doing and stared at him. "I think what made it easy for both Ula and Cavan to escape was love."

"Love?" he repeated, not certain he heard her right.

"Yes, love," she confirmed. "Ula's and Cavan's love for their families gave them the courage they needed to escape. It was the driving force that encouraged them never to give up."

And it was what propelled him to find Hope.

"I suppose love is more powerful than most imagine," he said. "Love endures where nothing else can."

"My father would have disagreed. He believed hate endured, and love never lasted."

"Then he never knew love."

"I often wondered the same myself," she said. "He hated so much that he never allowed room in his heart for anything else."

Not even the love of a young daughter.

The thought shocked but also tormented him. How could a bonny lass be raised on hatred rather than love?

She placed the buns in the hearth to bake and turned to Ronan with a smile. "I think I should make us a flavorful stew for supper."

"I'd like that," he said, and stood. "Tell me what you need, and I'll get it from Bethane."

"We should ask Bethane to join us," Carissa suggested. "She has been good to us."

While Ronan would have preferred to be alone with Carissa, he knew she was right. Bethane had been very good to them. She had given them time together, to discover and learn more than he ever imagined.

"I'll invite her," he said.

"Good," she said with an excited clasp of her hands. "I will bake fresh bread to go with the stew."

He walked over to her and took her hand. "Tell me what you need."

She stared at him for a moment, and he could see that she struggled to reply. And he knew that she wasn't thinking of her need in terms of baking, and neither was he.

The kiss was unexpected though desired by both. This time it lingered, as if sampling and finally realizing the taste was exactly what both favored, they drank deeply.

Their lips were the only part of them that touched as though if they went any further, neither of them could prevent what would happen.

It was a kiss that stirred their souls, and when it ended, their brows rested against each other's and both took deep breaths, though neither spoke.

When they finally broke apart, Ronan asked, "What do you need?"

Carissa answered before she thought, "You."

* * *

Carissa, her legs unsteady, plopped down on the chair at the table after the door closed behind Ronan. He hadn't replied to her response. He had simply walked out the door.

Something had changed between them, or had it changed in her? Had the fever robbed Carissa of her last bit of strength or had it helped Hope emerge? She didn't know, although she knew that she didn't want to live as Carissa any longer.

It wasn't who she was, and she didn't want to pretend anymore. She was so very tired of being who she wasn't. And with a taste of what she could have, it made her all the more eager to want it.

Fool. It can never be.

Not true, she could hope. Hadn't he kissed her? And there was no denying that they both enjoyed it. But then they had always enjoyed it, from the very first. Her skin continued to tingle from their recent kiss, just as it always had.

She still wondered how it was that they had so easily and quickly fallen in love and how it had seemed to endure even through separation and supposed death. Ronan hadn't stopped loving Hope even though he had believed her dead. It seemed that he loved her even more.

And she hadn't stopped loving him. She had no idea where their love had been born, but somehow it had been given life, and she so badly wanted to see it continue to live and grow strong.

She got a sudden chill, and she realized that the tingle from Ronan's kiss had dissipated, and she missed it. She missed him, and she wondered how she would ever live life without him.

Hope.

There truly was none for her, but there was Hope herself. If she could find the courage to let Hope live. But then, for that to happen, Carissa had to die. They both could not survive together. Only one could stay, the other had to go. And though she might be tired of Carissa, it was due to her strength and courage that she had survived. How then did she deny her?

She remained by the fire until Ronan returned, then she got busy preparing the stew while he once again joined her at the table.

"Bethane will be happy to join us," he said with a grin. "I boasted about your cooking."

"I'm not that good a cook."

"No, you are a *great* cook. I've never tasted such flavorful food."

Never had anyone ever boasted about anything Carissa had done, and that he took such pride in her skill touched her heart. But hadn't Ula told her that preparing a good meal could bring peace to the heart?

And right now, at this very moment, she felt at peace. Although she knew this was a rare moment, and more than likely she would never experience something like this again, she would enjoy it and cherish it and keep it strong in her memory.

"Tell me of your brothers," she said.

While she cut the potatoes, Ronan regaled her with stories of when he was young, and they both laughed at the antics of his youth. And the pleasant day continued when Bethane joined them hours later.

It turned into a pleasant evening among friends, and Carissa was grateful for it. She had always known that life was far different than she had lived it, though her father tried to convince her otherwise.

Bethane left sooner than Carissa would have liked, but the older woman insisted that Carissa still needed to rest. Though the fever was gone, she needed to regain her full strength.

Ronan agreed, and once Bethane was out the door, he ordered her to bed.

She was about to disagree when a yawn advised the same. Reluctantly, she retired to her sleeping quarters, Ronan promising to be close behind after he added more logs to the hearth and grabbed a couple to add to the small hearth in the other room.

She changed into her wool nightshift, grateful Ronan had brought her clothes with them, and climbed into bed, snuggling under the warm covers. She wished Ronan would join her. She missed him in her bed. There were times when they had shared a bed that she would wake and be in his arms. She would lie still and enjoy his warm embrace. She had gotten used to his being there and disliked the empty place beside her.

Ronan entered, and she watched him add dry logs that the flames quickly sparked to life. He stood and slipped off his shirt as he walked toward the bed. Could he be thinking of joining her? How she hoped he would. She would love to rest her head on his chest and sleep in his arms.

"You're all set?' he asked.

"I'm fine," she lied. And wished she could tell him she wanted him to sleep with her, but if she did, he would think her to be Carissa and wanting sex, when she simply wanted him beside her.

It wasn't that she hadn't thought of making love with him, even if only for one night, but at the moment it was him beside her that she wanted the most.

"If you need me—"

"I'll be fine," she said.

He nodded and turned away without another word, disappearing behind the curtain to the small sleeping nook.

Ronan woke out of a sound sleep and shot up in bed. Had he heard something? He listened, but only silence greeted him. He dropped back on the bed. He turned on his side and punched the pillow a few times while trying to find a comfortable position.

Damn if he didn't miss sleeping with Carissa.

He had gotten used to her body next to his, the familiar scent of apples drifting off her, the way she would snuggle next to him almost as if she couldn't get close enough. But he hadn't realized that until now . . . until he began to see Carissa differently.

He sprang up again.

This time he was sure he heard something. He

got out of bed, disregarded his nakedness, pushed the curtain aside, and walked over to her bed. She tossed in her sleep, a groan escaping now and then. She was obviously in the throes of a bad dream.

He didn't hesitate as he climbed in bed beside her and wrapped her in the safety of his arms.

She settled almost instantly against him, snuggling until she found a comfortable spot. Nosing her slim leg between his two warm ones, she fell into a peaceful sleep.

Chapter 21

Ronan grew thick and hard in the hand that stroked him. Damn, but it felt good, and it felt even better when her hand drifted down to cup him gently and squeeze lightly until he shivered.

"One night, just one night love me."

When he realized it wasn't a dream, he surrendered to his passion and captured her whispering plea with his lips. His hands tugged her nightshift up to explore her warm flesh, and it wasn't long before his lips followed where his hands had touched.

She tasted sweet, soft and silky and he couldn't get enough of her. He grew drunk with the taste of her, and he wanted more, so much more from her. He slipped her nightshift up and over her head, tossing it aside as his lips claimed hers once again.

She feasted on him as hungrily as he did on her. It was as if they were starved, and only the other could appease the gnawing hunger.

Her hands explored him with as much enthusiasm as his hands did her. There was no hesitation or shyness in her touch, she explored like a woman who knew what she wanted and would give as much as she got.

They rolled around on the bed like old lovers recently united, teasing and tasting until both could stand it no more, though it was Ronan who took control.

He slipped his arm around her waist and swung her beneath him, planting himself on top of her. He grabbed hold of her hands and stretched them past her head as he kissed her.

"Damn, but I love you, Hope."

"Now, right now, love me," she said against his mouth, and stole another fiery kiss.

He obliged. Not being able to wait any longer himself, he drove into her with a hungry need and she squeezed his hands hard as she gave a shout. He stopped abruptly.

"No, no, don't stop," she urged, lifting her hips.

She drove him deeper inside her and enflamed him even more.

He released her hands, and he braced himself over her and set a rhythm that had her moaning with pleasure and him near to exploding. But he waited, and it didn't take long before she screamed out his name; and then and only then did he join her.

They slept soon after, though they woke and made love again, Carissa once again initiating it and he obliging, until finally they fell into a sound sleep.

* * *

Carissa woke thinking she heard her name being called, but assumed it a dream when she listened and heard nothing. She smiled, turning in Ronan's arms to look at him.

"Thank you," she whispered, and kissed his lips gently.

He didn't stir, and she laughed softly. She had tired him out, but she would let him rest and not disturb him, for a couple of hours at least.

"Carissa."

She stilled, her body turning completely rigid. Someone had called her. It wasn't a dream. She carefully slipped out of bed, not wanting to disturb Ronan, dressed quickly, hurried into the next room, and came to an abrupt halt.

"Septimus," she said, and hurried over to him. "What are you doing here? Ronan is in the other room. You took—"

"It's Dykar."

She grabbed hold of his arm and kept her tone low. "What happened?"

"A ragtag group of mercenaries captured him and demands to meet with the leader of our group."

"Did you send for Hagen?" she asked.

Septimus shook his head, his expression troubled.

Carissa knew before he said a word. She was expecting this, though hoping otherwise. Her secret had lasted longer than she expected. How did she think she could simply walk away from it?

"They know our leader is a woman."

She nodded. "And they demand to speak to me."

"Or they threaten to kill Dykar," Septimus finished.

"Do you have any idea what they want of me?"

"No, but time is short. We must leave now if we are to reach the appointed rendezvous."

She nodded, knowing she had no choice. "Are the men ready?"

"They wait impatiently for your command."

"Then let's go."

"Are you sure?"

"How can you ask me that?" she said as she yanked her cloak off the peg.

"You have a chance at freedom."

"Not at the cost of Dykar's life," she said, and shoved him out the door before her. "And you knew that."

"It's just good to hear it."

"Now that you have, it's time to go," she said. "But first I need to speak with Bethane." Before she shut the door, she whispered softly, hoping somehow it would reach Ronan, and he would know. "I will return."

Ronan woke with a leisurely stretch and a grin. Damn, he felt good, and he'd feel even better when he made love to Hope again. He turned to do just that and bolted up in bed when he saw that she wasn't there.

He was about to call out for Hope, but stopped himself and shouted, "Carissa."

He shouted twice more as he quickly slipped into his clothes.

When he discovered the other room empty, concern struck his gut, and he grabbed his cloak as he headed out the door.

The day was overcast and cold, though it didn't look or feel like snow. At least he hoped not. He was suddenly eager to return to the security of his home. With hurried steps, he made his way to Bethane's cottage, and after a hasty knock, he entered.

"Just in time to eat," Bethane said, pointing at the table set with two bowls and tankards.

"Where is she?" he asked, closing the door behind him though not removing his cloak.

"She'll be back. She gave her word. Now sit and eat," Bethane said, and ladled porridge into the bowls.

"How do I trust the word of a barbarian?"

"That's a question only you can answer."

The scent of the food had him accepting her offer. He tossed his cloak over the back of a chair and scooped up a spoonful of porridge. Though it was good, it wasn't as tasty as Carissa's.

"I agree," Bethane said. "Carissa's porridge is much tastier."

He gave up trying to figure out how Bethane knew what people were thinking. Besides, it didn't matter. He wanted to know about Carissa.

"How soon will she return and where did she go?"

"I don't know where she went," Bethane admitted. "But she did tell me that you should return home, and she would come there when she can."

"What do you mean when *she can*?" he demanded angrily. "Damn, she tricked me again."

"Do you truly believe that?"

"What else am I to believe? We make love for the first time, and she disappears the next morning." He cringed. "I should not have told you that."

"Knowing that, I would surmise only something terribly important would have forced her to leave you."

"Or Carissa played me for a fool yet again," he said, pushing the bowl aside. "Getting what she wanted from me and escaping."

"What did she get that she wanted from you?" Bethane asked.

He couldn't say aloud what he thought. He couldn't admit to Bethane that Carissa wanted him to make love to her as he would have to Hope. But he did know what it had cost him. What she had taken from him.

He stood. "My pride. She took my pride, and I am going to take it back."

Bethane tried to speak, but he silenced her with a wave of his hand.

"No more advice. I opened my eyes as you suggested, but evidently not enough." He grabbed his cloak and swung it over his shoulders. "I leave for home now."

Bethane shook her head sadly. "You may have opened your eyes, but you failed to open your heart."

* * *

Ronan tried to make sense of Carissa's departure during the four days that it took him to get home. He wanted to believe what Bethane had told him, that Carissa would return. But why had she left in the first place? Why had she kept her departure from him?

Thinking on it, he probably would have objected to anything that would have delayed their return home. And it wasn't only because he finally felt ready to return home but because he wanted this matter concerning Carissa settled. Crazy as the thought was, and that he was even giving it consideration proved madness, but he wanted to spend time with Carissa to see if what he had begun to believe was true, that the woman he loved still lived within Carissa.

There was also another problem that tormented him. He would be returning home without Carissa, and Cavan had trusted him with the task of bringing her to justice. And that meant returning her to him for judgment.

Bethane had said that Carissa had given her word. But did he trust the word of a barbarian? Was there more to Carissa than he had first believed?

He had disappointed his brother once already when he had gotten them captured. It seemed unforgivable that he should fail him once again.

His thoughts remained troubled as he arrived home. A light snow dusted his cloak as he brought his horse to a halt on the moors and stared in the distance at the Sinclare village and keep. It had been what? Two years since he had been home? Two years since the battle that almost cost him and his brother Cavan their lives. Two years that changed him forever.

But he was here, and there was no turning back. And so he rode forward to finally fully reunite with his family.

Chapter 22

Ronan was surprised to find the village in the throes of preparing for battle. He was quick to dismount and leave his horse waiting outside the keep as he rushed inside. The great hall was a scene he had once been familiar with, clusters of warriors waiting for orders while the laird conversed with the leaders who would command each troop.

He was surprised to see Alyce, Lachlan's wife, huddled with his brothers, but then he recalled her acute awareness of the situation when they had first met and realized that Cavan would certainly put her unique abilities to work for him.

Before he could approach them, he heard a scream and didn't have to look to see who it was. His mother rushed to him with outstretched arms, and he welcomed her with a tight embrace.

"Finally," she cried through tears, though she wiped them away and, clasping his hand, raised it high. And with a distinct, clear voice she shouted, "Ronan of the clan Sinclare has come home!"

A cheer rang out so loudly Ronan could have

sworn the rafters trembled. His mother escorted him to the table in front of the hearth. The table the laird of the clan occupied with his family and the one that now belonged to the new laird, his brother Cavan.

Artair and Lachlan were quick to give him welcoming hugs, and his sisters-in-law sent smiles to him. Beside Cavan, there was a beautiful woman, with long black hair and lovely violet eyes, whose smile could melt the coldest heart.

She greeted him before they could be introduced. "I'm Honora, Cavan's wife, and I have so looked forward to your return."

"My brother is a lucky man," Ronan said.

"I often remind him of that," Honora said with a soft laugh.

Ronan had to smile. Honora was simply delightful. And he was so pleased to see that his brother had found such a wonderful woman. He wasn't surprised to see Cavan wrap a strong arm around Honora's waist and draw her near to him.

"Honora is a precious gift I will never stop appreciating," Cavan said.

"That's so romantic." Zia sighed.

"Now see what you've done," Artair said, pointing an accusing finger at Cavan. "Our wives are going to expect the same romantic gestures."

"My wife gets them all the time," Lachlan boasted with a grin.

"Morning, noon, and night," Alyce said teasingly.

Ronan's smile grew. "It's good to see that some

things never change. You still tease each other, and your wives now join in."

"And with great skill," Addie said proudly of her daughters-in-law.

A sprinkle of laughter circled the group, and Addie had her son sitting with food in front of him before he could finally ask, "What goes on here?"

"We received word that two groups of mercenaries are gathering on the fringes of Sinclare land," Artair said.

"How did you learn of this?" Ronan asked.

"One of our regular scouts informed us," Lachlan said.

"Do you know who leads each group?" Ronan asked, wondering if either were the group he had fought alongside.

"We believe we know one group though we don't know the leader," Alyce said. "We only know the man the leader sent to speak with us, Septimus."

"I know him," Ronan said, not surprised since the mercenary group was a strong force with an imposing reputation. "I rode with the group. A courageous and skilled warrior called Dykar seemed in charge."

"But didn't lead?" Cavan asked.

Ronan shook his head. "I don't truly know, since there were times he would disappear for days, and upon his return, new plans were implemented. I must say though that whoever is in charge of the group, he is an exceptional leader. He knew how to foster not only camaraderie in the men but an honor that was rare for mercenaries. And these men would do anything for him."

"I'd like to meet this leader," Cavan said, and his brothers agreed.

"He would be a good one to forge a friendship with," Artair said.

"I agree," Cavan said, and looked to Ronan. "Do you think you could speak to Septimus and arrange a meeting with his leader?"

"I haven't seen Septimus in some time, but I can try."

"Hagen can talk with Septimus. He can leave right away," Addie said.

Ronan noticed that his three brothers instantly bristled.

"Alyce can see to it for us," Lachlan said.

"I know Hagen," Ronan said. "He's a good man—"

"Yes, yes, he is a good man," Addie said, looking to each of her son's with a stern eye.

"And respected by the group," Ronan finished, wondering what perturbed his mother. "I'm sure he'll speak to Septimus on your behalf."

Addie stood. "Since it's agreed, I'll go ask him." She stopped and turned back to place her hand on Ronan's shoulder. "I am happy you are home, and we will talk when there is time."

"I look forward to it, Mother," Ronan said, and Addie kissed his cheek before she hurried off.

"I don't know why the three of you," Zia said, pointing from Cavan, to Lachlan and finishing with Artair, "must be so mean to your mother when it comes to Hagen. She has a right to fall in love again."

"Mother's in love with Hagen?" Ronan asked incredulously.

"You had to say he was a good man," Lachlan accused.

"He is," Alyce insisted. "If only any of you would take the time to talk with him."

"Does he love her?" Ronan asked.

"Don't even suggest it," Artair said.

"Why?" Honora asked. "Zia is right. Your mother has a right to love again, and I believe your father would want her to."

"Not with Hagen," Cavan said emphatically.

"Why?" Alyce demanded with a sharp tongue though she let no one answer. "Could it be because he's a mercenary?"

"She deserves better," Cavan said.

"She deserves to love whoever she wishes to love," Honora said. "And Hagen is a good man. Ronan knows him and can vouch for his character."

"Hagen is also an honorable man," Ronan said. "I fought beside him in battle and would stand beside him again in battle. He would keep Mother safe, and though his large size might frighten some, he is a gentle soul."

"I told you," Zia said, with a poke to her husband's arm.

"Not all mercenaries are what you think," Ronan said. "Most are forced into the life out of necessity, some are sold into it and must fight to buy their freedom, but many are good men."

"How did you come to be part of the mercenaries?" Lachlan asked.

"I was sold to them."

"Why didn't you contact us?" Artair asked. "We would have seen to your freedom immediately."

Ronan knew they needed answers as to why he hadn't returned home, and while he wanted them to have those answers, he wasn't sure if he knew them all himself.

"There were things I had to do," he said, hoping that for now his response would suffice.

"This discussion is better left for another time," Cavan said. "We need to speak of more pressing matters at hand."

Ronan was relieved though there was one more matter he felt he needed to address.

"You haven't asked me about Carissa," Ronan said, looking to his brother Cavan.

"I assumed you took care of the matter."

"I have discovered information that could be vital in regard to her punishment," Ronan said. "She took ill before we could return."

"Is she all right?" Zia asked with concern.

"With your grandmother's help, she got well," Ronan said. "Unfortunately, she left to attend to an important matter and promises to return to face judgment."

"You let her go?" Lachlan asked, stunned, while all remained dead silent.

"No," he admitted with a sense of guilt. "She left without my knowledge."

"Then how do you know she will return?"

Leave it to Artair to ask the most practical question. And while he had an answer, "she gave her word" would certainly make him appear a fool.

"This can also be left for another time," Cavan said. "We have more important matters on our hands. We don't know if these two groups are joining forces to attack us, or if they have a dispute to settle. Either way, I don't like the fact that they are close to Sinclare land."

Before the discussion continued, the women left to look in on the children, though Alyce was quick to return, assuring Lachlan that his son Roark was sound asleep and in good hands with Mia, the older woman who helped look after him.

Ronan wanted to take a moment to see to his horse, but Cavan had a lad see to it. And soon they were all in deep discussion again, arguing, anxious to decide on a suitable plan of action.

Hagen returned with Addie, and Ronan was surprised to see how their eyes sparkled when they looked at each other and how their hands remained clasped as Hagen spoke with the others.

Unlike his brothers, he was happy for his mother, but then he knew Hagen, and he knew that he would be good to Addie. He would protect her with his life.

Ronan stood as soon as Hagen and his mother reached the table and greeted Hagen with a bear hug.

"It is good to see you again," Hagen said.

"And you," Ronan said.

"I was surprised when Addie told me that you were her son."

"I was surprised when I learned that you care for my mother," Ronan said.

"I care for her very much," Hagen admitted, while his cheeks flushed bright red.

"How is it that Hagen didn't know who you were?" Cavan asked curiously.

"Where we came from and who we were is not important to our group," Hagen answered. "It is who we are as a group that matters."

Ronan couldn't agree more with Hagen. Not one mercenary questioned another about his past. None were judged by past deeds or misdeeds. It was what they gave and shared with the whole of them that mattered.

"Mother explained what we want of you?" Cavan asked.

Hagen nodded.

"Before you present our request," Cavan said, "can you find out why the two mercenary groups are meeting?"

"I already know," Hagen said. "My troop has contacted me."

"How?" Cavan asked, annoyed. "My sentries haven't alerted me to anyone entering the village."

Alyce laughed. "It could only be one of two people who could make it into the village without being detected. Evan your scout who remained behind at my village, or is it Piper, a young woman who knows the land as if she were born to it."

"They both were on a mission for Septimus," Hagen explained, "and learned of the problem before anyone else."

"What problem?" Cavan asked.

"That the other mercenary troop has captured Dykar," Hagen said.

"Your leader?" Cavan asked.

Hagen hesitated.

"Why has your leader's identity remained a secret?" Ronan asked.

Hagen nodded. "You knew Dykar wasn't our leader?"

"I surmised though I had no proof, only a gut feeling," Ronan said.

"I don't understand," Cavan said annoyed. "If Dykar isn't your leader, why was he taken captive?"

"They threaten to kill Dykar if our leader doesn't meet with them," Hagen explained.

"And how is that a problem?" Cavan asked. "Does your leader hide because he lacks courage?"

"I have known no other as courageous as my leader," Hagen said.

"Then there is no problem," Cavan said.

Hagen shook his head. "There is a problem. The men fear that the troop plans to capture our leader en route or while there."

"Why?" Cavan asked, shaking his head. "It makes no sense. And how could they with his men protecting him?"

"Our leader is to come alone to the meet, or they promise that Dykar will die and not quickly," Hagen said. "And as for why? There is a sizeable reward for our leader's capture."

"Who placed a reward on your leader's head?" Cavan asked.

Hagen hesitated, then finally said, "You did."

Chapter 23

Cavan shook his head. "I don't know what you could mean? I have placed a reward on only one person."

Hagen remained silent.

Cavan's mouth fell open in shock, and it took him a moment before he said, "Your leader is Carissa?"

Ronan glared at Hagen. "All this time the woman I searched for was the one who commanded me?"

Hagen nodded.

Ronan didn't know whether to be furious or relieved. Furious because he felt that once again Carissa had made a fool of him, or relieved because he knew she was safe with the mercenaries.

"Then there is no problem," Cavan said. "Once the mercenaries have her, they will bring her to me."

"Not before they do what they want with her," Hagen said.

Ronan looked to Cavan. "That can't happen."

"She has done worse to us," Cavan said.

Ronan shook his head. "Her father did; she had nothing to do with it."

"You defend her?" Cavan asked bitterly.

"Carissa is not who you think," Hagen said.

"She isn't?" Cavan laughed. "That's funny since I saw her smile every time her father had me whipped. And she was the one who insisted on tossing a bucket of God knows what on my wounds that caused me to pass out from the pain." Cavan slammed his fist on the table. "To me she is nothing but evil, so do not dare ask me if I care what becomes of her while in captivity of the mercenaries."

"I care," Ronan said.

"Why?" Cavan asked with a shake of his head. "Has she filled your head with nonsense since we left you at the village Black?"

"She escaped from the village and I had to go after her," he said. Another fact he had to admit to his brother that made him appear a fool. And before anyone could comment, he finished explaining. "We were stranded in a cottage in the woods due to the snowstorm."

"And she filled your head with nonsense and lies," Lachlan said.

Ronan hesitated to respond. He still wasn't certain who Carissa was. One minute she was the coldhearted Carissa, and another the kindhearted Hope. He simply didn't know how to reconcile the two.

"You're not sure who she is, are you?" Artair asked.

"Honestly, no," Ronan admitted, shaking his head.

"The only one who truly knows Carissa is Dykar," Hagen said. "And he does not share the knowledge with others."

Ronan felt a twinge of jealousy and before he could speak his mind, Cavan asked what he wanted to know.

"Who is this Dykar to her?"

"I truly don't know," Hagen said. "All I know is that Dykar protects her with his life and would easily die for her. But then there are many in the troop who know her that would do the same."

"Perhaps she bewitches men," Lachlan suggested.

"Not in the way you suggest," Hagen said defensively.

"The only way this matter can ever be settled," Artair said, "is for Carissa to be brought here."

"Unharmed," Ronan added quickly.

"Why such concern?" Cavan demanded of his brother.

How many times would he appear a fool this night? When he had told Bethane that Carissa had taken his pride, it was truer than he realized. But truth be known, his wounded pride would need to wait to be healed. He first had to think of Carissa.

He admitted a concern that had suddenly dawned on him when Hagen had suggested that Carissa could suffer at the hands of the mercenaries before she was turned over to Cavan.

"She may carry my child," Ronan said.

Faces couldn't have expressed more shock than those around him did, and silence hung so heavily that Ronan thought it just might crush all of them.

"I have no time to explain it all now," Ronan said. "My concern is to see Carissa safe, then I will discuss my dilemma with you."

"This changes everything," Cavan said standing. "An unborn child of a Sinclare could be in danger."

Artair and Lachlan nodded in agreement.

"I think Zia should come with us," Alyce said, "in case Carissa requires a healer."

"I agree, and I'll come along as well," Addie said.

"That's not necessary," Hagen said, and for once, the Sinclare men sided with him.

Addie, however, would hear none of it. "I'm going, and that's final," she said.

"Where are you going?" Zia asked, returning with Honora.

Once Alyce explained the situation, Zia said, "I'll get ready."

Cavan looked to his wife. "Don't dare tell me that you're coming too."

Honora shook her head. "No, though I would if I wasn't with child."

Cavan stared dumbfounded at her.

She went to her husband, took his hand, and rested it against her stomach. "I planned to tell you differently that you would be a father once again, but hearing about Carissa, I felt the need for you to know. And I ask that you protect Carissa, who may also be carrying a child, as much as you would me."

At that moment Ronan dearly loved his sister-in-law, for nothing he could have said would have had as much impact on his brother as Honora's words.

Cavan took his wife in his arms, hugged her, kissed her soundly, then said, "I give you my word."

Honora smiled and turned to Ronan. "It will be wonderful to have another woman pregnant along with me."

"I don't know for sure if she is with child," he said.

"We will know soon enough," Honora said. "Until then, we will all get to know her."

"Do not forget," Cavan reminded, "that she is our enemy."

Honora nodded. "Yes, but didn't you tell me that it is wise to know your enemy well?"

"And you did say you wished to know the leader of the mercenaries," Alyce said. "This would give you that chance."

"I would like to know her myself," Addie said.

"Her father was responsible for our father's death," Cavan said, annoyed.

"True, but not all the sins of a father," Addie said, "can be left on a child."

"The women have banded together," Artair said. "We don't have a chance."

Ronan felt his heart swell, realizing how good it was to be home among family. This was what he missed. This was what he feared he had lost and could never regain, but these women, two of whom he had only just met, had made his dilemma theirs and offered their help, as did his brothers, even though they doubted.

Cavan looked to Hagen. "We need to reach your troop before Carissa takes leave of them."

Hagen nodded. "I will show you the way."

Cavan then looked to Lachlan and Alyce. "You will both remain behind to see to the safety of the village and keep. This may be a ruse, and I want our home well defended."

They nodded. "You need not worry," Lachlan assured him.

"I know. That's why I leave you both," Cavan said. "Now for a plan of action."

Carissa rode alongside Septimus, six mercenaries behind them and a troop of thirty spread throughout the area. The remainder of men had not joined them. From the scouting report, the other troop totaled twenty and was a ragtag bunch that appeared thrown together with no clear leadership.

While it might appear an advantage to most, Carissa knew it was more a danger. Not one of them truly cared what happened to the other, and if one should fall, another one would step on him to get the prize, which was . . . her.

She wanted to be mad at Dykar for not informing her of the reward on her head. Septimus had explained that Dykar didn't want her to worry. And she certainly would have when she learned that it was Cavan Sinclare who had offered the reward.

While she was grateful for the one night with Ronan and the beautiful memories it had left her with, she feared it had only made matters worse. And she wondered if she was wise in returning to Ronan or better off simply fading into oblivion with the mercenaries.

She didn't want to cause Ronan any problems with his family. Her father had done enough to them. She didn't want to injure them any more. And with the mercenaries wanting her surrender in return for Dykar's life, it was obvious they intended to claim the reward. Though she didn't doubt she would suffer at their hands before they gave her to Cavan.

Once Ronan discovered that she was leader of the mercenaries, any trust they had been developing would be destroyed. He would not want to listen to her, just as he hadn't wanted to when he had first arrived at the cottage. He had trouble believing her then, and he would have even more trouble believing her now.

Her wisest choice was to disappear within the safety of the mercenaries and forget about Ronan. Her heart ached at the thought of never seeing him again, of never having him hold her again, of never making love, of never sleeping safely beside him.

She sighed and spilled not a tear. Her hurt felt like a knife to her heart, but then she had suffered many times throughout her life and had learned to survive. She would survive this though she couldn't help wondering how.

"Once you're alone, they will attack," Septimus said. "And they will not spare Dykar's life."

"I didn't believe they would though they will keep him alive until I see him."

"I agree," Septimus said.

"Are the bowmen in position?" she asked.

"They lie in wait according to plan," Septimus said. "The idiots don't even have sentries stationed near their camp, and such stupidity worries me."

"I agree," Carissa said. "They probably have no organized plan and intend to kill Dykar as soon as I make myself known to them."

"And you will have mere seconds to reach him if you are to save his life."

"I know," she said. "I will need to keep them distracted long enough to reach him."

"How do you plan to do that?"

"My cold heart and sharp tongue work magic," she admitted.

"But that isn't who you are," Septimus said.

"How long did it take you to realize that?"

"Longer than I care to admit," he said, "though I credit that to your ingenious ruse."

"I lived it every day," she said sadly.

"So I realized," he said. "We're almost there. Are you ready?"

She smiled. "I'm always ready. I won't let Dykar die."

"I know," Septimus said. "He told me how you saved his life once before, and he had no doubt that, if necessary, you would do it again, as he would for you."

"He knows me too well." She brought her horse to a halt. "We leave each other here."

"I won't be far."

"Keep your distance until Dykar is safe and—" She paused for a moment and shut her eyes, then opened them, strength and courage shining brilliantly in them. "If a choice must be made, you will save Dykar. Do you understand?"

Septimus looked ready to argue.

Carissa held up her hand. "I have no time to argue with you. You will follow my orders." Her horse pranced impatiently, and she easily controlled the skittish animal and looked once more to Septimus. "It's for the best, so please give me your word."

"I don't like it, but I will do as you order."

"Thank you. It eases my mind that I can count on you," she said, and she smiled. "Good-bye and take care, Septimus."

Carissa rode away, leaving Septimus staring after her. She didn't know if she rode to her death or perhaps a fate worse than death. She only knew that she would not let the only friend she had ever had, the only person who had ever cared for her, die.

She would see Dykar free, and whatever fate had in store for her, she would accept.

She spurred her horse on and rode to meet her fate.

Chapter 24

Carissa remained on the edge of the woods, the open field stretching out before her, and waited. Her opponents had made one intelligent move when they chose the open field for the place of exchange. Though her bowmen were hidden in the surrounding trees, it was still a good distance for an accurate shot. Some of the men could probably hit their target, they were that skilled, but if even one missed, it would endanger Dykar's life. So she had left orders that none were to release an arrow until Dykar was safe.

Five riders emerged from the woods on the far side of the field and, not wasting a moment, she rode forward. The sooner this was done the better for all. She kept her horse at a decent pace, not anxious or slow but appearing confident. Confidence, especially from a woman, seemed to intimidate men.

As she approached, she could see that Dykar had suffered a beating at their hands, and that made her angry. His lower right lip and chin were swollen, and the corner of his left eye had yet to finish bruising. She imagined he also had bruises elsewhere, and she was ready to take on these heathens herself for what they had done to her friend.

She slowed her horse as she reached them, seeing their smug grins, and knew they thought themselves victorious. How lucky that her father had taught her never to assume victory until you hold it in the palm of your hand.

She stopped a few feet in front of them. "Send my man to me."

"No," shouted the largest of the four mercenaries. "You come to us, then we will release him."

"That's not going to happen," she assured them in a sharp tone.

"You don't have a choice," a skinny fellow who looked in need of a good washing said.

"But I do," she said confidently. "I can turn around and ride away, or you can send my man to me."

The four men laughed, and the largest said, "We'd stop you."

"You could try," she said, her horse sensing that battle approached and prancing impatiently.

The men grumbled among themselves, which gave Carissa more time to assess the situation. No doubt they would meet her demand, though once they did, she would need to move quickly, for to her their intention was clear . . . they would kill Dykar once he was a distance from them.

With Dykar's hands tied, he wouldn't be of much help, and she would have to move swiftly. She had dirks and daggers concealed on her person and in easy reach. Speed and momentum were her best allies. She couldn't hesitate; if she did, all would be lost.

"You approach, and we'll send him to meet you," the skinny one ordered.

That was fine with her. It brought her closer to her targets.

She nodded, though her action was more a message to Dykar, and she knew he would read it wisely and be prepared. She had no time to free his hands to help her. The men would be on her before then, so he would do best to stay out of her way and out of the line of fire.

She moved forward, and one of them gave Dykar's horse a slap that sent him forward as well. She whispered to her horse to hold steady and kept a cold stare at the men beyond, so that they would not take their eyes off her, leaving her hands free to reach for her weapons.

Dykar had almost reached her when she saw the skinny one move. She yelled for Dykar to get down, and as he slipped off the horse, all hell broke loose.

Ronan and his brothers' group caught up with Septimus, who silenced them with a sharp-eyed reproach. He then motioned Ronan, Cavan, and Artair forward and pointed to the open field beyond.

Ronan couldn't believe what he saw. Carissa sat alone out in the open facing five riders. Though she was petite, she appeared tall and poised atop her horse. Her shoulders were squared, and she held her head high. He could imagine her tongue was probably sharper than her sword and would inflict more damage.

Septimus kept his voice to a bare whisper. "We wait."

Ronan looked ready to argue, but Septimus shook his head.

"Your impatience will endanger her and Dykar."

Ronan didn't like it, but he agreed and waited with little patience and a great deal of anxiety.

When Dykar began to ride forward, Ronan and his brothers were prepared to make their move, but once again Septimus cautioned their actions.

"Wait until I give the order," he whispered.

Ronan couldn't understand what he was thinking. Then he realized that Carissa had probably ordered him to wait until Dykar was clear before attacking, leaving her much too vulnerable. And there was something else that troubled him. He couldn't see Carissa allowing herself to be caught. She would know the consequences of being captured by the mercenaries.

That was when it struck him and he sent a heated glare to Septimus.

"She doesn't intend to be taken alive, does she?" Ronan said.

"Her orders," Septimus said.

"The hell with her orders," Ronan said, and raced his mare forward just as all hell broke loose on the field.

* * *●

Carissa's dirk flew from her hand, followed by another, and she didn't stop to see where they hit, though the skinny man and another toppled off their horses. She reached for her dagger and got another man before he reached her, the dagger going straight to his heart. She saw Dykar run for one of the fallen men and she knew he intended to retrieve a weapon and free himself to help her, but would there be time?

A large man launched himself at her before she could grab for another dirk, and they tumbled to the ground together. His weight was his biggest advantage, and he used it, pinning her to the ground with his girth.

"You did me a favor," he laughed, as she struggled helplessly beneath him. "Now you and the reward are all mine."

Arrows suddenly landed around them.

The large man released a string of oaths and hurried to his feet, surprisingly fast for a man his size, and grabbed her wrist. She saw Dykar struggling to cut free of the rope that bound his wrists while the last of the five men descended on him.

The large man paid him no heed. Instead, he began dragging her toward the cover of the woods, and when he whistled, his horse followed, providing some cover from the flying arrows.

She couldn't let him get her to the safety of the woods. Septimus and her men would be riding to her rescue, and Dykar would be in his own battle. She had to do something, but his grip was tight.

She swung at him with a tight fist that landed on his jaw and sent a pain racing through her hand. But it stopped him, and the look on his face told her she'd better brace for a worse blow than she delivered.

He raised a meaty fist and her eyes turned wide as she heard a bloodcurdling shout, and suddenly a man flew through the air and landed with a solid thud on her captor, sending him and her sprawling to the ground.

The large man refused to let go of her while he beat at the man with his free hand.

It took her a minute to realize that her rescuer was Ronan. For a brief moment, her heart soared. He had come to save her, and when he took a hard blow that knocked him to the ground, she grew furious.

She began pummeling the large man and scratching at him like a wildcat. It was enough for him. Before she could stop him, he sent a blow to her cheek that jolted her head back and sent her stumbling until she hit the ground hard.

Though not before she heard Ronan growl like an enraged animal, "For that you die!"

She saw nothing after that, for darkness claimed her.

It took Septimus, Cavan, and Artair to pull Ronan off the bloody man, and when they did, Ronan struggled free of them and rushed to Carissa's side. He was relieved to see that Zia and his mother were already there.

He ignored the chaos around him, never realizing that the other mercenaries with the motley five had emerged from the woods and were now engaged in battle. His only concern had been Carissa.

"You're bleeding," Zia said with concern.

He glanced down at his arm and saw that his sleeve was slashed and soaking up blood. He then recalled knocking a man from his horse to reach Carissa and recalled the feel of his sword slicing across his arm as he fell to the ground.

"It will wait," he said adamantly. "See to Carissa first."

"She has suffered a hit to her face and a blow to her head," Zia said. "I can do nothing for her now. It is more important that I see to your arm."

"Listen to her," Addie urged.

"After we get Carissa to safety," he said determinedly.

"It is not safe to move her in this melee," Zia said, nodding to the chaos around them. "Let me see to your arm, so that you will be able to help move her when we can."

Ronan agreed since he intended to be the one to see her to safety. He didn't particularly worry about the disorder surrounding them. Septimus and his men and his brothers seemed to have everything well in hand and were cleaning up after themselves.

Zia tore his sleeve off, and while she cleansed and announced the wound would need only a wrapping to have it heal, he noticed Carissa stir.

"She wakes," Addie said.

"That is good," Zia said with a smile, and they both turned to her.

Carissa felt the pain radiate from her jaw up along her cheek. And then there was the dull throb in the back of her head. Her hand pained her as well. She fought her way out of the dark, though as she did, the pain worsened, and she wondered if she should remain where she was. But something warned her against it, and so she fought.

"Carissa," the soft voice said. "Open your eyes. You're all right."

The soft voice kept urging her, and while she wanted to oblige, the pain held her back until . . .

"Damn it, Carissa, open your eyes!"

"Shouting at her isn't going to help," the soft voice said.

"I agree," Carissa said, her eyes fluttering open only to squeeze shut when the light hit them.

"Open your eyes," the strong voice demanded.

She was so annoyed with the command that she intended to open her eyes and tell him exactly what he could do with his order, but she slipped back into the peaceful darkness.

After a bit more of a struggle, she got them open and her mouth followed, ready to attack him with her sharp tongue when she saw that it was Ronan and she saw that the creases of worry around his eyes and mouth had deepened, and her heart melted.

"Ronan," she whispered softly, and reached out to him.

He took her hand and held it firm in his. "You should have never left me."

"My brother is right," Cavan said, coming up behind Ronan. "You gave your word to my brother and had an obligation to return home with him."

Carissa bristled at Cavan's scolding tone and struggled to sit up, though pain shot through her head and cheek, and she winced at the sharp ache.

Ronan tried to stop her, but she would have none of it. She grabbed hold of his arm and hoisted herself up, though he helped once he saw that she wouldn't be dissuaded.

"I had an obligation to my friend," she snapped.

"I would have taken care of it," Cavan said.

"Since I couldn't be sure of that, I couldn't take the chance." Carissa held on to Ronan as she struggled to stand.

"We can discuss this later," Ronan said, slipping his arm around her waist and practically lifting her off the ground to rest against him.

She allowed him to support her weight, not feeling strong enough to stand on her own just yet. But lacking strength or not, she would not cower to his brother.

"It makes no difference to me if your brother wishes to speak now," she said. "I expected no less of him."

"And I expect no less of you . . . a barbarian," Cavan spat. "The only reason I give you any quarter is because you may carry my brother's child."

Carissa was stunned silent. While she should have considered the possibility, she hadn't. Too much had happened too fast for her to have given it a thought. Not that she would mind having Ronan's child, truly she would love to. But if it was the only reason Cavan would not see her punished, or that Ronan had come to her rescue, then her fate rested on whether or not she was with child.

She had waited long enough. She intended to wait no more.

"I will face my fate with you whether with child or not," she said.

"It is not your choice," Cavan said, and looked to Zia standing beside Artair. "Is she fit to travel?"

Carissa pushed away from Ronan though she wavered before finding solid footing and brushed away Ronan's helping hand. "It is me you ask, not her."

Cavan glared at her. "If Zia tells me you need to rest, you will rest."

Carissa laughed. "You may command the Sinclares, but you don't command me." She stepped forward, and shouted. "Dykar!"

He maneuvered his way through the Sinclares to stand before her.

"Ready the men to leave," she ordered.

"My warriors can easily stop your small troop," Cavan said.

She laughed again. "Do you think me a fool to

come here with only a few men?" She looked to Dykar again. "Call the men out."

Dykar let loose with a mighty roar, and before they knew it, they were surrounded with a fighting force that surpassed Cavan's warriors.

Ronan stepped forward. "This has gone far enough." He looked to Cavan. "I told Carissa you are a fair laird, and she agreed to return with me to face whatever fate you decreed."

"And then she took her leave without a word to you," Cavan said.

"That is for her and me to settle," Ronan said with a hint of a challenge.

Artair stepped between his brothers. "This matter should wait to be settled when we get home." Artair leaned over to whisper to Cavan. "And remember what you promised your wife."

Cavan cringed. "We wait on the matter."

Dykar took Carissa's arm, ready to help her to her horse.

Ronan put a hand on his arm. "She'll ride with me."

"No," Carissa said. "I ride with my men."

"You return with us," Ronan said.

"She will not go without us," Dykar said.

Ronan looked to Cavan, for it was the laird's decision, not his, as to what would be done.

"You may come with her, no more," Cavan said. "Elsewise, there will be a battle."

Before Dykar could protest, Carissa said, "Accepted, though my men will follow to the border of your land before they depart."

Cavan nodded and walked away in angry strides.

Ronan looked to Carissa. "I ask that you ride with me. We need to talk."

While she knew they did need to talk, she was not up to it. There was so much to be said between them, so very much. She didn't even know where to start. She felt terrible about leaving him without a word, and she was angry with him for confiding in his brother that she could be with child.

She put her hand to her head. "Not now, Ronan."

"Yes, now," he insisted.

She looked at him, wanting to tell him she just wasn't up to it right now. But he seemed to move away from her, far away and she wondered where he was going.

She heard him call out her name and she reached out to him to try and grab hold of him before he slipped completely away. And just as she thought she grabbed hold of his hand . . . the darkness swallowed her.

Chapter 25

Ronan held Carissa close in his arms, an extra cloak wrapped around her, and guided his mare slowly along the snow-covered path. After he had caught her as she crumpled in a faint, he wouldn't let her out of his arms. She had reached out to him, called out to him, and he was damned if he was going to let anyone take her from him.

She could be obstinate and sharp-tongued, but when she had called out to him, he heard only Hope calling to him for help. After that, he had made it known that Carissa would be riding back in the safety of his arms. No one protested, but then he had been insistent.

Carissa stirred in his arms, and her eyes opened slowly.

"You're safe," he said. "I'm taking you home."

Her brow wrinkled, and he could tell that she was attempting to make sense of what he meant.

"You're going home with me, Carissa," he assured her again.

She didn't open her eyes when she said, "I have no home."

"You do now," he said adamantly, and drew her more tightly up against him.

He didn't know why he had to reassure her. A few days ago he was angry with her for leaving without a word, and now he was offering her a home. Many would think him crazy.

He laughed. He even thought himself mad at times. How could he not after discovering that the woman he loved was actually his enemy? And how did he accept his enemy as his love?

He shook his head. He was crazy.

"Are you all right?" Cavan asked, riding up alongside him.

"I don't know," he answered, still shaking his head.

"Women can do that to you."

"That's not reassuring," Ronan said.

The brothers laughed.

"Tell me how this came about," Cavan said with a nod to Carissa sleeping soundly in his arms. "I don't understand. It makes no sense. You wanted revenge against her for killing the woman you loved and now . . . "He shook his head. "The same woman may carry your babe."

"I don't know how to explain it," he admitted. "I'm confused myself and yet"—he stared down at her—"I believe she is the woman I love."

"What of the other one?"

He looked from Carissa to his brother. "They *are* one."

Ronan could see that he confused his brother even more, and so he attempted to explain. He started at the beginning and told him what had happened after they were separated. How badly he was beaten and unable to see. How he had fallen in love with the slave who had seen to his care. How before his sight healed, he was sold to the mercenaries.

"You remained at the barbarian stronghold after we were captured?" Cavan shook his head. "They told me you weren't there. At times they tried to make me believe you were dead."

"I almost felt that I was. I couldn't see, couldn't care for myself, and didn't even know if someone was there with me. I only knew that the slave, I named her Hope, was my salvation. If it hadn't been for her, I would never have survived."

"And now you believe that all along Hope was actually Carissa?" Cavan asked.

"I know how it must sound."

"It sounds what it is," Cavan said. "A sadistic woman who will stoop at anything to have what she wants."

"Or perhaps a woman who found a way to survive a sadistic father."

"I find that difficult to swallow," Cavan said.

"I thought the same at first. But then I got to know Carissa while stuck in that cottage. There were times I glimpsed a different side of her, a good side I never imagined possible. And I began to wonder if perhaps Carissa wasn't who she appeared to be."

"And what did coupling with her prove?"

Ronan winced.

"You brought this on yourself," Cavan said.

"When I left you, I felt assured that you would put to rest the last of the barbarians who owed *us* a debt. *You and me.* As I mentioned earlier, Carissa was cruel, and I for one didn't intend on forgiving her. She is the last obstacle if we are ever to lay this all to rest and finally be free. I believed you felt the same."

"I thought I had. But then I also wondered if I could ever come home again."

"I understand. I thought the same myself," Cavan said.

"You did?"

"I had been treated and lived like an animal for near a year, and I doubted I could ever be the man I was. I was bitter and angry and disappointed that I had failed you."

"Me?" Ronan asked stunned. "But it was I who failed you."

"You did nothing."

"I cried out like a coward for you to save me," Ronan said, and felt the pain of his spinelessness down to his soul.

"I didn't hear you cry out," Cavan said. "I saw that you were in trouble and rushed to help you. If I had been more attentive to the situation, I would have approached it differently and saved us both. But my only thought was to save my little brother."

Ronan laughed bitterly. "And my only thought was to reach out to my big brother."

"We both should have kept our wits about us," Cavan said.

"It was a difficult battle."

"It was a horrifying one," Cavan admitted. "I still dream about it."

"I do too," Ronan admitted.

"She is the key to ending this," Cavan said, looking to Carissa.

"What if it turns out that I truly love her?"

"She is our enemy," Cavan advised. "Make certain how you truly feel before you invite the enemy to join our family."

Carissa woke in bed with a start. An arm was draped over her waist as she lay on her side, and she smiled, causing a pain to shoot along her cheek, though she noticed her head didn't throb any longer.

She rested her hand over his, placing her small fingers between his large ones. They were mismatched in more ways than one, and yet she thought them a perfect fit.

She snuggled her back closer to him, and his fingers instinctively locked with hers. She felt safe, then it came to her.

They weren't in the cottage, and if they weren't there, where was she? And how did she get here? The last thing she did recall was . . .

Dykar and her men.

She reluctantly eased out of bed and, finding her clothes, dressed and slipped out the door. She entered a narrow hallway and had no idea which way to go. Since it was quiet, she knew it had to be night; whether near dawn or not, she didn't know.

She only hoped she had sufficient time to scout the area and see where she was and if her men were nearby.

She finally made her way to the great hall and to the large front doors. With her cloak wrapped around her, she opened the doors and walked out into the night. Dawn had yet to appear on the horizon, and she was relieved, knowing that the darkness of night would afford her time to prowl.

She didn't have to go far when she heard, "Rissa."

She turn with a smile and hurried over to Dykar peeking from around the side of the keep.

"I knew if I waited long enough, you'd wake and come in search of me."

"You are all right?" she asked anxiously, reaching out to gently touch the bruising around his eye.

"Do not worry about me," he insisted. "It is you I'm concerned for."

"I am fine," she assured him, though eager to clear her foggy memory. "Was I taken from you and the men?"

"No, Cavan told you that I could accompany you here, but not the men—"

"Now I remember," she said interrupting him. "I was going to ride with you when I—" She shook her head. "Damn, I fainted."

"You reached out to Ronan, and he wouldn't let anyone touch you after that. You rode with him on his horse, wrapped in his arms."

"I did?" she asked with a sigh.

Dykar shook his head. "Why did you have to fall in love with a man who swore to see you dead?"

"I don't know, Dykar. What I do know is that I can't stop myself from loving him. It's like it was meant to be, and no matter what I do, or he does, I continue to love him."

"Even if he hates you?" he asked incredulously.

"He doesn't hate me. I know he doesn't."

"Do you know how foolish you sound?" he asked.

"For once," Carissa pleaded, "let me be foolish."

"It could cost you dearly," he warned.

"What hasn't cost me dearly? Nothing has ever come easy for me except this love for this man. I don't know where it will take me. I don't know if I will suffer more for loving him, but I want to find out."

"I'll be here for you either way, though if he breaks your heart, you know I'll want to kill him," Dykar said, though he did so with a smile.

Carissa laughed softly. "You're the only one I could ever count on in my life."

"I wouldn't have a life if it weren't for you."

"But you do now, and soon, when this is all finished, there'll be no more worry about hiding me," she said.

"And what if the laird decides that it is your life you must forfeit to satisfy him?"

"Then you will have to rescue me, and I will have no choice but to leave Scotland, leave you, leave everything I've ever known." Carissa shook her head when Dykar went to protest. "Let it be for now. There's no sense in worrying until we need to."

"I will stay right here with you until a decision is made, but in the meantime, I will make plans for a hasty escape."

She nodded. "Where are the men?"

"Far enough away not to be detected, but close enough if we should need them."

"You've done well, Dykar."

"No, you are the one who has saved all these men and given them hope. And when the news spreads to the rest of the troop, they will feel the same and pledge their allegiance to you."

"That's not necessary," she insisted.

"It is to them."

Carissa didn't argue. She much preferred to use the time so Dykar could familiarize her with the lay of the land so that when she sneaked out at night, she knew places to meet him. Even though Dykar told her that the laird had made a cottage available for his use, she didn't want them to think she was meeting with him. Some things were better kept private.

After she was done, she hurried inside and, with quiet steps, headed for the stairs.

"What takes you outside in the dead of night, Carissa?"

She stopped and turned with a defiant tilt of her chin to face the laird of the clan Sinclare.

Chapter 26

"**M**y men," Carissa answered, walking over to him with a confident stride, though her innards trembled with concern.

"Join me," Cavan said, pointing to the bench opposite from him at the table.

It wasn't a request, and while she would have preferred to retire upstairs and snuggle next to the laird's brother and talk with Cavan another day, she knew that, out of respect, she could not deny him.

"You've satisfied your concern?" he asked once she sat.

"I spoke with Dykar, and he assures me that all is well." She didn't intend to lie. There was no point to it. If he had guards lurking in the shadows, they would tell him what they had seen, and he would trust her even less than he did, which at the moment was almost not at all. "What has you up so late?"

"You."

"Why is that?"

"You've presented me with a very difficult situation," he admitted.

"You and Ronan have talked," she said.

Cavan nodded. "Unlike my brother, who wishes to give you a chance, I believe you are who you are, and that cannot be changed."

"You believe you know me."

"I saw who you are with my very own eyes," he said.

The hatred flared like flames in his eyes, and he fought to control the anger in his voice. Would anything she could say make a difference?

"It would seem that you have already condemned me, and nothing I could say would change your decision."

"At the moment, your life is in my brother's hands, and I wait for him to come to his senses."

"I understand," she said. There was no way this man would ever accept her, and she had been a fool to think any Sinclare would, not that she could blame them, but she had hoped.

"You are not only a skilled warrior for a woman, but an impressive leader, and believe me when I tell you that I don't and never will underestimate your abilities or your talents."

"You're warning me that you don't trust me and intend to keep a close watch on me."

"At all times."

"Even when your brother sleeps beside me," she asked bluntly.

"That arrangement will change starting now,"

he informed her. "There is a small cottage beside the keep. It will be your home while you are here and a guard will be close by."

"This is not my home," she said with a cutting curtness. She had been a stupid fool to think that anything would ever come of loving Ronan.

"And it would be wise for you to remember that."

Carissa stood. "Be careful, Cavan. Hate is a powerful weapon that can easily destroy."

"I'm sure you know that better than anyone."

"More than you'll ever know," she said, and turned toward the stairs, wishing she could return to Ronan and yet knowing . . .

"The cottage waits for you," Cavan said. "I will have one of my warriors escort you there."

She simply nodded, knowing it would be senseless to argue with him. He was the laird and would have his way, though she wondered over Ronan's reaction when he discovered what his brother had done.

"You what?"

Ronan's shout had everyone in the great hall stopping and glancing at the closed solar door.

"The choice of who I sleep with is *mine*," Ronan said with a slap to his chest.

"When your choice of sleeping partners affects this clan, then it becomes my choice," Cavan said, his hands splayed flat on his desk as he leaned across it to glare at his brother. "If I allow this to continue between you and Carissa, then she will be with child for certain in no time. And then she will never answer for her crimes."

Ronan wanted to lash out at his brother, but he was right. He didn't want to keep his hands off Carissa. He ached to make love to her again.

"Did you ever stop to think that this was her plan all along, that if she became pregnant with your child, she would be immune to punishment?"

"I'm not an idiot," Ronan said. "I want time with her so that I may finally find the truth."

"Coupling with her isn't going to help you find it."

"No, but it sure in hell feels good."

Both brothers suddenly grinned and laughed.

"I don't do this to hurt you," Cavan said.

"I know that," Ronan said, rubbing his chin in frustration. "And if part of me wasn't blind to Carissa, I would have realized the same thing."

"It cannot be denied that she is a beauty, but beauty bewitches, so be very careful," Cavan warned.

Ronan nodded.

Cavan walked around his desk and looked his brother up and down. "Finally, you're dressed like a Highlander. Welcome home."

The guard had knocked on Carissa's door early and instructed her that he was there to escort her to the keep for the morning meal. She was tired and not at all hungry, but she knew she couldn't refuse. After all, she was a prisoner of the Sinclares.

She donned her cloak and wondered if Ronan had brought along the meager belongings she had left behind in the cottage at the village Black in her haste to help Dykar. She needed a good washing and change of garments. And she prayed that he had thought to bring them with him.

The day was gray and the air biting cold as she walked the few feet to the keep. A sharp, icy wind whipped her through the open door, and when she turned and got her bearings, the sight near stole her breathe.

Ronan stood dressed in the Sinclare plaid, dark green and black. A white linen shirt lay beneath the strip of plaid that crossed his impressive chest, and black winter boots trimmed with fur and secured with leather strips crisscrossed his thick calves and shins. His long dark brown hair shone as if it had been washed. And she knew then that Ronan had finally returned home.

He was a Highlander.

She suddenly felt more a barbarian than ever. And though she wished she could have improved her own appearance, she walked with the dignity her father had forever demanded of her.

She was disappointed when it was Zia who rushed to greet her. She had expected Ronan to be the first to welcome her, and when he failed to do so, she knew that her situation had changed. And she had no doubt Cavan had been the cause.

"How are you feeling?" Zia asked.

"I am fine," she said.

"Good. I worried that perhaps your head might

continue to pain you," Zia said, walking her to the table.

"No pain," Carissa said.

Ronan said nothing while Zia proceeded to introduce Carissa to those she was not familiar with.

A lovely woman with dark hair and a generous smile was first.

"This is Honora, Cavan's wife," Zia said.

"Welcome," Honora said with a nod.

Carissa noticed that Honora's arm rested on the table and her husband's on top of it. She wondered if he had prevented her from standing and greeting her.

"And this is Addie," Zia said.

Carissa heard the caution in her voice and needed only to see the older woman's eyes, so familiar to her, to know who she was. "You're the mother."

Addie looked at her oddly. "Yes, and a proud one."

Carissa wasn't sure what she saw in the woman's eye—contempt, uncertainty, hatred, and she had no time to digest it. A large dog suddenly charged into the room, and when he caught sight of Carissa, he hurried over to her and began licking her hand. She froze and made no move to respond to his friendly gesture.

"He won't hurt you," Addie assured her. "As you can see, he licks rather than bites."

Carissa said nothing, and Addie ordered the

dog to her side. He obeyed instantly, plopping his butt beside her.

Ronan finally walked over to her and held out his hand. "Join us."

She looked around at the Sinclares. Zia sat leaning into the crook of Artair's arm. Lachlan had his arm wrapped around his wife Alyce's waist, and even Addie had a loving dog beside her. She would never be accepted into this devoted family, and she'd be a fool to join them and pretend otherwise.

"I'm not hungry," she snapped. "I'd like to know if you have my clothes."

"Your clothes?" Ronan asked.

"I left them at the cottage," she said.

Ronan shook his head. "I didn't realize—"

"Obviously, there is little you realize," she snapped, and turned to leave.

Cavan's commanding voice stopped her. "I'd prefer that you join us."

She'd had enough and was about to turn and snap at him when Hagen entered the hall. "Hagen," she cried, and hurried over to him, throwing her arms around the large man, not that they fit.

As soon as he wrapped his arms around her, she whispered in his ear, "I need to get out of here now."

Before the large man could do a thing, Cavan spoke.

"It is good you're here, Hagen. You can join Carissa at the table with us."

Carissa saw the torn look in Hagen's eyes, and she turned and saw that Addie had stood to make room for him and that she wore a radiant smile.

"She loves you," Carissa whispered.

"I hope so," Hagen murmured, "for I love her like no other." He sighed. "What should I do?"

"Go to her," Carissa said.

"But—"

Carissa didn't let him finish. "I can defend myself."

He was about to protest, when Carissa gave him a slight shove, then turned and walked to the door.

"Carissa," Cavan called out.

She didn't look back. She simply shouted. "I am not hungry."

The room remained silent after the door shut behind her. Then Ronan turned to his brother Cavan, glared at him, turned around, and stormed out the same door.

Honora pulled her arm away from her husband. "That was no way to treat a guest."

"She's a prisoner," Cavan argued.

"I don't see her confined to the dungeons," she said.

"She's not that kind of prisoner, and this is not the place to discuss it," Cavan said, the others at the table wisely remaining silent.

"How do you ever expect to find out anything about her if you don't give her a chance?" Honora demanded, and before her husband could answer, she turned to Hagen. "What say you of Carissa?"

"Honora," Cavan warned in a clipped tone, which she proceeded to ignore.

"Tell us, Hagen, what say you of Carissa," Honora repeated.

Addie took his hand. "Yes, tell us, for strangely she seems familiar to me."

Hagen shook his head. "I mean no disrespect to Cavan, but I owe allegiance to Carissa and am not at liberty to speak about her."

"But it may help," Honora said.

"Then I suggest you watch her, for it is in her actions you will find who Carissa truly is," Hagen advised.

"Why does she fear dogs?" Addie asked.

"She doesn't," Hagen said, giving Champion a pat. "She loves them."

Zia looked to Cavan. "If we do as Hagen suggests and watch her actions, then we would have to assume that if she asked Ronan about the clothes she had left behind, it would mean that she had every intention—"

Honora finished with a glare at her husband. "—of returning."

Chapter 27

"**C**arissa, wait," Ronan said, hurrying after her.

She stopped a few feet from her cottage and swung around.

Ronan took a step back and held up his hands. "You could kill me with that look."

"Don't tempt me. How could—"

"I'm sorry," he said before she could finish.

She stared at him befuddled.

He approached her cautiously, though confused that she should appear so surprised by his apology. "I was wrong."

She took a step away from him and shook her head.

He had to smile at her bewilderment. "Hasn't anyone ever apologized to you?"

"No."

She said it with such blunt honesty that it startled him. "Never?"

"Never," she repeated.

He reached out and took hold of her hand to draw her near. "Then hear me well, for though this may be the first, I am certain it will not be the last time I apologize to you. I am sorry for not defending you against my brother, and I am sorry I did not greet you immediately when you entered the hall."

She drifted into his arms. "Why didn't you?"

"You looked at me so strangely, as if you didn't know me, and for a moment I thought perhaps—"

"That I was what your brother claimed . . . a barbarian who cannot be trusted?"

He shook his head. "No, that you changed your mind and didn't love me."

She sighed and rested her head to his chest. Looking up at him, she said, "When I saw you dressed in your plaid, I realized that you were a Highlander, and I was . . ."

He lowered his lips to hers, and before he kissed her, he whispered, "The woman I love."

The kiss left her head spinning, and she had to shake it to clear it. "You love Hope."

"You are Hope."

She shook her head again. "I am Carissa, daughter of Mordrac the Barbarian and your enemy."

He slipped his hand inside her cloak, then beneath her blouse, until it rested over her heart. "Your heart is too kind to be a barbarian or my enemy."

"I want to trust you, believe you, but—"

He smiled. "My brother feels the same about you and warns me that you only pretended to be Hope for your own selfish purposes. He forbids me from sleeping with you until we see if you are with child, and if not, you can then be judged."

"Your brother truly hates me."

He heard the regret in her voice. "He only knows Carissa."

She pulled away from him. "I am Carissa."

"No, you are Hope," he insisted, and reached out to take hold of her. But she moved away.

"Look at me, Ronan. I am Carissa, daughter to Mordrac your enemy, leader of the mercenaries, hated by most," she said, and took a fortifying breath before continuing. "That is what people see when they look at me, as much as I want it not to be that way, it is. It will never change. They have nothing but contempt for me."

He could see how the weight of her words hung heavy on her shoulders, and he wanted to comfort her, but he knew she needed much more than comfort. She needed him to accept her as Carissa and for a brief moment . . .

She smiled, though sadness filled her eyes, and she shook her head. "I can see it in your eyes. You can easily love Hope, but you don't know if you can easily love Carissa."

He stepped forward.

"No," she said firmly. "Your brother is right. It is best we keep our distance, and if I am not with child then . . ."

"I'm not going to lose you," he said adamantly.

"You never had me," she said, pounding her chest. "I am Carissa, not Hope. Carissa, do you hear? *Carissa.*"

He reached out, but she turned away and hurried inside the cottage, slamming the door behind her.

He stood staring at the door. How was he going to make this right for them both? How was he going to reconcile Carissa and Hope? That he loved this woman was not the question. It was defining the woman that was the problem.

He was about to turn and walk away when the door creaked opened.

"My clothes?" she asked, peering out. "You never brought them with you?"

"I'm sorry, I didn't," he said, glad he had fore-warned her that his first apology certainly wouldn't be his last.

Before she closed the door, he said, "I'll see about getting you fresh garments."

"I would appreciate it."

"Would you like a bath?" he asked. "I had one this morning."

She smiled. "I would love one."

"I'll arrange that too."

"Thank you," she said, and closed the door.

He went to see to both, then suddenly stopped, a thought hitting him. If she had left her clothes behind, then that meant she had planned on returning. He smiled broadly and rubbed his hands together, finally realizing that he had never grabbed his cloak and was cold. With a hasty step, he hurried to the keep.

"Damn," Carissa said, plopping down on the narrow bed in the cottage. Just this morning, when she woke in Ronan's arms, for a brief time, she had thought that there would be many similar mornings to follow. Then, in an instant, her hopes and dreams were gone.

She knew she had asked for just one night of love with him, but having sampled it, she realized she wanted more, so much more.

"Idiot," she scolded herself, and fell back on the bed. "He's a Highlander, and that was clearly defined for you when you saw him in his plaid."

She sighed. He looked so good, so handsome, and so courageous. And then he apologized. No one had ever apologized to her, not ever. It had shocked her to hear him say it, and he went and said it again in regards to her clothes.

"Damn," she repeated. "Why couldn't he simply love *me*?"

No one loves you, Carissa. Remember that, no one.

Her father had repeatedly reminded her of that, yet somehow she had managed to hold on to the hope that she'd be loved. She always believed that her mother had instilled that hope in her. Even though her mother was just a slim shadow in her memory, she believed that it was because of her love that she was able to survive her father's cruelty.

There was a knock at the door, and she jumped off the bed, thinking that perhaps Ronan had returned. But Dykar stood there, and he didn't look happy.

"Septimus needs to speak with you."

She grabbed her cloak and ordered Dykar to leave first. She would meet him in one of the designated spots they had agreed upon once she was certain no one followed her.

She smiled, for her it would be simple to sneak off. She had learned how when she was young and had sharpened her skill through the years. She'd have no trouble slipping out of sight of the guards. Of course, there was always a chance of being caught, and there would be consequences to face, but there was no point in concerning herself with something that might never be. She needed to see to this matter, then . . .

She prayed that bath would be ready.

Ronan rejoined his family, taking part in the morning meal, and realized that a decisive tension filled the air. Conversation was limited, and it was obvious that the laird and his wife were not on good speaking terms, since Honora got up in the middle of the meal and left.

Cavan followed shortly after, and the others took their leave one by one to see to their respective tasks until only he, his mother, and Hagen remained.

Ronan turned to the one woman he had and would always trust, and who he could count on always to be honest with him.

"What do you think of Carissa?" he asked Addie.

"I would like time to get to know her," Addie replied.

"She's an excellent cook," Ronan said with pride.

"That she is," Hagen agreed with a grin.

Addie frowned and shook her head.

"You don't like her?" Ronan asked, upset.

"It isn't that," Addie said, and thought a moment. "There's something alarmingly familiar about her, and I can't place what it is."

"How could that be? You've never met her," Ronan said.

"True, but I feel as if I have," his mother said with a confused shake of her head.

"She may remind you of someone," Hagen suggested.

"The question is who?" Addie tapped her head as if trying to force the answer.

Hagen took hold of her hand. "We will go for a walk and talk about it and see what sparks your memory."

Ronan's shoulders slumped. He wanted to speak with his mother, but he didn't want to keep her from what appeared to be the man she adored. He was glad for her, but he needed her at that moment.

Addie slipped her hand from Hagen's and patted his face. "We will take a walk later. Right now I'd like to speak with my son."

Hagen nodded. "Just let me know when you're ready."

Addie leaned over and kissed his cheek. "Thank you."

She turned to Ronan when the door closed behind Hagen. "I never thought I would love again after losing your father. I didn't think it was possible. I loved your father so very much, I could never imagine loving another with the same intensity."

Ronan remained silent, listening.

"Then Hagen smiled at me." She laughed. "Can you imagine, just a smile and I felt something in my heart flutter. He is different from your father, and yet . . ." She shook her head. "I found myself falling in love with him." She laughed again. "He's a gentle giant, where your father was much like Cavan." She took her son's hand. "We can't dictate love. We can't ignore it. We can't beg for it. But we can recognize it and embrace it when it finds us, no matter how crazy it may seem."

Ronan hugged his mother's hand. "I do feel crazy. How does one fall in love with one's enemy?"

"How *did* you fall in love with her?'

Ronan told his mother all about it. From the very first time he had met Hope to his discovery of the true possibility that Carissa and Hope were one and the same, to his utter confusion and utter hope that the matter would somehow miraculously resolve itself.

"Perhaps the question you need to ask is," his mother said, "is Carissa truly your enemy?"

"That is the way I have thought of her for the last two years. And it is the way Cavan continues to think of her."

"You and Cavan are no longer captives. You are home in the safety and love of your family. Think as you wish and reach your own conclusion. It is what your family expects of you, as does your laird."

He took her hand. "Somehow you always manage to make it seem as though things will go well."

"And you," she said proudly, "somehow always managed miraculously to solve your problems." She smiled. "You not only need to know who Carissa is, you need to remember who you are."

Chapter 28

Carissa couldn't believe what Septimus was telling her. Cregan, a warrior whose heritage was
in dispute, as some believed he came from nobility
while others believed him no more than a bastard,
had surfaced once again. Cregan had battled on her
father's side on occasion, though remained far removed from the battle with the Sinclares. She had
known that some of her father's warriors had fled
to Cregan's stronghold following Mordrac's defeat,
while others had left beforehand, having lost confidence and respect for their leader.

"You're telling me that in these past two years,
he has been building his fighting force?"

"It seems that way," Septimus said, warming
his hands by the campfire flames. "And he's on the
move."

"How has he managed to build such a force with
no one hearing about it?" Dykar asked.

"He resides on the fringes of the northernmost
regions of the Orkney Islands, an isolated area and
not an easy place to live or to reach. It would take
time for news of his activities to reach here; and

then only if word was sent from the inhabitants themselves," Carissa said.

"Which means Cregan has purposely sent word that he's headed this way," Dykar said.

"I don't like this," Carissa said.

"There's more," Septimus said reluctantly.

"What is it that you've obviously been hesitant to tell me?" Carissa asked.

Septimus rubbed his hands together and peered across the flames at Carissa. "It's rumored that Cregan comes for *you*."

She snapped her head back as if she'd been slapped. "Why?"

Septimus explained. "From what I've learned, it seems that your father had made plans for you and Cregan to wed. And Cregan plans to claim his intended."

Carissa could only shake her head. She had worried that the time would come that her father would choose a mate for her, with no consideration to what she wished. She couldn't believe that her father reached from beyond the grave to continue to command her life. And to a man who in many ways was similar to him.

"How did you come by this information?" Carissa asked.

"One of Cregan's men appeared at our camp seeking protection," Septimus said. "It seems that he doesn't want to remain part of Cregan's group any longer."

"Or as I've said"—Dykar nodded—"Cregan sent someone."

"And I suppose this man acts as if he doesn't know that I lead the group," Carissa said. "That he believes you simply a strong group of mercenaries."

"It appears that way, but, like Dykar, I don't believe him," Septimus was quick to say.

"Are Evan and Piper still with you?" Carissa asked.

Septimus nodded. "Yes, they plan to visit with Alyce and Lachlan before they return home."

"See if they would be willing to scout for us before they go, and explain how they must keep it a secret," Carissa instructed. "And send some of our men out to see what they can discover."

"Are you going to discuss this matter with Ronan?" Dykar asked.

Carissa gave his question thought. If she confided in Ronan, she could very well place his life and his family's lives in danger. Cregan was after her, and if anything, he wasn't stupid. While he might have amassed a small army, she didn't believe his intention was to defeat the Sinclares though that didn't mean that one of them wouldn't be caught in the conflict. Undoubtedly, he sent someone, or more than one person ahead to find out where and how accessible she was. Only then would he decide on a plan of action. Thus it gave her time to wade through this mess and decide on her own course of action.

"Time will tell whether I do or not," Carissa answered. "I need to know more about Cregan's whereabouts before I share any information with the Sinclares. With that said, it is best we return. I have been gone long enough."

Dykar agreed, and Septimus promised to let them know when he heard anything new.

The guard that had followed her to the stable and saw that she intended to see to her horse's care was still outside talking with two of his friends. She was grateful her absence had not been noticed, but then she had kept her time with Septimus short though she had wished for more. Cregan was not a man to dismiss lightly, and she would have preferred to linger and discuss possible scenarios that Cregan might consider and their options in preventing them.

She did wish that she could confide in Ronan, but presently she wasn't sure if that was the wisest decision. She didn't wish to place anyone in any danger, though danger lurked either way. It was just that until she knew more, she felt it was best she say nothing. And at the moment, she wanted nothing more than to steep in a tub of hot water and wash her weariness and worries away.

The guard followed her to her cottage, and when she entered, she was disappointed to see that no bath awaited her. Frustrated and tired, she reluctantly left the cottage and went to the keep.

Addie was the only one in the great hall and she hurried off the bench and walked over to Carissa. "I've been waiting for you. Ronan asked me to see to a bath and some clean clothes for you."

"I would truly appreciate both," Carissa said sincerely.

"Follow me," Addie said.

Carissa couldn't help but notice the odd way Addie looked at her. She wasn't certain if the woman was trying to peer deeper into her or if she struggled to keep her hatred from showing and her mouth from speaking. She continued to wonder over it though she made no comment.

She was surprised when Addie took her to Ronan's room. A tub waited and was soon being filled by a bevy of servants. A dark blue wool dress gathered beneath the breast with light blue ribbon lay on the bed waiting for her. It was lovely and reminded her of gowns she once wore and a life she once lived, but now she preferred simpler garments, a simpler life.

Carissa would not disrobe in front of any of them, and so she waited for the servants to leave. When they finally did, and Addie was just about to, she turned to her and asked, "You treat me so kindly, and yet you look at me as if . . ." Carissa shook her head. "I can't define it, I just know there is something there you wish to say, and I prefer you say it."

"You are a puzzle to me, dear," Addie said walking over to her. "And I will admit that it is all because Ronan has fallen in love with you. At least he believes it is you he loves. Before that, I would have believed you like your father, heartless and selfish, but if my son thinks otherwise of you, then I must learn for myself what it is he sees that others don't, or haven't been allowed to."

Carissa raised her head proudly. "I am who you see standing here."

Addie smiled. "What we see in front of us isn't always the truth of things." Addie laughed. "Take Hagen. He's a large man, tall and broad who at first glance could frighten the devil out of you and yet—"

"He is the kindest of souls and his speech more articulate than one would expect," Carissa finished.

"So then he isn't what he appears to be, and I daresay my son saw the same in you."

"Ronan hates Carissa," she said sadly.

"He doesn't know Carissa, nor do I," Addie said. "Therefore, I must get to know you before I am to judge you. And the reason I stare so oddly at you?" She shook her head. "You look startlingly familiar to me and yet I—" She continued shaking her head. "I cannot recall where it is I could have seen you."

"I doubt you have seen me anywhere. My father kept me cloistered as much as possible."

That got Addie to stop shaking her head and instead laughing. "If you were like most children, you would have found a way to sneak off on your own."

Carissa grinned. "I did, and I had the best adventures."

"Then you and Ronan have something in common, for he did the same when he was young."

"But he had brothers to share it with."

"Not all the time," Addie said. "He often sneaked off on his own, to have his own adventures. He would return and confide his secret endeavors, and I, in turn, would keep them secret."

"As you do now with what he has confided to you about me?" Carissa asked.

Addie nodded. "Why don't you tell me why you love my son?"

"You believe I love your son?"

"At times I catch a glimpse of it in your eyes," Addie said, "though you try hard to hide it. Tell me how you fell in love with my son."

With that Addie began to help Carissa undress, and Carissa didn't protest. She felt the need to tell this woman, the mother of the man she loved, just how she had so unexpectedly fallen in love with her enemy.

"He was hurt and frightened," Carissa began, "and he reached out to me, not knowing who I was, not judging me, simply needing someone to hold on to. I empathized with him since I often felt the same myself. From there it was easy to pretend I wasn't Mordrac's daughter, and the more I got to know Ronan, the more my heart went out to him.

"I was accustomed to demanding, domineering men; never had I known a man to reach out to me in need, to be vulnerable and yet so brave." Carissa shook her head. "It sounds strange that a needy man could be brave."

"As I said, what we see isn't always what is."

"Ronan is like no man I have ever known," Carissa admitted. "He may have hated Carissa and wanted her dead. But when he did finally capture her, his intentions were to see that she was treated fairly and presented before his laird for judgment. Unlike my father, whose judgment often came swiftly at the end of a sword."

Their conversation twisted and turned in many directions, and it wasn't near to ending by the time Carissa stepped from the bath. But after a preponderance of yawns, Addie insisted she nap.

Carissa didn't argue; she felt tired down to her very bones, and she wanted nothing more than to sleep.

Addie tucked her in Ronan's bed, and while Carissa knew she should have protested and returned to her appointed cottage, she was simply too tired. She would nap and be gone before Ronan, or—heaven forbid—Cavan, knew she rested in this bed.

The last thing she heard as her eyes closed and sleep claimed her was the click of the closing door as Addie took her leave.

Ronan couldn't believe that he had three nephews and a niece. The little fellow, the one twin who was his namesake, had a similar nature to his own. And the one named for Ronan's father, Tavish, was as temperamental as *his* namesake. And at two years old, the little lads appeared inseparable, one always looking to see where the other was and both enamored of their mother.

Blythe, Artair and Zia's daughter, was a little beauty, with a sweet smile that could charm the coldest heart. Over a year old, though with the confidence of one much older, she eagerly climbed onto his lap and into his arms when he reached down for her, and her vibrant green eyes startled, since it seemed that she could see right inside you.

Then there was Roark, Lachlan and Alyce's son, who was yet to turn one, though he made himself known with his broad smile that so reminded Ronan of Lachlan. However, he seemed to have his mother's strategic mind, for his eyes followed everyone, he knew what each was up to, waving frantically at the twins when one crept up on the other, and he was alert to when someone left the room.

This was his new family, and he hoped with all his heart that Carissa carried his child and that their child could not only join this happy clan but unite enemies.

Ronan was as disappointed as the children when naptime was declared by the mothers, though when his mother advised him that Carissa was presently napping peacefully in his room after a soothing bath, he hastily took his leave.

While he could have joined his brothers, who were in Cavan's solar discussing clan matters, he much preferred to join Carissa. He was well aware of Cavan's warning about keeping his distance from Carissa, but he was only going to check on her, or so he told himself.

The door opened with a creak, and he winced, not wanting to wake her. He knew she must be tired, having woken before dawn, then having to deal with his brother and him. It was good she rested, though damned if he didn't want to rest alongside her.

He took careful steps over to the bed. She was lying naked on her side beneath the covers, one slim leg resting on top of the blanket, her arm exposed as well, and her lovely breast peeking out from the covers.

Naturally, he reacted as any man in love would. He grew hard as a rock.

He warned himself to take his leave, get out of there right away, run if he had to, but get his legs moving. His feet refused to budge. It was as if he were stuck to the floor and his glance stuck on her.

He ached to make love to her once again. One time just was not enough, he wanted more. He wanted to hold her, kiss her, love her, lose himself in her and hear her moan with the pleasure he brought her.

His passion spiked even more, and he moaned in discomfort and had to fight to keep himself from stripping naked and rushing to her side. One taste of her had him starving for more, and he was having a difficult time denying himself and her, for he doubted she would turn him down.

He finally got his feet moving, though not toward the door—the wiser direction. He walked to the bed and stopped next to it, staring down at her. She sighed and turned, the blanket slipping farther off her and fully exposing one breast as she stretched her arm up above her head.

Her gentle movement also gave a peek at the

blond hair that nestled between her legs. It fired his loins even more, more so than if she had lain fully exposed, since the slight peek tempted and teased him beyond reason.

He should pay heed to his brother's command and allow Carissa and him time to learn more about each other. They needed to reach a reasonable solution to their dilemma, and being intimate right now would not be the wisest thing. He couldn't be selfish and think only of himself. He had to think of Carissa and what his self-indulgent actions would do to her.

If she didn't deny him, as he knew she wouldn't, it would appear to his brother that she was having her way of things, winning the battle Cavan believed she waged. It was only proving to his brother, and he supposed to himself, that she played no ruse, that her nature was of hope, not cruelty.

He smiled. He might not be able to make love to her, but it didn't mean he couldn't, if only briefly, hold her. He pulled the blanket over her, a shield against her nakedness and his desire, and stretched out on his side beside her.

Chapter 29

Ronan nestled his face in her hair, a hint of lavender teasing his senses as the soft, silky curls tickled his face. He rested his arm across her waist though he kept his hand from touching her, afraid that if his fingers simply brushed her flesh, he would want more. And he did not intend for his raging desire to interfere with the pleasure of holding her close.

She turned around and snuggled up against him as she had done so many times when they were at the cottage. His arms closed around her instinctively. When had he begun to protect her? When had he begun to realize that she belonged in his arms? When had he realized that Carissa was the woman he loved?

"It doesn't matter," he whispered. "I love you."

As if she heard, she rubbed her cheek over his heart, then rested firmly against it. Her simple action made him shiver to his soul, for he felt as if she had claimed him for herself more potently than words.

He should have been wise and left then, but

love appeared to be more foolish than wise, and at the moment he wanted to be more foolish than anything.

Carissa stirred, and her eyes suddenly sprang open.

And he couldn't, he simply couldn't, resist a kiss.

Her lips were warm, her taste familiar, and when she responded so willingly, the kiss slipped from his control. Need and yearning took over, and they both surrendered. He struggled to keep his hands to himself, while they itched to touch and explore.

She didn't help matters, pressing her body firmly against his. He was disappointed though grateful that he could feel only a shadow of her body through the blanket. If he felt any more of her, he'd be sure to surrender to his passion, and she would obviously have trouble not submitting to her own.

He had no choice, he had to end the kiss, but he did so with extreme reluctance. He rested his brow on hers, giving them both time to catch their breaths and, hopefully, still their yearnings.

"We shouldn't," she whispered

"We won't," he said.

"But I want to," she admitted breathlessly.

"As do I, but we must wait."

"Yes, we must wait," she said sadly. "We must make certain that your brother is assured that I play no game but truly love you."

Ronan was surprised she didn't turn away from

him, for her remark had left him feeling guilty that, yet again, he had failed to come to her defense, or was it their defense? Instead, she returned her head to his chest, and he took his leave when once again she fell asleep.

When Carissa woke a short time later, she was hungry, not only for food, but for Ronan. Since only one was possible, she dressed and found her way to the cook area. The servants seemed reluctant and a bit uncertain whether to serve her, and she wasn't surprised. Gossip among villagers traveled fast, and if the laird had yet to approve of her, then the villagers certainly weren't going to accept her.

She was relieved when Addie appeared, and though in a hurry, she took a moment to instruct the servants to provide Carissa with whatever food she wished.

Addie's cheeks glowed red and her green eyes sparkled. After she grabbed a flask of wine and crusty loaf of freshly baked bread, she hurried out. Carissa smiled, knowing that Addie and Hagen were about to rendezvous.

After tasting what was available and finding it not to her liking, actually barely tolerable, she gathered ingredients needed to make a tasty meal, to the bewilderment of the servants, and went to her cottage. If anything, the cooking would keep her thoughts from Ronan.

She cut, chopped, and kneaded, thinking of nothing but the task at hand. Her thoughts had been occupied of much lately, and she longed for time away from her problems.

She had just set a pan of apple buns on the wooden table to cool when a gentle knock sounded at the door.

Knowing it was senseless to think she could keep anyone out, she bid her guest enter. She was surprised to see that it was Honora.

"It smells heavenly in here," Honora said, and smiled. "Forgive me, I forget my manners. I should have given you a greeting first."

"That was the best greeting I have ever received," Carissa said.

"It's a truthful one." Honora sniffed at the cooling apple buns. "If they smell this heavenly, I can only imagine how they taste."

"Please sit," Carissa said, pointing to a chair at the table. "I'll heat some cider for us, and you can have a taste."

"I certainly won't turn down that invitation," Honora said, and sat.

"If you don't mind, I need to finish this bread while you visit," Carissa said.

"Please do. I didn't mean to interrupt, though I never expected to find you cooking."

"It's something I enjoy."

Honora took a bite of the bun Carissa sat in front of her, and her eyes opened wide. Before she took another bite, she said, "And something you do with great talent."

"Thank you," Carissa said, "and forgive my bluntness, but why are you here?"

"I've experienced your bluntness firsthand," Honora said.

Carissa nodded. "I remember when my father had you kidnapped and brought you to his stronghold."

"I remember how coldhearted you appeared," Honora said. "But what surprised me was when you first arrived here, it was as if I was seeing a different woman, and I began to remember more."

Carissa continued kneading the bread.

"When food was brought to me, you always accompanied the slave who brought it and the platter was always full, much too full for a prisoner . . . and the food much too tasty. And you always managed to calm your father's anger when he spoke with me, or more often redirected it to yourself."

Carissa shrugged. "Those things mean nothing."

"My husband would probably agree with you," Honora admitted. "But there is one more thing that defies reason, as Artair would say. I had prayed and hoped to find a way to escape your father so that he could not use me as a pawn when my husband came to rescue me. I had all but given up, not being able to find any way out of your father's stronghold, then . . ."

Carissa remained silent.

"Cavan arrived to lay siege to your father's land and, while chaos erupted around me, I spied you on your horse taking a path I had never noticed before. It would have only been noticeable to one who knew it was there. I followed you and made my escape, and to my surprise, a horse waited along the path, which made my escape easier."

"Why do you tell me this?"

"Because the more I thought about it, the more I realized that it wasn't luck that helped free me from your father—it was you."

"No one would ever believe such nonsense," Carissa said.

"I thought perhaps my husband would."

"But he didn't, did he?"

Carissa shook her head. "He recalls only pain when he thinks of you, and yet somehow I wonder about that too."

"Your husband's suffering and pain were real when held captive by my father."

"I have no doubt of that," Honora said sadly. "But I do wonder if perhaps you helped him, and possibly others, without any of them realizing it."

Carissa punched the dough and gathered it up and slapped it down on the table. "I am who I am."

"That's the problem I have, Carissa," Honora said softly. "Who are you?"

Carissa never got to answer Honora, who was summoned to the keep by her husband and, for once, Carissa was grateful for Cavan's interference. Besides, how did she answer the question? She had spent far too many years protecting herself to suddenly begin to trust strangers. And to her, Honora was a stranger.

She sat on the chair she had moved near the

hearth and watched the bread bake. Now that she was done cooking, her thoughts rushed forward, and she wished for a reprieve from them.

The heavens answered when another knock sounded, and this time it was Zia who entered, wearing a huge smile.

"Mind if a visit for a while?" she asked, and pulled a chair near the fire before Carissa could respond.

"I'm glad you're here. It gives me a chance to thank you for all you've done for my men."

"I know we don't know each other well, but my grandmother speaks so highly of you that I am pleased finally to have the chance to get to know you myself."

"Your grandmother is a remarkable woman," Carissa said. "She helps so many."

"From what she's told me, you do the same."

"I look after my warriors—"

"More than just your warriors" Zia said.

Carissa felt uneasy with compliments. She did what she did because it was the right thing to do. She needed no praise for it.

"Can I offer you a hot brew?" Carissa asked, wanting to change the course of the conversation.

Zia popped up off the chair. "I'll get it. You rest." She talked while she worked. "It seems that everyone is wondering about you."

"What you mean is that gossip has begun to spread, and tongues are wagging wildly," Carissa said. "I have no doubt villagers are already aware of why judgment against me has been delayed and that most, if not all, believe I tricked him to couple with me."

Zia nodded as she handed a mug to Carissa.

"With barely a day since my arrival, I can't imagine what further time here will bring for me," Carissa said.

"I find that time can be a friend rather than an enemy, which is another reason I stopped to visit. Can you tell me how long it will be before you know if you are with child?"

"About two weeks," Carissa answered.

"You are feeling well?" Zia asked.

Their conversation continued about birthing and babes, and Zia regaled her with stories of the Sinclare deliveries and babes and how Carissa would meet the little darlings later at supper. And then she left.

When the door closed, Carissa's hand went to her stomach. She hadn't given much thought to being with child. Perhaps it was because she had thought it only a distant dream that would never come true. But now there was a possibility that it might.

She didn't know what she would do if she was carrying Ronan's child. However, she did know that it would present problems, one being that Cavan would not pass judgment on her.

The thought disturbed her, for then she would never be free. And the Sinclares would be forced to accept her.

She shook her head. She didn't want to be forced on anyone, least of all Ronan.

The solution to her dilemma came easily. If she was with child, she would not let anyone know. Then she realized it could possibly cause her another problem. Cavan just might punish her, and that could harm the babe. And what of Ronan? Didn't he have a right to know that he would be a father?

She stood and paced before the hearth.

It would be so much easier if she wasn't with child, yet she had so wanted children. And she would probably long for one of her own even more after meeting the Sinclare babes tonight.

She shook her head. She couldn't do it. She couldn't participate in a family meal with the Sinclares and watch the love and happiness they all shared and know they had yet to accept her.

She didn't wait for Ronan to come collect her for supper. She notified the guard that she wasn't feeling well and wouldn't be taking supper with the Sinclares. He looked ready to remind her that Cavan had ordered her to the meal, so she gave him two apple buns and hot cider, spiced with her own flavorings.

A short time later he knocked on the door and told her he would deliver her message and that he hoped she was feeling better, and by any chance did she have another apple bun to spare?

Chapter 30

Ronan got finished tumbling on the floor with his twin nephews and stood, brushing the rushes off the little lads, then himself. Blythe had clapped with glee, and Roark had kept steady eyes on them all.

He couldn't believe his family had grown so much and in ways he had never imagined but loved nonetheless. He had never given much thought to children, his brothers and he too busy enjoying the pleasures of being young and free. But his ordeal had made him view life much differently.

He had never realized how very important his family was to him. And though he had worried that he would feel estranged from them, they had not changed. It was he who had changed, or at least thought he had. And while he might look at some things differently, he was who he always was—a Sinclare.

"More!"

Ronan laughed at his namesake, who stretched out his tiny arms to him. "Time to eat." He snatched the little fellow up in his arms and pretended to chomp at his cheeks. The lad laughed with glee until his mother, Honora, took him, which then had him crying in disappointment.

Ronan grabbed the lad's chin. "We'll play again, but first you must eat."

The lad seemed appeased and went with his mother.

Ronan turned and joined Cavan where he sat alone at the end of the table.

"Ronan loves his uncle Ronan," Cavan said with a smile.

"What's not to love?" Ronan teased.

Cavan shook his head and laughed.

"I thought one day there would be children to carry on our name." Ronan shook his head. "But I can't believe that day is already here."

"I look at my sons and think the same," Cavan said.

"As I do," Lachlan said, joining them near the hearth.

"Sons?" Artair asked as he approached. "Wait until you have a daughter, then you will know what it is to worry, especially when you recall your own wicked ways."

Lachlan slapped Artair on the back. "Look on the bright side. Blythe has three male Sinclare cousins to protect her innocence."

"Knowing her mother's spirited nature, do you think that consoles me?" Artair asked with a grin.

"It will have to do for now," Cavan said.

"Truly?" Artair asked. "I wonder if you will feel the same if it is a daughter you have next."

Cavan cringed, then swore then said, "Daughters obey their fathers."

His remark was like a punch to Ronan's gut. Had Carissa obeyed her father whether she liked it or not?

"Will you consider that when you pass judgment on Carissa?" Ronan asked.

"I will consider it all, including how I screamed, then passed out when she threw water on my open wounds after I had been whipped mercilessly," Cavan said. "And I certainly will remember how she laughed and told me to embrace the darkness."

"Wise advice," Zia said, walking over to the table, her daughter reaching her tiny hands out to her father and Artair taking her with a smile and snuggle.

"What do you mean?" Cavan snapped.

"If Carissa told you to embrace the darkness, then she knew you would pass out from her action. It is how you felt when you woke," Zia said, "that matters the most."

Cavan looked perplexed.

"How did you feel?" Zia asked. "Were you in pain? Or was your suffering bearable?"

Cavan looked ready to answer, then held his tongue, and his brow crinkled in thought. "I was on my stomach when I woke and someone, a soft, caring voice, ordered me to remain that way. And the pain—" He paused and shook his head. "The pain was minimal."

"Hope," Ronan whispered, though not quietly enough.

"Hope?" Cavan reiterated. "Of course I kept hope strong."

Ronan shook his head. "No. Hope helped you as she helped me."

"You're suggesting Carissa helped me?" Cavan asked irritably.

"If you weren't so stubborn, you might see that it is a strong possibility," Honora said, returning with one of the twins, who looked as if he wore his food rather than ate it.

"Your namesake is a fussy eater," Cavan said, ignoring his wife's accusation.

Ronan leaned down and playfully pinched the lad's cheek. "I know someone whose food you'd enjoy."

Honora smiled. "I had one of Carissa's apple buns. It was delicious."

"She made apple buns?" Ronan asked. "I need to get some."

"Carissa won't be joining us for supper," Cavan informed him. "She isn't feeling well."

Ronan turned on him with a sting of anger. "You just inform me of this now?"

"I only learned of it a short time ago," Cavan said.

"And you didn't think to inform me?" Ronan asked annoyed. "Especially knowing she could be with child?"

Zia was already walking to the door. "I'll see if she's all right."

Ronan joined her.

The others stared at Cavan.

"I am laird," Cavan said.

Honora huffed. "Then act like one."

Carissa had just taken the cauldron from the hearth to cool. She was looking forward to the rabbit stew that had simmered for hours. The scent was delicious, and her mouth watered for the first bite.

She had managed to calm her thoughts and intended to enjoy a tasty supper and retire early and hopefully meet with Dykar at sunrise to see if Septimus had unearthed anything new about Cregan.

Therefore, her door bursting open was completely unexpected and startling to say the least.

Ronan was at her side when he asked, "Are you all right?"

"I'm fine," she said.

"Are you sure?" Zia asked, having hurried in behind Ronan.

Carissa nodded, still startled by their appearance.

"We were informed you were ill," Ronan said.

"More tired than anything," Carissa said, which was the truth. She was simply fatigued by her whole ordeal.

Carissa saw that Ronan surveyed the room, and she knew he'd reach the obvious conclusion.

"You planned to eat alone," he said.

Zia gasped. "You shouldn't be alone if you aren't feeling well."

Ronan agreed, and before Carissa knew what

was happening, she was hurried to the keep, where Zia, with help from Honora and Alyce, had her tucked at the table with a soft wool blanket wrapped around her.

Ronan had seen to her rabbit stew being brought along with her as well as the fresh bread she had baked and the remainder of the apple buns, to the disappointment of the guards.

She was tucked and snug against Ronan as the Sinclares began to fill their bowls with her stew and share the bread she had made, while the twins happily ate the apple buns.

Carissa listened though she did not partake of the banter among the Sinclares. They were family, and while she sat among them, she still could not claim herself one. But she wished she could. They loved and laughed. They teased and tormented. But always, always, they were family.

She could even see how the Sinclare brothers—all but Ronan—tried hard to accept Hagen. Ronan had no problem with Hagen since he had fought by his side and knew him well. And Ronan trusted that his brothers would discover Hagen's worth for themselves.

This, she realized, was family. Something she had never known and what she had always hoped for and dreamed of, and yet never found. Now that it was in her reach, she ached to be part of it.

Carissa ate very little and hadn't realized that Ronan urged her to eat more. She had been too consumed by what went on around her.

"More! More!" the lad Ronan yelled, and his brother Tavish joined in.

"They love your apple buns," Honora said.

"I do too," Cavan said, splitting the last one to share with his twin sons.

"I'll make more tomorrow," Carissa said.

"Only if you're feeling well enough," Ronan insisted.

"Ronan's right," Cavan said, "only if you feel up to it."

Carissa remained silent, the whole night remaining strange to her. Laughter mixed with chatter. Praise for her cooking circled the table, and when Cavan suggested that she share her cooking talent with the cooks, she thought for sure she was in a dream.

But it was when Ronan walked her to the cottage and closed the door behind him and took her in his arms and kissed her that she believed a dream.

"Do you know how much I want to make love to you?' Ronan asked.

"You can't," Carissa said, telling herself it had to be this way. There was no choice. It was for the best.

"Why?"

"Your brother dictated as much," she said.

"My brother cannot dictate love."

Carissa managed to regain some of her senses, his kiss having rendered her vulnerable. "But who do you love, Ronan?"

"I love you," he whispered in her ear before nibbling along it and sending shivers down her spine.

"Who am I?" she asked, surrendering to his hands, which had managed to find their way beneath her garments to tease and tempt.

"The woman I love."

Carissa groaned when his mouth attacked her neck with nibbles and nips that tormented her beyond belief.

Somewhere reason assaulted her as he continued to taste her. "We can't do this."

With a strong arm wrapped securely around her waist, Ronan lifted her against him and carried her along to the bed. "I have let far too many people dictate my future. You are mine. You belong to me. And no one, not even my laird, will tell me that I can't make love to you."

Chapter 31

Ronan went down on the bed with her, and she sighed with the pleasure of his body covering hers. And though he felt so very good, and it felt so very right for him to be there with her this way, a nagging voice warned her against it.

"Ronan—"

He captured her mouth with his and kissed her senseless. It took her a few minutes to gather her wits, and the moment she did, he kissed her again, leaving her breathless.

"We need to talk," she said quickly before he stole another kiss.

"No," he said, and claimed her mouth again.

When he finished, she caught her breath, and said sternly, "Enough, we must talk."

He was off her in a flash, but not before she caught a hint of anger in his eyes. She didn't have to wonder over it. She knew what had caused it. He had recognized Carissa in her commanding tone.

He turned his back to her when he had stood and had yet to turn around and face her. No doubt he attempted to compose himself, but it didn't truly matter. Even though it was for a brief moment, she had clearly seen anger in his eyes where only moments before she had seen love.

That brief flare of anger was sparked by the hatred he felt for Carissa, and she wondered if he could ever truly love her as she was.

He finally turned around, and she sat up on the bed.

"What else is there to say?" Ronan asked.

She stood and placed her hand to his chest and with a soft, kind voice said, "There is much for us to say."

He smiled, and his eyes brightened. Gone was the doubt and anger, replaced by sheer joy, and he wrapped her in his arms. "Let's love first and talk later."

She would have loved to do just that, but she needed to know if what she had seen in his eyes lay dormant and would rear its ugly head whenever Carissa spoke.

"Do you truly love me?" she asked snappishly.

There it was again, that flare of anger that seemed to deepen the color of his green eyes. And was that tightness around his mouth? And where was his response? Stuck in his throat? Or was it the truth that he simply could not love Carissa?

The thought hurt her terribly, but then she had been a fool. How could she think that he would love her? His love was all for Hope, not a shred of it was for her.

"No answer?" she asked softly.

Again his anger dissipated, and he cupped her

face in his hands, warm, tender hands that sent shivers racing through her.

"I love you." He kissed her gently. "Only you."

"Is that Hope or Carissa you speak of?" she asked, her tone reflecting Carissa.

She was relieved he simply frowned and that no anger flared in his eyes.

"I wish the answer was that easy, but it's not," he admitted truthfully.

"Isn't it?" She walked away from him, making certain the table separated them.

Ronan rubbed at the back of his neck and seemed reluctant to speak.

"Talk to me, *Carissa*," she demanded.

He fisted his hand and shook it at her, his green eyes blazing with anger. "I've hated you for two years. And that hatred grew when I believed you killed the woman I loved. When I hear that familiar tone and recall her—" He stopped and dropped his fist to his side releasing his tightly curled fingers and shaking his head. "You can't expect me not to react to Carissa's voice. I'm still trying to make sense of it all."

He turned away from her for a moment, then swiftly turned around, throwing his arms wide. "I loved Hope more than anything in this world. If I hadn't, I wouldn't have searched so hard for her. I would have returned to my family, my home. But all I could think about was saving Hope and building a life with her." His anger returned though not as bitterly. "And what of you? You could have told me the truth."

Carissa laughed. "And what would your response have been?" She answered for him. "You would have never believed that Carissa could have a heart. You had known only her cruelty. And like your brother, you would have believed it all a ruse, a plan of mine to learn more about the Sinclares and eventually destroy them. After all," she said defiantly, "I am my father's daughter."

"Then where did Hope come from?"

"From you," she snapped.

He lunged forward, and though the table separated them, she stepped back, for his face raged red, though his words startled her.

"No, love created Hope," he said, pointing a finger at her, "your love and mine."

She stared at him, bewildered.

"Somehow," he implored, "somehow in the melee of anger and hate, love was born, our love. And if we don't fight against all odds to save it, hatred will win, and love will have lost."

"Father warned that love never lasted."

"Help me prove him wrong," he said. "Love me, no matter what. Love me as I will you. Love me until there is nothing left between us but love. Hatred will have no choice but to vanish forever."

"You believe love can do that?" she asked, hoping he was right.

"I believe *our* love can do that," he said, slowly walking around the table. "I already love Hope with all my heart. Give me a chance to love Carissa."

"You don't fear as your brother does that it's a trap?"

A slight smile played at the corners of his mouth as he got closer to her. "How do you know I'm not trying to ensnare you?"

She could tell by the glint in his eyes that he teased her. She reached out and took hold of his shirt and drew him closer. "You already have."

He brought his head down, bringing his lips close to hers. "I'm glad you realize that, since I'm never"—he kissed her—"ever"—he kissed her again—"going to"—he grabbed her around the waist and held her tight as he kissed her again, then whispered hotly in her ear—"let you go."

She threw her arms around his neck and pressed her body hard against his, and their lips found each others yet again, and they feasted.

Breathless when the kiss ended, she pressed her cheek to his and after a moment, said, "I want to make love with you."

He grabbed her chin and wore a wicked grin that only served to excite her more.

"Who do I make love to, Carissa or Hope?" he asked with a devilish glint.

"Can you handle Carissa?" she challenged.

He chortled and lifted her up to plop her down on the edge of the table. "The question should be, can she handle me?"

Carissa grinned and slipped her hand beneath his plaid to stroke the hard length of him and damn if he didn't feel like velvet in her hand. "You appear the right size, Highlander, but . . ." She paused, and her grin grew. "We'll have to see if you have the stamina."

"That's a challenge, my love, I'm definitely up to."

He tossed up her skirt and she pushed his plaid aside and when he grabbed her around the waist and yanked her forward, he slid into her with ease.

He rested his brow to hers. "Perfect fit."

"I agree," she said, and she slipped her arms around his neck. "Now let's see how much stamina you have."

He laughed, dropped his hands to her bottom, and lifted her just enough for him to move in a motion that had her moaning and groaning with pleasure in no time. And when she thought she would climax, he stopped and altered his rhythm, whether long or short strokes, it didn't matter, for it quickened her passion and her moans grew louder.

"Now," she begged after what seemed like forever.

"No, not yet," he whispered, and carried her to the bed, still inside her.

"Strip us," he whispered as he nibbled at her ear.

She did with haste, and he lowered them to the bed, where he proceeded to drive in and out of her with such exquisite torture that it wasn't long before she was begging him for release.

And he gave it to her with a forceful suddenness that had her screaming his name. But he wouldn't let it end there. When she thought it was done, the ripples past, they started all over again. He raised her legs so they rested on his shoulders and drove even deeper into her, igniting her passion all over again.

It was as if he had set her soul to burning, and only he could extinguish the never-ending flames. The heat poured through her and her body sparked and she wanted nothing, absolutely nothing, but him inside of her stoking, firing, and finally bursting until the fire completely consumed her.

She cried out when the burst came upon her, and it spread in ripples of pleasure as he made sure she enjoyed each and every one. Then she felt him burst and moan with pleasure, and she smiled.

She thought they would sleep the night, but their bodies thought differently, and she woke to his hand teasing her nub, already wet with the want of him. But he took his time, hardening her nipples with his flickering tongue, kissing down the center of her until his tongue replaced his hand, and she arched from the thrill that raced through her.

She was ready to climax in no time and he didn't stop her, though when she was almost finished, he entered her and caught up her ripples once again and drove her to another climax, in which he joined.

She snuggled in his arms afterward, feeling more content and complete than ever before. But that wasn't the end of it. Dawn had yet to arrive when she woke to him gently stroking her body, soft and subtle as if he barely touched her, and yet his faint touch created magic. It teased and tempted and made her shiver with desire. And when he was done with the front of her, he rolled her over and went to work there and she buried her face in the mattress to stifle her loud moans.

She heard him laugh, and as she turned to confront him, he wrapped his arm around her waist, swung her completely around, kissed her, then entered her slowly and with a damn grin.

She rose up to meet him, but he held back.

"Tell me you want me," he teased.

"You know I do."

"Tell me," he said, and eased out of her, though not completely.

"Don't make me beg," she snapped.

"Ah, my sweet Carissa," he said, his green eyes intent. "Tell me, Carissa, tell me you want me."

He had called her Carissa, and there was no anger in his eyes, so without hesitation she said, "I want you, Highlander, I want you so very badly."

"Damn if I don't feel the same about you," he growled as he set them in motion and within minutes sent them both reeling from the explosive release that left them breathless and completely spent.

The next time they woke they both lay exhausted wrapped around each other.

"I'm tired," she said on a yawn.

"So am I"—he grinned—"but it's a sweet exhaustion that I savor."

She smiled. "I wholeheartedly agree."

"We should sleep more," he said with a yawn.

"Again I agree," she said, as her eyes closed.

The final time they woke it was to be startled out of sleep by a vicious pounding on the door.

"Ronan, get out here," Cavan yelled from out-side the door.

Carissa had no intention of letting Ronan face his brother alone. She was just as guilty as he, though Cavan probably thought her more guilty. He probably assumed she had seduced Ronan.

"What are you doing?" Ronan asked as he wrapped his plaid across his chest to tuck in at his waist.

She tucked her blouse in her skirt and stuck her chin up. "I will face your brother with you."

"You'll do no such thing," he ordered. "This is between Cavan and me."

She stopped herself from protesting, realizing that it was as Ronan said, something that could only be solved between brothers.

"You're right," she said. "I will wait here for you."

"Thank you," he said, and kissed her, then smiled. "You have to admit. I do have stamina."

She chuckled. "And glad I am for it, Highlander."

"Ronan, get out here, or I'm coming in," Cavan shouted.

"I'm coming," he yelled back.

"You will not fight your brother, will you?" she asked, worried.

He laughed. "It may be what we need." He kissed her then, and said, "Make me some apple buns while I see to my brother?"

She nodded. "I'll have them waiting."

As soon as Ronan walked out the door, she hurried to the window and peered out. She was disappointed to see that they took their argument to the keep. With nothing left for her to do but wait, she hurriedly washed her face with water she heated at the hearth and tied her hair back with a strip of cloth.

She then got busy with the apple buns and just as she set them to cool a knock sounded at the door, and she sighed with relief, though she wondered why Ronan didn't just enter.

But it wasn't Ronan at the door. It was Dykar.

"Don't tell me, more bad news," she said after closing the door behind him.

"Septimus received a message that Cregan wishes to speak with you."

"Well that sounds promising," she said. "I can tell him face-to-face that I have no intentions of honoring any agreements my father made with him."

"I hope it's that simple."

"Is there some reason you don't believe it will be?" she asked.

Dykar shrugged. "Why didn't he come for you right after your father died? Why did he wait?"

"I'll find out," she said. "When does he wish to meet?"

"He won't be here for at least a week, and he asks that you choose where and when."

"He seems to be accommodating."

"Too accommodating," Dykar complained. "And I still think it would be wise to inform the Sinclares about his approach."

"If I can handle this without them knowing anything about it, it just might be better for all."

"And what if they find out about his approach and think you have planned something with him?" Dykar asked.

"You do have a point," she said. "No doubt they will discover his approach when he draws near enough."

"And then it will be too late, and you will appear guilty."

"You've always looked out for me when possible," she said with a smile

"That's especially important now since you've gone and fallen in love," he said, grinning wide.

"I have, Dykar," she said joyfully. "I have truly fallen in love."

Just as they threw their arms around each other and hugged tight, the door flew open and in walked Ronan.

Chapter 32

Ronan stood frozen in the doorway, never expecting to see the woman he loved in another man's arms. They broke apart, and Carissa hurried over to him, greeting him with a blissful smile and a kiss, but still, he did not like the scene he had burst in on.

"Dykar has come to visit," she said. "He can join us for the morning meal."

Ronan nodded, though reluctant, preferring time alone with her. He closed the door behind him. "The twins asked for more apple buns."

"Would you like to take some to them?" she asked, walking over to scoop out a couple.

"You take them," he said, sitting at the table. "It will give Dykar and me a chance to get better acquainted."

Dykar responded before Carissa could object. "Go, Rissa. I'd like a chance to speak with Ronan."

Carissa looked from one man to the other, shook her head, then scooped the buns in a basket and placed a cloth over them.

She gave Ronan a kiss, and as she walked out

the door, she said, "You obviously survived the encounter with your brother, please do the same with Dykar, since I love you both."

Ronan glared at Dykar and wondered what she meant that she loved them both. He should be the only one she loved. Who was this man who had earned Carissa's love? Suddenly he remembered something Carissa had mentioned at the cottage. Just a brief reference when they had spoken about siblings . . .

"She loves you like a brother, doesn't she?" Ronan asked.

Dykar nodded. "And I love her like a sister."

"Do you know her like one?"

"Better than anyone," Dykar said.

"Not quite," Ronan said with a smile.

Dykar didn't smile. "I know things about her you will never know, for she will never speak of them to you."

"Tell me," Ronan said. "I truly want to know Carissa."

"If you love her, what difference does it make?"

"It's not *if* I love her, I *do* love her, but—"

"But what?" Dykar snapped annoyed. "If you love her, nothing else should matter."

"Nothing does matter," Ronan shot back. "But I have a family that needs convincing that she is kind and can be trusted."

"She needs to know the same of you, though I can tell you that her father made sure that trust did not come easily to his daughter," Dykar said. "He was a cruel, cruel father."

"So it would seem from the few things she has told me," Ronan said. "I'm surprised her father allowed you two to become so close."

"He didn't. Carissa learned early on that he would not allow her to love anyone or thing, and with me being a slave—"

"You were a slave of Mordrac's?" Ronan was shocked.

"I was, though Carissa made certain that I wasn't treated badly." He laughed. "The only way she could be sure of that was to treat me badly herself. She made it appear that she hated me, then we would sneak off to the woods together, where she had food hidden for me. We would talk and play."

His smile faded.

"What happened?" Ronan asked.

"I matured, became a man, and couldn't stomach the way Mordrac treated her. I foolishly spoke up to him."

"What did he do?"

"He ordered me whipped to near death and left on the post to die slowly."

"Carissa saved you?"

Dykar nodded. "That she did. She got me out of there before the whipping. I wanted her to go with me, but she refused, reminding me that Mordrac would search the world for his daughter, then brutality kill the man she fled with, but a mere slave he would not waste his time on."

"So she remained behind and you—"

"I fled, though not far, and Carissa brought those she helped flee to me."

"Which started the mercenary troop?"

"Yes, that's how we got started," Dykar said.

Ronan thought a minute. "So Carissa made me think I was being sold to mercenaries when she was actually freeing me."

"She hoped you would simply return home and forget about her."

"And when I didn't—"

"Her only choice was to remove the reason why you remained with the group," Dykar said, shaking his head. "She didn't realize that your love for Hope was so strong that it would demand revenge against her."

"Carissa seems to have sacrificed a lot for others," Ronan said.

"She has lost more than you will ever know."

Ronan was beginning to realize that there was a depth to Carissa that defined not a cruel nature but rather a selfless one. It made him want to protect her, cherish her, and love her all the more.

"This may seem an unimportant question, but why is Carissa frightened of dogs?"

Dykar sighed and slowly shook his head. "Rissa loves dogs."

Ronan stared at him oddly. "Not from what I've seen. She froze when my mother's dog raced over to her to lick her hand, and I watched her shove a puppy away from her when all he wanted to do was play."

"I'll tell you a story no one knows, and I only know it because I watched from a hiding spot, fearful that Rissa would suffer her father's rage." Dykar paused and took a breath. "At a young age, Rissa became attached to a puppy while her father was away warring. The little fellow followed her everywhere. They were inseparable. When her father returned, he flew into a rage when he discovered that she cared for the puppy. He screamed at her about love being foolish and not lasting and he would not have a daughter of his being foolish. He took that puppy and in front of her . . ." Dykar couldn't finish, his eyes filled with tears.

Ronan sat speechless, feeling as if his heart had been torn out of his chest.

"Rissa learned that day never to let her father see that she cared for anyone or thing. She pretended to steel her heart to keep others she cared for from suffering, but somehow she still managed to hold on to hope." Dykar pointed at him. "And you arrived beaten, bruised, and bloodied, and you reached out to her and called her Hope, and she lost her heart to you."

Dykar pointed his finger at Ronan. "Don't break it. Her heart has been damaged enough. She does what she does to protect people, not to hurt them."

Ronan was stunned. He almost wished Mordrac was still alive so that he could kill him all over again. But then Carissa had experienced enough hatred; what she truly needed now was to be loved.

"I'm glad we got to talk," Ronan said.

"So am I," Dykar agreed. "And just remember that whatever Rissa does, she does out of love."

* * *

"Thank you so much," Honora said, pulling apart the apple buns for her sons to share. "That's all they have asked for since they woke this morning."

"I'm glad they like them," Carissa said, wanting to return to the cottage, worried that Ronan and Dykar might not get along.

Tavish screamed when Lachlan stole a piece of the bun from his plate.

Honora sent him a scathing look.

Lachlan licked his fingers after finishing the piece. "They're too tasty to ignore."

"I'll bake more," Carissa said, pleased that everyone enjoyed them.

"Lots," Lachlan said.

"Carissa!"

She jumped at the unexpected shout of her name, though turned calmly to glare at Cavan.

"I wish to speak with you," he said.

It was a command, not a request, and she nodded.

"Can't this wait?" Honora asked her husband. "She has yet to eat, and neither have you."

Cavan glared a moment at his wife, then turned and walked away.

Carissa knew it was a silent command for her to follow, and so she did, with a quick smile to Honora for her concern.

She entered Cavan's solar, he closing the door behind her. And without waiting to be invited to sit, she took a seat in one of the chairs before the hearth. He joined her, and she could see that he was none too pleased with her actions, or perhaps he was unhappy with his confrontation with Ronan. Either way, he was annoyed.

"My brother believes you a good, kind woman," he said.

"And you don't?"

"According to Ronan, my opinion of you is misconstrued and, therefore, I would not be able to judge you fairly. He feels that you should be given time to prove how kind and generous you are before I pass any judgment on you."

She was ever so pleased that Ronan had defended her. "And how do you feel about that?"

"I feel I should judge you and end this farce since it's obvious my brother has no intention of obeying me," he said angrily.

"Would you obey such an order?"

"He is not my laird."

"No, he's your brother," she reminded. "And the both of you have suffered enough because of my family."

"I agree," he said bluntly.

"Then judge," she said, her shoulders back and her chin high.

"Here and now?"

"I'm ready," she said.

He shook his head. "You are entitled to be heard by all before I pass judgment."

"I waive that right. Judge me as you will, you have the right."

He shook his head. "You are a bold one."

"If it is bold to speak the truth, then I am guilty of being bold," she said. "So say what you will, and I will do the same."

"Fair enough," he agreed.

"Tell me what I am accused of so that I may challenge the accusation."

"You and Ronan are of the same mind," he said. "He reminded me that you have committed no crime. You may be guilty of being cruel while we were prisoners of your father, but your only crime is being Mordrac's daughter. He also pointed out that we haven't always been kind to prisoners ourselves and have never been punished for it."

"But you still seek revenge against me," she said. "I can see it in your eyes."

He leaned toward her. "Give me a reason not to. For my brother's sake, give me a reason."

Carissa hesitated. Did she take the chance and trust this man? Could he truly want to help his brother, or did he somehow wish to trap her? In the time she had spent with Ronan and in the short time she had been here, she had learned one thing. The Sinclares truly loved each other, and if she believed that, then she had to believe that Cavan loved his brother and wanted to see him happy.

"I could tell you how very much I love him. How nothing would make me happier than to carry his child, the first of many. But I don't believe that would appease you," she said. "The problem is, you think of me as your enemy."

"Yes, I do," he said.

"Until you believe me your enemy no more, there is nothing I can do to convince you."

"For my brother's sake, I urge you to try," he insisted.

Her brow puckered. "Why the urgency?" Before he could respond, she gasped. "Ronan gave you an ultimatum."

"He did. I either make peace with you or you both will leave and find a place where you will be accepted."

Her heart soared, then plummeted. She did not want to see Ronan give up his family for her. Family was much too important, and she would not let him do that.

"He can't do that," she said.

"I told him the same, but he is stubborn, or I suppose, stubbornly in love."

She smiled then, finally understanding. "You are trying to give him what he wants."

"If I don't, my wife will stop speaking to me, as will my mother, not to mention Zia, and Alyce has mentioned several times that it is wiser to keep an enemy close."

"The women defend me?" she asked surprised.

He shrugged. "I can only assume they see something I don't." He grinned. "Though my wife is a good judge of people, and I trust her opinion. Besides, I would miss talking with her."

Carissa held back her laugh.

"So tell me, Carissa, daughter of Mordrac, why I should allow you to join my family and my clan."

"If I confide in you, Cavan, laird of the clan Sinclare, will you give me your word not to share what I tell with anyone?"

"Does that include Ronan?"

"Yes, it does," she said softly.

"I give you my word as laird and as a warrior."

Carissa did the only thing she believed she could do. She trusted Cavan. She shared stories with him that she had never told a soul. She told him about her father's cruelty from when she was young. And then she explained how she had helped Ronan and how she fell in love with him. Finally, she finished by explaining why she had treated him as she did when he was a captive, how it was all a ruse so that she could help him without her father knowing. She told him how the water she had thrown on his wounds had contained herbs that had helped to heal him. And she explained how she had planned and executed the escapes of many prisoners and slaves, including him. And then she detailed how she had formed the mercenary troop and finished with a surprise that left him speechless; she explained how she had helped his wife escape so that her father could not use Honora as a pawn against him.

Cavan sat staring at her.

"I can't make you believe me," she said. "But I must tell you that I have never entrusted anyone, not even Ronan, with all of what I just told you. And while I don't know if you will believe me, I have spoken the truth to you."

Cavan sat silent for a few moments, then finally

found his voice. "I am grateful and honored that you trusted me. And oddly enough, I do believe."

"And now do you know enough about me to pass judgment?" she asked, her head held high.

"I do," he said.

"Wait," she said making a decision that she felt was for the best. "There is one more thing I must confide to you." She told him about Cregan, and that she had not confided this for fear of placing the Sinclares in danger.

"Thank you, Carissa," Cavan said. "You have given more than I needed to make a wise decision, and I do agree that we tell no one about Cregan just yet, not until we find out more. And I'm very proud to welcome you to my family and my clan. You are truly a Sinclare warrior."

Carissa jumped out of the chair with a cry of joy.

Chapter 33

Ronan didn't wait long after Dykar had taken his leave to hurry to the keep. Carissa had been gone too long, and he was worried. He shouldn't have sent her there alone. Not after the heated discussion he and Cavan had.

He had tried to get his brother to understand how he felt about Carissa and that there was nothing he could possibly say that would change his mind. He had surprised Cavan and himself when he told him that if Carissa wasn't accepted into the family, he would find a place that would accept them. And he had meant it.

After last night he knew that Carissa belonged to him and always had. The more they made love throughout the night, the more he watched as Hope and Carissa blended together as one. At times he heard the sweet kindness of Hope, then the bluntness of Carissa, until after a while he could barely tell the difference. Hope and Carissa were one and he loved that one . . . he loved Carissa.

That realization had made it easy for him to confront his brother. While he had no desire to leave his family, he also didn't want to lose Carissa. His ultimatum to his brother had been for Cavan to realize just how determined he was to keep the woman he loved.

Ronan understood Cavan's anger, for it had once been his own, but he was certain that once Cavan truly got to know Carissa, he would feel differently toward her, and all would end happily. At least that was what he hoped.

Ronan entered the great hall, and the twins went running to him. He scooped them up, one under each arm, and walked to the table with them, giggling. He was about to ask where Carissa was, concerned that she was nowhere in sight, when he heard her screech.

He plopped the lads down by their mother and ran to the solar, flinging the door open and rushing in. He was shocked to see Carissa hugging a grinning Cavan.

Honora rushed in behind him, skidding to a stop beside him.

"You've finally come to your senses," Honora said, walking over to her husband.

Carissa moved away from Cavan and hurried to Ronan's side.

He wrapped his arm around her waist; her smile was jubilant.

"I'm free," she said. "I'm truly free."

Honora slipped her arm around her husband's waist and kissed his cheek.

"Is that all the thanks I get," he whispered.

She kissed his cheek again, then murmured, "When the twins nap, I'll show you just how appreciative I am of such a wise and fair husband."

Cavan swung his wife around in his arms to rest securely against him. Then he looked to Ronan and Carissa. "Since you owe me, please take the twins and keep them occupied for a while."

"Cavan!" Honora scolded, her cheeks blushing red.

"I'd love to have the twins for a while," Carissa said.

"We'll play in the snow with them," Ronan said, pleased with the turn of events. That Cavan entrusted the twins with Carissa meant that he did truly accept her and possibly even forgave her. And by playing in the snow with the lads, the villagers would see that Cavan approved of Carissa.

"Keep them as long as you'd like," Cavan said, and grinned at Ronan.

Ronan laughed.

And before Honora could say a thing, Cavan's mouth found hers and while he hungrily kissed his wife, he waved Ronan and Carissa away.

After Ronan shut the door, he did the same to Carissa, kissing her.

"It's done," Ronan said. "You are free, and you are now protected by the clan Sinclare."

"I can't believe it," she said, smiling. "I never thought this day would come. I never thought it possible."

"We will celebrate," Ronan said. "What would you like to do?"

"I want to do as you told your brother. Play with the twins in the snow."

"We will, but what else?" he asked, wanting her to have what she never did, a choice of her own.

"For now that's enough," she said. "To play freely with children and truly be able to enjoy it means much to me."

"Then that's what we'll do," Ronan said, and took her hand to go gather the twins.

Tavish and Ronan squealed with delight each time their uncle Ronan hit one of them with a snowball. And they enjoyed it when, each time they hit him, he fell to the ground. His namesake would then run over and drop scoopfuls of snow on him. Then Tavish and Carissa would join in until, with a growl, Ronan would rise, and the twins would run off laughing.

The only way that Carissa and Ronan could get the twins inside was for Carissa to tell them that they could help her make more apple buns. And that's what they did. First they went to the kitchen, and the twins and Ronan helped her gather what she needed, then they went to the cottage where Carissa stayed and, before making the buns, she set a broth to brew for them to have while the buns cooked.

Carissa had never had such a wonderful time cooking. The lads were covered with flour and apple bits stuck to their cheeks and fingers. It was a delightful time, and while the buns baked, the twins sat eagerly eating the broth and bread she had spread with soft cheese.

A knock came at the door just as Carissa joined them at the table. Ronan bid them to enter with a shout, and the twins mimicked him.

Honora entered, Cavan following behind her.

"You didn't have to keep the lads this long," Honora said.

Cavan grinned. "But we're glad you did."

Honora playfully slapped his arm, then went to hug her sons.

Tavish started crying. "No go. No go," he said through tears.

Ronan smiled. "Looks like your son found a new home."

"Join us," Carissa offered, standing to give her seat to Honora. "There's plenty."

Cavan scooped up Tavish and sat him on his lap. "It smells too good to turn down."

They ate and talked and between them all they finished the buns, and by the time they were done, the twins were sound asleep in their parents' arms.

Before Cavan left, he turned to Carissa. "Maybe you could teach our cooks to cook like you. Otherwise, you're going to have the whole Sinclare family eating every meal here."

Carissa agreed, and when she shut the door, Ronan slipped his arms around her waist and rested his cheek next to his.

"It's been too long since I've held you," he said.

"Much too long," she agreed.

"And too long since I kissed you," he said, and turned her around in his arms to do just that.

She sighed when it ended. "I've known no other kiss but yours, but I do know that no other kisses could satisfy or entice me as yours do."

He traced her moist lips with his finger. "You're telling me that these lips have known no others but mine?"

She nodded. "Yes, you are the first ever to kiss me."

He grinned. "And I'll be the only man ever to kiss your lips."

"I want no other but you, Highlander," she said softly.

He lifted her up in his arms and carried her to the bed, and for the next few hours, they lost themselves in love.

Snow fell for the next few days, though not heavily. While Carissa and Ronan found time to be alone, often in bed, she also started becoming part of the Sinclare family.

She was amazed at how easily she got along with the three wives and shared their interests. She'd spend time with Honora stitching and even showed her how to improve on a stitch or two. When visiting with Zia at her healing cottage, she discussed herbs and potions that helped heal. And when with Alyce, they discussed battle strategies. The only thing the other women knew about that she didn't was birthing babes, and they freely discussed each of their experiences with her.

It was the first time in her life that she felt that she had a family, and she cherished every moment spent with each of them. She much enjoyed talking with Artair, for he was pragmatic, and Lachlan? He made her laugh. He was a charmer. But there was no doubt that each Sinclare man was a warrior, and a courageous one at that.

Then there was Addie. While Carissa wished to get to know her better, the woman was rarely around. She spent much time with Hagen, to the chagrin of all of her sons, except Ronan.

"Mother's been gone for three days," Cavan said, as they finished the morning meal in the keep.

"She told us where she'd be," Artair said.

' "With Hagen, don't worry,' is not telling us where she is," Cavan said.

"Cavan's right," Lachlan said. "We should know where she is."

"Hagen would never let anything happen to Mother," Ronan said.

"There's no need to worry," Carissa said. "Hagen and your mother are with my men."

"What?" All four sons bellowed.

The wives chuckled.

"What is my mother doing with mercenaries?" Cavan asked perturbed.

Carissa shook her head. "I couldn't tell you that. I only know that they are with my men, and they are safe."

"Why are your men still here?" Artair asked curiously. "With you in no danger, I assumed they would return home."

"There are some matters that must be seen to first," Carissa explained.

"A new leader being appointed for one," Ronan said.

"Let's get back to Mother," Cavan said. "Carissa, can you please get word to our mother?"

"I thought to go see my men today," she said.

"I'll be going with her," Ronan said, "so I'll see how Mother is."

"I'll go along," Alyce said. "I'd like to visit with Septimus."

"Evan and Piper are there as well," Carissa said.

"Then I'm going too," Lachlan said.

"Maybe all of us should go," Cavan said. "And the keep can take care of itself."

"You should spend more time with your wife," Lachlan suggested. "You're less cantankerous when you've spent time with her."

Cavan shot him a look that should have had him cringing, but instead Lachlan laughed.

"I'll be here," Artair reminded his brother.

"Though I may need him to help deliver a litter of pups later," Zia said.

Cavan stood. "I've had enough." He looked to Carissa. "I need to talk with you."

Ronan stood along with her.

"I will speak to Carissa alone," Cavan ordered.

"We don't keep secrets," Ronan said.

"I do," Cavan said. "And while it appears at times you all fail to treat me as your laird, make no mistake that I am."

Things had just turned for the good, and Carissa didn't want to be the reason the brothers argued. She placed a gentle hand on Ronan's arm, and said, "Why don't you see to getting the horses ready? We can leave as soon as I'm done."

She could tell he was annoyed, but he nodded.

Carissa smiled and tugged at his shirt so that he would lean down, and she kissed his cheek, and whispered, "I'll confide all to you when we're done."

He was instantly appeased, and Lachlan and Alyce joined him to see to their horses.

Carissa didn't give Cavan a chance to speak once he closed the door to his solar.

"I assume this meeting pertains to Cregan," she said.

"It does," he answered. "I'd like to know what else your men have learned about his approach. How many men in his troop? If there is any further indication of what he wants and so on. You have commanded your men long enough to know what information I'm looking for."

"I don't like keeping this from Ronan," she admitted.

"I can understand that. But I know my brother, and when he learns that a warrior who had fought alongside your father heads this way wanting to meet with you . . ." Cavan shook his head. "I will not be able to contain him. And in a sheer moment of foolishness, he could very well lose his life."

"I don't believe Ronan would do anything fool-ish," she said, though she secretly wondered.

"Are you sure of that? After all he's gone through to find the woman he loves, do you truly believe he wouldn't do anything to protect you?"

"I see what you mean," she admitted. "I suppose it is better we don't take the chance."

"It is better we find out what Cregan wants from you before we alert Ronan to the situation."

She nodded. "Agreed."

"So what are you going to tell him I said to you?"

"How did you know I'd tell him?"

Cavan grinned. "I have a wife who expects the same."

She laughed and shook her head. "I'm not sure what to tell him."

"I am," Cavan said. "Tell him I wanted to know if he asked you to marry him yet."

Chapter 34

Carissa rode beside Ronan, while Alyce and Lachlan rode in front. A fur-lined cloak and hood, along with fur-lined boots, a wool skirt and blouse did much to keep her warm against the bitter cold.

"I've waited long enough," Ronan said. "Tell me what my brother had to say."

Carissa hesitated. Things had been going so well, and while she would love to be Ronan's wife, she didn't want to suggest it to him. She much preferred he'd ask her on his own. And yet Cavan had asked the question. Dare she?

"You hesitate," he said, concerned. "What's wrong? Did my brother upset you?"

"No," she said quickly, not wanting him to assume the worst. "Cavan has been very pleasant with me."

"I truly believe he has grown to like you"—he laughed—"though I wonder if it has something to do with your delicious cooking."

"It's possible," she said, though she knew it was because she had shared the intimacies of her life with him that caused him to see her in a different light.

Ronan smiled and reached his hand out to her. She took hold of it, and though it was warm, it sent shivers racing up her arm and throughout her body. It was always that way with him. All he had to do was touch her, and she wanted him.

"*We're* home now. It isn't only me who has come home; it is I and the woman I love who are finally home."

She had never thought she'd have a true home, and she let him know how much it meant to her. "You could have given me no greater gift than the gift of being welcome in your home."

"It is just the beginning of the gifts I will give to you," he said, squeezing her hand. "And we will have a lavish wedding with clans coming from far and wide to honor our special day."

Her heart quickened and her breath caught and she glared wide-eyed at him.

"What's wrong?" he asked, alarmed. "Don't you feel well?"

"You wish to wed me?" she asked, as if not believing her own question.

It was his turn to look startled. "Of course I do—" He stopped suddenly and shook his head. "I should have approached our getting wed differently. This is neither the time nor the place to discuss the matter. Instead, let us talk about what Cavan had to say."

Carissa laughed.

"My brother was humorous?"

"No," she said, trying to stop from chuckling, "it's just that Cavan wanted to know if you had asked me to marry you yet."

They both smiled and continued holding hands as they rode along.

Ronan went in search of his mother, Septimus having told him she had recently returned with Hagen and they were warming themselves by one of three campfires.

Septimus took Alyce and Lachlan to see Evan and Piper, and Carissa went off alone with Dykar. She informed him that Cavan now knew of Cregan, but following his advice, though she was aware it was more an edict, she had yet to tell Ronan.

"I could see where Ronan would be upset if he knew Cregan was coming for you," Dykar said.

"Have you found out why yet?" she asked.

Dykar shook his head. "His man has been vocal in his reasons for leaving Cregan's crew, too vocal, but he remains tight-lipped when it comes to important information. He foolishly thinks we believe that he wishes to join our group."

"Perhaps he simply bides his time until Cregan arrives."

"Either way, I believe he knows much more than he says," Dykar said.

"How long before Cregan arrives?"

"A small contingent of his men should be here soon enough," Dykar said.

"He sends an advance group?" Carissa asked curiously. "I wonder why?"

"I've wondered the same myself."

"I don't like this," Carissa said. "I need to discuss this with Cavan, and, like it or not, Ronan needs to know about this."

"I agree."

"Keep the men on battle alert," Carissa said. "Have the scouts reported any unusual movement in the area?"

"Nothing of note."

"I want to speak with Evan and Piper," Carissa ordered. "They see things others don't."

Dykar nodded and went to find them.

Ronan spotted his mother sitting next to Hagen in front of the campfire. Her smile was wide and she practically beamed with joy. He was pleased to see her so happy. His brothers had told him how much she had grieved for their father. He was glad to see that she would always love his father, but also that she found happiness for herself with a good, trustworthy man.

She jumped with a cry when she spotted him and ran to him. He caught her in his arms and hugged her tight, just as she had done so many times to him when he was a lad.

"I have news I want to share with you and Carissa," Addie said. "It will make Carissa so happy."

"Tell me," Ronan said,

Addie shook her head.

"No, the news is for Carissa, and she should hear it along with you."

"I'll go get her," Ronan volunteered.

"Let me," Addie urged. "I've spent little time with her."

"But you won't tell her anything without me, will you?"

"I promise," Addie said. "I will tell all when I have you two together."

Ronan nodded as his mother hurried off, then he turned and sat next to Hagen on the thick fallen tree by the campfire.

Hagen shook his head. "I'm not saying a thing."

"Just give me a hint," Ronan cajoled.

"Your mother remembered who Carissa reminded her of."

"Who?" Ronan asked anxiously.

"Would you break a promise to the woman you love and intend to marry?" Hagen asked.

"You got me on that one—" Ronan glared at Hagen. "You intend to marry my mother?"

"I do," Hagen said firmly. "I love her, and I will have her as my wife if she agrees."

Ronan grinned. "You do realize that you're going to have to speak to Cavan first. And then there's Artair and Lachlan. Now if you were to share just a bit of information with me, I might be able to ease the way for you since you have no worry from me. It's obvious that my mother loves you and that you love her, so I have no problem with the union. Besides," Ronan said with a slap on Hagen's back, "I know you're a good man."

"I appreciate the offer, truly I do," Hagen said, "but I gave your mother my word, and I will not go back on it. And your brothers don't frighten me."

Ronan rubbed his chin. "I was afraid of that. There isn't much you fear."

"Only losing your mother," Hagen said.

"I'm pleased and proud to welcome you to our family," Ronan said.

Hagen smiled. "Thank you, Ronan. I appreciate that."

Ronan held his hands out to the campfire to warm. "Now that we're going to be family, at least tell me where you and mother went."

Hagen shook his head.

"Do you need help?" Addie asked, as she approached a thin-faced man leaning against a large boulder. He looked to be in pain.

"My stomach," he said, his hand pressed against it. "Must be something I ate."

When she reached him he leaned on her, draping his arm around her shoulder.

"I can fix you a brew that might help," Addie offered.

"You're already helping," the man said, leaning his face close to hers and placing the tip of his dirk to her stomach. "Keep quiet and keep walking."

Addie did as told.

Carissa saw Addie approach with the man leaning on her. She didn't walk forward to meet them. Instead, she studied them, since the man didn't look familiar to her. She had made certain to know the faces of her men, not that they knew her. She had always watched her troops from a safe distance and trusted only those she knew she could.

Something wasn't right with Addie, she could see it and she placed her hand on the dirk at her waist. She cursed the fact that she had chosen to remain removed from the men while waiting to speak with Evan and Piper. While she could see some of her men, they were too far to take note of her, and even if they did, nothing would seem amiss.

"Take that dirk out slowly and drop it nice and easy to the ground," the man ordered. "Or I'll cut this woman good."

"Then I'll be of no help to you," Addie said.

"I'm not stupid," the man whispered harshly. "I'll cut you to hurt you, not to kill you."

"Enough," Carissa said softly though anxiously when his hand looked ready to stick Addie in the gut just to prove his point. After she dropped her dirk, she asked, "What do you want?"

"For you to come with me," he said.

"Let her go and—"

"I give the orders," the man said. "You're both going with me. Now move."

Carissa didn't argue. She would do as she was told until a chance presented itself; and then . . . the man would find a knife at his gut.

Unfortunately, that chance never materialized, and the situation worsened rapidly. The man never let go of Addie, so there was always the threat of his hurting her, which would make an escape even more difficult, for there was no way Carissa would leave Addie behind.

They were soon joined by three other men, garbed in monks' clothing. It didn't take Carissa long to realize that they were no monks but rather experienced scouts, who knew how to cover their trail. She only hoped that Evan and Piper were more knowledgeable.

Carissa knew Dykar had sentinels posted around the camp, alerting him to anyone's approach, but she had no doubt that the so-called monks had seen to removing that obstacle. And with the sentinels not being changed for another few hours, Dykar would not know immediately of their absence. Not that they wouldn't be missed soon, but not soon enough for a good head start.

They soon met up with three more men, and these had horses.

"Let her go," Carissa said in such a commanding tone that the men looked startled. "Cregan wants me. Let her go, and I will go with you."

The thin-faced man laughed. "You'll go with us anyway." He poked Addie in the stomach with the tip of his dirk. "She'll make sure you obey."

Carissa walked up to the man so fast he had no time to react. "Cut her, hurt her in any way, and I'll make sure you die a slow, agonizing death." Before he could respond, she continued with bravado. "And if you doubt me, know who I am, Carissa, daughter of Mordrac the *merciless*."

The man quickly moved his dirk away from

Addie and ordered everyone on their horses. Carissa was glad that they intended for her and Addie to share a horse. It would give them time to discuss their situation though they were ordered not to speak.

Whispers would do, since she made certain to ride behind Addie and warned her to say nothing, respond only with a slight nod or turn of her head.

While they rode single file, Carissa whispered to Addie, telling her all about Cregan and that Cavan was aware of the situation. No doubt they would be rescued; but, not wanting to take a chance, they would need to do what they could to procure their escape.

Addie agreed.

Carissa explained that the sooner they tried to escape, the better, since they would probably meet up with more of Cregan's men, which would make an escape even more difficult. And, since Addie was familiar with the area, it would behoove them to do it immediately.

Both women were excellent riders; they knew their chance was now. Carissa held on tight to Addie. Addie gave the horse a kick, and both women started screaming, upsetting the other horses and startling the men so badly they didn't know what to do, which gave the two women time to make their escape.

"What do you mean Carissa and my mother can't be found?" Ronan demanded of Dykar.

"We don't have time to explain it all," Septimus said. "We need to find their trail and follow."

"They wouldn't leave the camp," Ronan argued.

"My brother's right," Lachlan said, Alyce standing beside him.

"They didn't," Septimus said. "They were abducted."

Ronan felt his heart pound mercilessly in his chest, and it took him a moment to speak. "What do you mean? Who would abduct them?"

Dykar gave him a quick explanation about Cregan, finishing with, "Carissa was going to speak with Cavan right away and see that you were informed about the situation."

"We need to leave now," Septimus said.

Lachlan agreed fast enough.

Hagen stood beside Septimus. "We can't let them get too far from us."

While Ronan agreed, there were also other things to consider, and though he wished Cavan hadn't kept this from him, there was no time to waste being angry at him.

"Lachlan, you and Alyce return to the keep and tell Cavan. He will have our warriors ready in no time. Dykar, Septimus, Hagen, and I will take some men and find and follow the trail."

"Evan and Piper are already on it," Septimus said. "If they can't pick up the trail, no one can."

"We'll leave men along the way so you know where to follow," Ronan said.

Lachlan nodded and stepped up to his brother.

He put his hand out and their hands locked on the other's arm.

"See mother and Carissa safe," Lachlan said.

"You have my word on it," Ronan said.

Lachlan and Alyce rode off, and Ronan joined the other men.

There was no way he would lose the woman he loved now that he had just found her, and there was no chance he would allow any harm to befall his mother.

This Cregan would pay for abducting the two women who meant the most to him. He might look a Highlander, wearing his clan plaid, but at the moment he felt more a barbarian, ready to kill without thought or reason. And he would do just that to save the ones he loved.

Chapter 35

Carissa and Addie put as much distance between them and the men as possible, but two riders slowed the horse down, and the men caught up with them in no time. Not that she and Addie gave up. They maneuvered their way through the men until the thin-faced one called Sully struck out, hitting Addie and knocking her off the horse. Carissa went with her, having no intention of leaving Addie alone to face Sully's anger.

When he jumped off his horse and rushed toward the women, Carissa scrambled to her feet as Addie confirmed she was all right and stood protectively in front of the woman, her feet braced, her head high, and her hands fisted in front of her.

"Touch her, and I'll kill you," Carissa said through gritted teeth.

Sully wisely halted and glared at her. "Try that again, and I will kill her."

Carissa marched right up to the man and rapped him in the chest. "Do that, and I'll see that Cregan doesn't get what he wants."

"What do you mean?"

Carissa snatched the dirk so fast from the scabbard at Sully's waist that he had no time to respond, especially when she placed the blade at her throat.

"Do Addie harm in any way, and you'll not have me to hand over to Cregan."

Sully quickly tried to take the dirk from her, but he could not budge her hand, and he paled.

Carissa was wise in the ways of men like him and knew he did not pale simply because she threatened to take her life. He paled because he feared something more than her threat.

"Tell him, Cregan," she called out. "Tell him I will do it, and he will have failed you."

"I knew you would grow to be your father's daughter," the deep voice boomed.

Carissa threw the dirk to the ground, the point sticking deep into the soil. Then she turned and looked upon the man she had not seen in some time.

He sat astride his stallion. He was sizeable in girth and height, with thick black hair braided at each side and falling past his shoulders. He was not a man of good features, with a nose that had been broken in several spots and scars that ran down one cheek and his neck. He had thick hands that she remembered recoiling from.

She had just turned fifteen, and he had run his hand up the sleeve of her dress in a way that had disturbed her, grinning in a way that had turned her stomach.

And his words that day, she had pushed from her mind. "One day, Carissa, you will be mine."

"Let the woman be," Cregan ordered.

Carissa leaned down and helped Addie to stand. Her chin was darkening from Sully's blow.

Carissa turned to Cregan. "She stays with me."

He laughed. "You don't trust me."

"Not the least," she said bluntly, "though I also don't believe you a fool. If you kill the mother of the laird of the clan Sinclare, they will hunt you until their dying day."

"True enough," he agreed, "which is why she will be released soon enough. After all, it is only you I want."

"You can't have me. I am promised to another."

Cregan laughed again. "I think not. Your father promised you to me."

"Then why didn't you come for me sooner?"

"You were not easy to find," he admitted. "It took the man who claimed to love you two years finally to track you down. I have no love for you, only the desire to mate with a woman born of Mordrac. And watching you handle my man, I can see that you are your father's daughter."

"I am not like my father," Carissa argued.

"You are more like him than you know," Cregan said. "Now it is time for us to leave."

"You need Addie no more, let her go," Carissa demanded.

"In time," Cregan said. "And, while I admire your courage, do not think to dictate to me, for I will teach you your place fast enough."

Carissa laughed in his face. "If you truly believe me Mordrac's daughter, then you know that is not possible."

"Mount," Cregan shouted. "We leave now."

Carissa helped Addie onto the horse.

"You won't ride with her," Cregan said.

She ignored him and mounted behind Addie.

Sully marched over to her and reached out to grab her. She kicked him hard in the chest with her booted foot and sent him sprawling to the ground.

"Have you learned nothing from dealing with her?" Cregan asked, shaking his head at the man.

Sully looked from Cregan to Carissa as if at a loss as to how to handle the situation.

"I ride with Addie," Carissa said. "It will be no other way."

"I could force—"

Carissa never let Cregan finish. "Do you truly wish to try?"

"As I've said." Cregan smiled. "You are your father's daughter."

Ronan never saw anyone traverse the terrain with such familiarity as Piper. Though Evan was an excellent scout and tracker, Piper was beyond excellent. Evan agreed, and said so with evident pride in the woman he loved.

She stood only about four inches over five feet and had a thatch of wild red hair pinned haphazardly to the top of her head though several strands didn't always remain secure, and she was slim and wiry. And her face always had a smudge of dirt somewhere on it that Evan took delight in removing for her. They were a perfect pair.

He was a good four inches taller than she and his long, pale brown hair forever appeared unkempt, though his face bore no signs of dirt. His brown eyes lit with love every time he looked upon Piper, as hers did when she looked upon him.

Watching them made Ronan fear all the more for Carissa's safety though he knew she was far more capable of taking care of herself than his mother. Not that his mother wouldn't try, it was just that Carissa had more experience in so many ways.

She would certainly show her abductors not an ounce of fear, and she would do whatever it took to escape. He knew without a shred of doubt that she would protect his mother, even with her life, and that frightened him. Not that he wished to trade his mother's life for Carissa's. He wanted them both alive. It was just that Carissa took chances others would not and, if she did, she might forfeit her life in an attempt to free them.

"They found the trail, though it won't be an easy one to follow," Dykar advised, riding up beside him. "It seems that someone is good at covering their tracks."

"But we will be able to follow it?" Ronan asked concerned.

"It's a challenge that Piper doesn't intend to lose," Dykar said, shaking his head. "That woman knows the woods as if they birthed her."

"Thank the lord for that," Ronan said.

"I know you're worried about Rissa, but she can take care of herself."

"That's what worries me," Ronan admitted.

"Don't let it," Dykar said. "I have seen her extract herself from situations I thought impossible."

"There's always that one time . . ."

Dykar nodded. "That one time was you. No matter how hard she tried to free you, you kept coming back. And I believed that she hoped you would."

"I don't give up easily."

"For her, I'm glad you didn't," Dykar said. "Rissa needs and deserves someone to truly love her, someone to finally free her of Mordrac."

"I would have thought her freed once her father died, but now, knowing how he treated her, I understand what you mean."

Septimus joined them. "We have a good trail, and Piper and Evan move ahead to keep us on the right one."

"Then let's not waste another moment," Ronan said, and followed the two men.

Carissa knew that the farther away from her men and Sinclare land they traveled, the more difficult a rescue would be. She did believe that Cregan wouldn't harm Addie. It made no sense for him to do that; after all, she was leverage in his game.

"Do you really think he'll come for you?" Cregan asked, pulling his horse up alongside her. "Or will he come for his mother and surrender you for her?"

Addie laughed. "You don't know my son. He will see us both released, or you will die."

"Shut up, old woman," he snapped.

Addie ignored him. "Then there's Hagen to deal with. He'll rip you limb from limb for taking me."

It was Carissa's turn to laugh. "She's right about that. I've seen what happens when he's enraged, which isn't often, but when it does." She shook her head. "Not a pretty sight."

"A worthy opponent, since my rage is much like your father's, Carissa," Cregan said. "And I'm sure you recall his."

How could she forget it? Mordrac had been an uncontrollable madman when enraged. No one could speak to him, let alone speak reason to him. One warrior who'd tried lost his life quickly enough. After that, no one spoke when Mordrac flew into a rage, and all scattered, none wanting to become a target of his fury.

She had learned to avoid him at those times, and if she couldn't, she had learned how to agree with him unless it meant someone's life, then she spoke up—often suffering the consequences.

"Your silence and obvious deep thought tells me you recall," Cregan said.

"A madman is often hard to forget," Carissa said.

"Your father was no madman," Cregan said. "He was a brave and powerful warrior."

"He was a fool," Carissa argued, "as are you for taking on the Sinclares."

"She's right about that," Addie agreed.

"I have no intentions of taking on the Sinclares," Cregan said. "You were promised to me, documents were signed, and I have the right to take you."

"I have given myself to another," Carissa said, hoping once he heard that he would not want her any longer, but he simply smiled.

"It matters not," he said with a shrug. "What I want is children born of you and me, children of Mordrac's bloodline. And I will have it." He rode off.

Once he rode away, Addie whispered, "Do you think he would let you go if he discovered you weren't Mordrac's daughter?"

Ronan was hunched on the ground, studying the tracks and shaking his head. "How many men and horses do you think were here?"

"Several horses and three more men," Piper said.

"I don't know how we failed to detect their presence," Dykar said, to show his annoyance.

"You couldn't have," Piper said. "We had to have seen them but for some reason thought them no threat, and—" She paused and turned to glare wide-eyed at Evan.

"Monks," he said before she could. "We spotted three monks, and they seemed no threat." He looked to Dykar. "I told you about them."

Dykar chastised himself. "I am a fool."

"It matters not," Ronan said. "What concerns me more is that Cregan may very well have split his men up purposely."

"Which means they'll all come together, and we do not know how many we will face," Dykar said.

"Leave a man here," Ronan ordered, "and make certain he advises Cavan of this matter. We continue on."

"That's a good idea," Carissa whispered. "If I can get Cregan to believe I am not truly Mordrac's daughter, he would not want me any longer. But it would have to be a believable tale."

"Why don't you tell him that your father captured your mother in a raid on a village?" Addie asked.

"It has been whispered that is what happened though my father saw it differently. Strange as it may seem, I think that my father believed my mother loved him. But somewhere he must have realized the truth, for he often commented that hate endured while love never lasted."

"Love endures," Addie said softly. "I can attest to that, as I am sure you can."

"I have loved Ronan from the moment I laid eyes on him, and never has my love for him weakened or faded throughout this whole ordeal."

"Such an enduring love usually brings suffering and a good touch to add to the story. Convince Cregan that your mother had such a love for your true father," Addie said.

"I have often wondered if my mother loved my father."

"According to the story, she loved your true father beyond all reason, as you do Ronan," Addie said, adding to the tale. "She and your father knew each other since they were young and were inseparable. Where you found one, you would find another, and it seemed only natural that the two would be together forever."

"What a lovely story," Carissa said. "And it truly sounds believable."

"That it does," Addie said, "but I must finish it. You must use names to make it more convincing. Cormack, your father, and Shona, your mother, wed, and they were happy. She got with child after a short time and they both looked forward to the birth and hoped for many more."

"Now comes the suffering," Carissa said sadly.

"Yes, it does," Addie agreed. "Their village was ravaged by barbarians."

"My father," Carissa whispered.

"No, my dear, remember that your father is Cormack. Mordrac is nothing more than the barbarian who brought suffering upon your family. He killed your true father and took your mother for his own."

"And she never let Mordrac know she was with child," Carissa said, adding her own touch to the tale.

"That's right," Addie said. "She wanted to secure her unborn child's future, and by making the mighty Mordrac believe the child his, she had that chance."

"But she couldn't live without my true father's love, and she perished from a broken heart," Carissa said, ending the sad tale.

"Would you not do the same?" Addie asked.

Carissa thought on it, knowing that her situation mimicked that of the tale. Only she knew the circumstances of the child left behind, for she had lived through them. And she could very well find herself in the same situation. Soon she would know if she carried Ronan's child and that, if no escape was made or rescue accomplished, then she would live the tale herself.

"While my love for Ronan is beyond measure," Carissa said, "I could not nor would I leave my child with Cregan, for that would be a fate more cruel than its death."

"Perhaps, then," Addie said softly, "you are stronger than your mother."

"Circumstances made me strong."

"Then, in a sad way, your mother gave you the strength to survive," Addie said.

"I would have preferred that my mother remained with me."

"Loving someone from the time you were very young and having him die in your arms is a tragedy that not only breaks the heart but tortures the soul."

Carissa closed her eyes for a moment, imagining how she would feel if Ronan lay in her arms dying, but then he would have died if she had not struggled to keep him alive and safe from her father. She could not imagine the excruciating pain and helplessness she would suffer if Ronan lay dying in her arms with nothing she could do to save him.

"I am glad this is just a tale, for it is a very sad one," Carissa said. "But it is one I am sure I can make Cregan believe."

Chapter 36

Night fell, and they had to make camp. Ronan sat staring at the campfire flames. He felt helpless, and he didn't like it. He had felt helpless far too much in the last couple of years. The only thing steadfast in his life had been his love for Carissa.

A smile teased the corners of his mouth.

Carissa, not Hope.

When had he fully merged the two? He couldn't say. He only knew that he no longer thought of them as two separate women. While he had once believed there were distinct differences between the two, he had come to learn that there were distinct reasons for those differences. Once he understood them, he was finally able to see the whole woman that Carissa truly was, and he loved her all the more for it.

"She will survive," Dykar said, joining him by the fire.

Ronan nodded. "I have no doubt of that. From what I have learned, she has survived far worse. But there is a big difference now."

"A difference?"

"Yes, a very big difference," Ronan said. "Carissa now has me to love and protect her. And I intend to make Cregan pay for taking what is mine."

Dykar smiled. "It is good to hear that you will fight for her."

"I would die for her."

"Do not do that," Dykar warned. "While Carissa has survived much, I do not believe she would survive your death. She would want to join you. And I selfishly do not wish to lose my best friend."

"Worry not," Ronan advised. "I have waited too long to find the woman I love, and I intend for us to enjoy many, many, many long years together."

Carissa sat by the fire with Cregan. Addie lay curled up in a blanket sound asleep not far from them. His men patrolled the area, and sentinels were posted for the night. Cregan was diligent about keeping anyone from finding them.

But Carissa knew that Piper and Evan would be tracking them, with Dykar right beside them. And she also knew that Ronan would come for her, she had not a doubt that he would.

Hate and love were close companions. It was hatred that had driven Ronan to find Carissa, and it would be love that drove him to rescue her. The thought filled her with soothing warmth that rippled over her entire body and filled her with a sense of peace.

She loved and was loved in return.

"I'm not Mordrac's daughter," Carissa said bluntly.

Cregan simply laughed. "Who are you then?"

Carissa conveyed the tale that Addie had concocted with such belief that, with every word she
spoke, the lines between Cregan's eyes and around
his mouth grew deeper, until he was left with a
heavy frown.

"When did you learn of this?" he demanded.

"When I was young."

"Who told you—certainly not your father?"
Cregan challenged. "He believed you his."

"As my mother intended." She and Addie had
considered everything Cregan might question, so
she would be prepared to answer, and she did. "It
was a slave who told me the truth about my heritage, told to her by my mother."

"Mordrac would have heard such stirrings of
untruth."

Carissa scoffed and shook her head. "Who would
have dared to say such to Mordrac? He would have
had him killed for such lies."

Cregan rubbed his chin, and she could see that
he agreed, though didn't like it.

Suddenly his frown turned to a smile. "It matters not."

While his abrupt change concerned her, she did
not show it. "Why is that?"

"If it is true, and I'm not saying it is," he empha-
sized, "then Mordrac did a good job in making you
his daughter in every sense."

Carissa was glad Addie had thought of everything, and she was prepared with a more-than-

adequate response. "That he did, but what of the children I would bear? From what I know, my father was a kindly man; therefore, any of my children could be like him."

"I would beat the kindness out of him," Cregan said, shaking a fist at her.

He was just like Mordrac, for that is what her father tried to do to her, and she would not have it done to a child of hers.

"I would not allow it," she snapped angrily.

"You have no say in it."

"You're a fool if you believe that."

"I will be your husband and you will obey me," he said, his face growing red with anger.

She laughed, which only made his face burn red all the more. "You will not be my husband, and I will certainly not now or ever obey you. And whether you believe me Mordrac's daughter or that he raised me to be such, you know I speak the truth."

"You will learn," he said, his anger ebbing.

"You truly are a fool."

"A tongueless wife would suit me just as well," he threatened.

Carissa's smile turned carnal. "How then would I please you?"

She didn't get the response she expected; he laughed.

"You will be a worthy wife and a worthy opponent."

"I will be neither."

"Do you not wish to grant your father his last

wish, that you and I form a strong alliance and breed a family of true warriors?"

"My father is dead, and I finally have my freedom. Why would I want to relinquish that?

"To honor your father's name," Cregan said.

"There is no honor to my father's name," she said with a shake of her head. "He was a cruel, horrible man who deserved to die."

"Mind your tongue, woman or—"

"You'll cut it out," she scoffed. "I've been threatened with far worse, and I doubt any man would want a tongueless wife."

"At least a man would not have to put up with a woman's harping."

"But he would lose far more when it came to pleasure," she reminded. "So which do you choose?"

"You bait me."

"Most men are easy to bait since they put their concerns above those of others, especially women. It takes a fearless warrior to love a woman, faults and all," she said.

Cregan laughed. "Any man who doesn't fear a woman is a fool. They are cunning creatures who can never be trusted."

"And a man can be trusted?"

"We have our honor."

"Which few of you live up to," she said.

"Your barbs leave scars that do not always heal."

"I do not care if my words offend you," she said. "I speak my mind, and I tell you clearly that I will not wed you."

"It is what your father wanted."

"Mordrac was not my father, and I will no longer follow his dictates," she said firmly.

"You have no choice."

She grinned. "You truly believe that?"

Her confidence unsettled him, and he shifted where he sat. "I've had enough. I could take you here and now and settle this matter once and for all."

"Then you will never know if I carry your child or another's."

Cregan shrugged. "Then I will wait and see if you are with child." He grinned. "What do you think your father would have done in this situation?"

Her stomach turned, for she knew full well what her father would have done. He would have waited for the child to be born and killed him. She silently chastised herself for her own stupidity, though it gave her more of an impetus to escape. If she did carry Ronan's babe, she would not see anything happen to him.

She found the courage to respond. "The same cruel thing you would do. The only difference is that I'm not a weak sniveling woman who would sit by and allow that to happen. I would see you dead first."

Cregan laughed and rubbed his hands together in front of the flames. "We will make a good pair, you and I."

"We need to slow them down," Carissa whispered to Addie the next morning, as they rode at a good pace.

"How?" Addie murmured.

"An attempted escape."

"We've tried that once already. I don't think it will work again."

"Not with the both of us," Carissa said. "While the one leads them on a chase, the other can make a mad dash into the woods and hide there. Cregan will not linger long to look for her. He will want to put as much distance between him and his enemies as quickly as possible."

"You're talking about me," Addie murmured.

"He will search forever for me. You are no longer useful, other than leverage when your sons arrive. He will not waste time on retrieving you. And you can alert Ronan and the others to what they face."

"What do they face?'

"I imagine Cregan has a large contingent of troops waiting for him somewhere up ahead, which explains why he's rushing us forward. The more warriors he has, the better chance of outrunning or outfighting your sons should that become necessary. He will probably leave with me, and perhaps a handful of his men, while leaving the others to delay our rescuers."

"But he leaves them to face a certain death or surrender," Addie argued.

"He does, but he does not care. He copies what my father often did."

"But why would his men obey knowing they would meet death or worse?"

"The 'or worse' was facing my father's wrath,"

Carissa said. "And believe me when I tell you that death was preferable, though perhaps a slim chance at freedom made them obey."

"I don't like leaving you," Addie said.

"It is the only choice we have if we both hope to survive."

"You are wise for one so young," Addie said.

"Wisdom knows no particular age, but it does know suffering and, with that, comes many lessons. I have grown wise by no choice of my own, but since I am, I choose to use that knowledge to my benefit and others' when possible."

"I am proud to have you as my daughter," Addie said, choked by tears.

"And I am so grateful finally to have a mother," Carissa said. Although she knew this was a time for joyful tears, she could not cry.

"What do you want me to do?" Addie asked.

"I will tell Cregan we need to stop and have a moment of privacy," Carissa said. "Once in the woods, I will run. There will be chaos, and Cregan will direct his men to follow after me. No doubt there will be a moment when no one watches over you. It is then you must run and not look back. Find a place to hide, even if it is not far from here. Cregan will not bother to spare his men to search for you."

"And you?"

"I will be caught eventually."

"Are you so sure?" Addie asked.

"Cregan would never stop searching. He believes

that I am signed and sealed by the agreement he made with my father. He intends to have me. My only chance is you."

"I will not fail you, my dear daughter," Addie said.

"I believe you won't, and I will wait impatiently for your return."

The escape went more smoothly than Carissa had expected. The two men sent with her and Addie into the woods immediately took off after her, and that provided Addie with ample time to escape.

Carissa was out of breath and her legs bone weary, but she kept running. The longer it took for them to find and catch her, the longer the delay and the better chance for Ronan and her men to catch up with them.

She ducked under a heavy brush when she heard Cregan call out.

"I will find you, Carissa, and you will suffer for this."

He did not frighten her though she would suffer no punishment willingly, which would provide more of a delay. The escape was going better than she had imagined.

Addie was no fool. She had watched the direction they had traveled and as soon as she could, she retreated in that direction, though she did so carefully. She had no intentions of getting caught by Cregan's men. Her new daughter had surrendered herself to provide both women with a means of escape, and she would not fail Carissa.

She traveled between the brush and trees, careful not to make noise, the cover of soft snow helping her. She didn't know how long she had traveled when she thought she heard a noise, and she quickly ducked under a snow-covered bush.

She kept as still as she could and thought herself safe when she didn't hear another sound, then booted feet appeared by the brush, and she feared she was caught.

"It's Piper, you're safe."

Ronan thought he was furious seeing the dark bruise on his mother's jaw. It was nothing to the fury he saw on Hagen's face. Still, the large man remained calm in front of Addie and held her shivering body tightly to his, ordering a fire built for her.

While men scurried to do his bidding, Ronan spoke with her and Hagen continued to hold her tight, seeming to believe that if he didn't, someone would once again snatch her away.

"You are sure you are all right, Mother?" Ronan asked again for what seemed like the hundredth time.

"I truly am," she said. "It is Carissa that concerns me."

She went on to explain everything to Ronan, from when they were first captured, to the tale Carissa told Cregan. Then she spoke of Carissa's courage and strength, qualities that Addie insisted she had never known any woman to display to such a degree.

"Carissa is a remarkable woman," Addie finished.

"She truly is," Ronan agreed. "But tell me, did Cregan believe this tale you concocted?"

Addie looked to Hagen.

"Tell him," Hagen urged. "He needs to know."

Ronan looked from one to the other, and asked anxiously, "Tell me what?"

"I had hoped to tell you and Carissa together," Addie said.

"It is better that Ronan knows now," Hagen encouraged. "It will help him to help Carissa."

Ronan was growing upset with the exchange between his mother and Hagen. They obviously knew something about Carissa that would startle or upset her, or could it be much worse?

"Tell me," Ronan urged.

His mother reluctantly left Hagen's arms and walked over to Ronan and took his hand.

Her comforting touch didn't help; it made him feel worse. What was she about to confide in him?

"You know how I have been wondering why Carissa looks so familiar to me."

He nodded.

"I realized why," Addie said. "She reminded me of a woman in a village a bit east from here. Your father and I would stop there after visiting neighboring clans. A woman spun the most beautiful wool yarn, and I would purchase some from her.

It was that woman Carissa reminded me of, and so I went to speak with her."

Ronan continued to listen.

"Her name was Kate, and I told her of a young woman I had recently met who bore a striking resemblance to her. She began to cry and she told me a tale about her sister Shona." Addie took a breath. "That tale was the one Carissa thought I concocted."

Chapter 37

"**C**arissa is not Mordrac's daughter?" Ronan asked, wanting to make certain he understood what his mother had just told him.

"No, she's not," Addie confirmed. "Kate told me in full detail how Mordrac plundered their village and how she had watched from a hiding spot in the woods as Mordrac killed Carissa's father. Kate told me that Shona knew she was with child and probably didn't let Mordrac know for fear he would harm her babe."

Ronan shook his head. "Why would Mordrac care so much for a slave?"

"He didn't want her as his slave; he wanted her as his wife. Kate told me that he had passed through the village on several occasions, no one knowing he was a barbarian leader and had expressed interest in Shona, a kind and beautiful woman. An elder of the village told him that Shona was pledged to another and he grew furious. When they didn't see him after that, everyone assumed he had simply gone his own way."

"But he didn't," Ronan said. "He planned to have Shona for his own."

"Kate told me that Shona loved her husband Cormack and could have never lived without him. She assumed that Shona perished with the child."

"While this should make Carissa happy," Ronan said, "I believe it will also make her sad, and perhaps hate Mordrac all the more. I will tell her about it at the appropriate time. Now we must rescue her."

"Cregan is a determined one," Addie said.

"And I," Ronan said with a pound to his chest, "am a man who intends on saving the woman I love."

Cregan dragged Carissa by the back of her hair along the ground. Her eyes stung from her hair being pulled so tightly. Stones and branches dug into her backside and legs as he was unrelenting in his efforts to get her back to the horses.

She knew he worried that he had lost precious time, and no doubt the Sinclares were drawing closer. If he didn't reach the contingent of men she was certain waited for him somewhere up ahead, he and the few men with him would find it impossible to defend themselves.

He released her suddenly, then grabbed her by the back of her cloak and dragged her to her feet. Once she stood, he backhanded her across the face. The blow sent her head reeling back, but she dug her feet into the ground, refusing to stumble.

When she felt the trickle of blood at the corner

of her mouth, she smiled at Cregan before spitting a wad of it in his face.

He wiped it off, his face red with fury. "I do not know if you're worth the trouble."

"Then release me and avoid more trouble for yourself."

"You think me afraid of the Sinclares?" he scoffed.

"It isn't only the Sinclares you'll face. It's my men, and they are more barbarian than civilized."

That bit of knowledge infuriated him all the more, and he lashed out at her once again, only this time she deflected the blow with raised arms.

"Hit me again, and I'll kill you," she said.

He laughed. "You have no weapon."

"I don't need to kill you now, but I promise you that if you strike me again, you will die."

"We need to leave here," Sully dared to say.

"My men will be here sooner than you think," she said with a grin.

"She's right," Sully said. "We have wasted time searching for her."

"Get the other woman, and we'll leave," Cregan ordered.

Sully took a step away from Cregan. "The other one escaped."

"What?" Cregan yelled. "Did you search for her?"

"We were too busy going after *her*," Sully said with a nod toward Carissa.

Cregan grabbed Carissa by the throat. "It appears that your plan has worked."

Carissa fought to smile though breathing was difficult.

"I should kill you and leave you for the animals to feast upon and for your love to find what is left of you," he said, releasing her.

"If I can defend myself against an animal like you," she said hoarsely, "then I certainly can manage the animals of the forest."

"You belong to me," Cregan shouted.

"Are you certain that you want me?" she challenged.

He approached her again, and Carissa did not move away in fear. Instead, she proudly stood her ground. He grabbed her chin.

"With my men and your men combined, we could be an unstoppable force. Just think of the power we would have. The fear we could instill in people, the places we could conquer, and our children could carry on our supreme reign."

She looked at him oddly as if suddenly realizing something. "That's why you waited to come for me. You knew I was amassing a troop of mercenaries, and you wanted them as well as me."

"I'm no fool. There is power in numbers."

"My men would never serve you," she spat.

"They would if you ordered them to."

"That will never happen," she said.

"I think otherwise."

"Think all you want. It will never be so," she said.

He squeezed her chin tighter. "I will have what I want."

She opened her lips to protest, and he slammed his mouth over hers in a savage kiss.

Ronan was annoyed to see that Cavan had arrived. They had just come upon Cregan, and he wanted no interference from his laird. It was his to choose what he would do.

Lachlan and Alyce were also there, as was Zia, who was busy fussing over his mother.

"Where's Artair?" Ronan asked annoyed. "Isn't this a family affair?"

"Someone had to protect the keep in case Cregan had other ideas in mind. Zia wanted to come in case Mother or Carissa needed tending. Now tell me what goes on here."

Ronan was quick to explain that they had just come upon the spot where Cregan's crew had stopped. No sentinels were posted, and it seemed that the chaos their mother had told him about was still going on.

Loud voices had him and Cavan suddenly dropping to the ground, and they watched silently through thick branches as Cregan dragged Carissa into camp. Ronan would have jumped up if not for his brother's heavy hand on his back.

"Don't be foolish," he whispered. "We need to surround them."

"Then hurry and have it done," Ronan murmured, "for I will not wait long."

When Cregan landed a hard blow to Carissa's jaw, he was ready to jump again, but this time

Dykar stopped him. "We're almost ready, and she can take it."

"I don't care. I'll not see her suffer like that."

"If it were you, she would strike when the time was right," Dykar said.

Ronan said nothing. He watched and when Cregan's mouth hungrily connected with Carissa's he jumped up, shoving away Dykar's arm and marched straight into the camp.

"Get your hands off her and get ready to die!"

Carissa smiled. Her Highlander had come for her. He stood proud and strong in his plaid, with his claymore planted in front of him waiting for his opponent to face him. She wanted to run to him and throw her arms around him and tell him how very much she loved him, but she restrained herself. She worried that such actions could do him or even her harm, and she would not chance losing her love.

Cregan turned around, planting himself in front of her. "She's mine."

"Not likely," Ronan said with a laugh. "She belongs to me. She *always* has and *always* will."

"I've already marked her with my lips," Cregan boasted.

Carissa scoffed and craned her head past Cregan's back. "You can't call his smashed mouth against my lips a kiss."

Ronan roared with laughter. "I guess you just don't know how to kiss, Cregan."

Cregan stepped forward. "But I do know how to kill."

Ronan raised his claymore and stepped toward him. "What I've been waiting for."

Cregan sidestepped him and gave a signal. His men surrounded Ronan in a flash.

"You idiot," Carissa cried.

"See what she thinks of you now," Cregan said on a laugh.

"Carissa doesn't mean me," Ronan said.

Cregan turned to glare at Carissa.

"Are you truly foolish enough to believe he has come here alone?" she asked.

"My men would have warned me—"

"What men, you fool? All your men were busy chasing me."

Cregan froze as he finally realized what she was telling him. Just as he did, Cavan, Lachlan, Septimus, Dykar, and more stepped from behind bushes and trees and surrounded them.

Cregan shook his head, as if he could not believe what was happening.

"Carissa has a way of making a fool appear even more the fool," Ronan said. "But don't feel too bad. You were doomed as soon as you captured her."

Ronan stepped forward until he was so close to Cregan that he could hear the man's rapid breathing. "No one takes what belongs to me and, as I've told you, Carissa always has and always will belong to me."

"Then she is yours," Cregan relented wisely. "I'll take my leave."

"Not that easily you won't," Ronan said. "Carissa, go with my brothers and wait for me."

She looked ready to object, and he glared at her. Surprisingly, she obeyed, though she detoured to give him a kiss first.

"This one time I obey you, Highlander, but don't get used to it."

Ronan laughed. God, he loved that woman. Life would never be dull with her around to challenge and to love him.

Cavan ordered the men to go and take Cregan's men with them.

Ronan could see that Cavan was reluctant to leave him, but he didn't need his big brother to help him this time. In the two years he had been away, he had become a man in his own right. He had matured with confidence.

He smiled, and Cavan bowed his head, acknowledging his brother's ability and determination to handle Cregan on his own. So, with a smile, Cavan turned and left his brother to fight his own battle.

"There's no need for either of us to die," Cregan said. "I had thought that once I spoke with Carissa, she would see the wisdom of us uniting. Without her men, my troop pales in comparison to your warriors. I pose you no threat."

"That we both know," Ronan acknowledged. "But you dared to abduct not one, but two women I love, and for that you must suffer the consequence."

"Death seems a harsh consequence when I meant them no harm."

Ronan tossed his claymore aside. "True enough."

Cregan grinned and threw his weapon aside. "What if I win?"

Ronan laughed. "There's not a chance of that."

"There is blood on your skirt," Zia said. "Let me have a look at your legs."

Carissa would not sit still long enough for Zia to have a look. "Ronan is taking too long. Someone should go see if he is all right."

"He's fine," Cavan said, walking over to her. "Now sit and let Zia tend you."

"No," she said, and went to walk past Cavan.

He grabbed her arm, and she winced.

"That's it," Cavan said. "Ronan will have my head if he finds out you've been injured and not tended to."

"You're the laird, he can't have your head," Carissa said.

"But I can have yours, now sit," Cavan ordered.

Her eyes turned wide, and she yanked her arm free and sped past him.

Cavan turned just as she reached a battered Ronan, and he smiled.

Carissa didn't care if Ronan was bloody and bruised, she ran into his outstretched arms, and as they closed around her, she attempted to kiss him. They both winced from the pain of their split lips.

"I thought . . ." She could not vocalize her fear.

He cupped her face. "I'm not going anywhere. You are stuck with me."

"It is you who are stuck with me," she said.

"Good, then we're stuck together."

"Forever?" she asked softly.

"Forever," he repeated, and placed a gentle kiss on her lips.

"It is done?" Cavan shouted to him when their lips parted.

Ronan nodded. "Send his men to collect him. He will bother us no more."

"Good, then we can finally all go home," Cavan said.

"Home," Carissa whispered.

"Yes, home," Ronan said, then whispered in her ear, "and when I get you there, do you know what I'm going to do to you?"

She giggled as he poked her playfully, but gently, in the ribs. "Tell me."

He wrapped his arms around her waist, drew her near, and whispered exactly what he intended to do to her. Her face flushed bright red, her body tingled, and she wished they were already home.

Chapter 38

It wasn't until later that evening that Carissa and Ronan got to be alone, and only then because they sneaked away. First, Zia insisted on tending their wounds, which only amounted to minor abrasions and bruises. Then Artair and Honora wanted a detailed description of what happened, which Addie happily supplied while wrapped in Hagen's arms. Later, when Carissa and Ronan were about to take their leave and have a quiet supper to themselves, Dykar and Septimus arrived, and Cavan invited them to the table.

The abduction was discussed again in more detail, and Dykar told them all that a contingent of mercenaries was only too glad to join Sinclare warriors in escorting Cregan and his men off Sinclare land.

Dykar assured them that Cregan would return home, lick his wounds and stay put, knowing he had been soundly defeated.

It was during this constant chatter that Carissa and Ronan managed, separately, to slip away and reunite in their cottage.

A light snow fell as Carissa hurried along, and for a moment she stopped and looked up at the night sky. Clouds kept the half-moon from shining through, and with the air having turned crisper, more snow was bound to fall.

She smiled and drew her cloak around her. This time she and Ronan wouldn't mind being stranded in a cottage together. They truly would delight in the prospect.

The door to the cottage opened, and Ronan stood silhouetted in the doorway. Her smile grew, for he wore only his plaid, which meant he had been busy undressing.

"Carissa," he called out, and held his hand out to her. "What kept you?"

She hurried to him, her hand ready to grab his. "I've been thinking about how lucky I am."

He took her hand and swirled her around right into his arms and kissed her. Not hungrily, but lovingly.

"And you're about to get even luckier," he said playfully when the kiss ended.

"Promises, promises," she said, as they drifted together inside the cottage, Ronan shutting the door with his foot.

"Promises, I will always keep," he said with a gentle kiss, and rid her of her cloak.

Her hands easily found the end of his plaid and in no time she rid him of it, letting it fall to the ground.

"Now that's the way I like you," she teased.

"And I you," he whispered in her ear as he set to work undressing her.

Of course his lips had to trail where his fingers touched, and when Carissa shivered, he moved them closer to the warmth of the hearth and finished until finally they both stood naked together.

"You are so very beautiful," Ronan said, his hands roaming lovingly over her.

Every part of her body tingled, and she quickly grew wet with the want of him. "I don't want to wait," she said, and took hold of him. She chuckled. "Obviously, you don't either."

"I'll not have you only once tonight, woman," he teased.

"You would disappoint me if you did."

He laughed as he lifted her about the waist, and she locked her legs around him to rest on his hips.

"I will not disappoint you," he said, and lowered his lips to her hard nipples.

She dug her fingers into the back of his head as he suckled her and made her moan with pleasure. His mouth continued to torture her until, finally, she could stand it no more.

"I will come here and now, Highlander, if you do not stop."

He chuckled and, while his mouth continued to feast, his fingers found their way inside her, and in mere moments he had her screaming out in pleasure. But as ripple after ripple claimed her body, he hurried her to the bed and came down on top of her, delving inside to set her flesh tingling again.

She wrapped her legs around him to take

him deeper inside her, and it didn't take long for them both to cry out as they exploded in pleasure together.

When calm returned to them, Ronan rolled to the side, taking her with him to lie close beside him, his arm wrapped snug around her.

She laid her head on his chest and settled contentedly against him.

"Rest, for it will not be long before I want you again," he teased.

"I will be ready before you."

"How lucky am I to have found an insatiable wife."

Wife.

Carissa had never thought to be a wife to a man of her choosing, and she silently thanked the heavens for this miracle.

"Are you all right?" he asked with concern. "You tense in my arms."

"It is I who am lucky," she said softly, placing her hand over his heart. "I never thought I would be a wife to a husband of my choice and that he would truly love me."

Ronan lifted her chin for her to look at him. "Hear me well, Carissa. I love you with all my heart, and I intend to have you as my wife because of that love and for no other reason."

She had to ask, "You want Carissa not Hope?"

"You are hope," he said. "You gave hope to me and you have given hope to many. Hope resides in you whether you want it to or not. And I love every part of you, Carissa."

She smiled. "You can love any part of me any-time you want."

"Do you know what that smile of yours does to me?"

She shook her head, and he took her hand and guided it down over him.

"I'm going to have to smile all the time."

"You may just kill me if you do that"—he laughed—"but what a way to die."

She climbed on top of him. "I'll temper my smiles since you have trouble keeping up with me."

"A challenge?"

She ran her hand over his hardness. "You seem to be up to it."

He laughed again, but before he could take charge, she slid down over him, and he cried out with the exquisite feel of her.

"My turn," she said, and proceeded to love him.

They lay snuggled together, Carissa yawning.

"I tired you," Ronan boasted.

"The night is still young," she challenged, and yawned again.

"You are tired and need to rest."

"I have not had enough of you yet," she said, draping her leg over his and snuggling closer.

Ronan hugged her tightly. "We have the morn-ing and the day after and the day after that. We have forever."

"That sounds delightful." She sighed and couldn't help recall a time she thought differently.

"I once believed that I would never have you, that it was an impossible dream, and now I can't imagine not being with you, not having you hold me, not growing old with you."

Carissa looked up at him. "That tale your mother made up for me to tell Cregan was so sad. While I suffered greatly when I sent you away, at least I knew that you were alive and well."

"About that tale, Carissa," Ronan said with a tender stroke of her cheek. "It was no tale. It was the truth."

Carissa popped up in bed, her long blond hair falling over her bare breasts as the blanket fell away from her. "What do you mean?"

"My mother told you that you looked familiar," he reminded. "She finally realized who it was you reminded her of, and had Hagen take her to the village. The woman, Kate, whose fine yarn my mother favored is who she thought you resembled and it was Kate's sister, Shona, who was your mother."

Carissa shook her head. "Are you saying that Mordrac truly wasn't my father?

"That's right. You are not the daughter of Mordrac."

"Mordrac killed my father?"

Ronan nodded and reached out and took her hand.

Carissa grasped tightly to him. She couldn't believe what he was telling her. The news brought a mixture of relief and heartache. And it explained so much. She had often wondered how her nature was so different from that of her supposed father."

She smiled and squeezed his hand. "I am like my true father."

"I would say that you are."

She gasped. "Do you know what this means?"

"What?"

"I have family other than yours. I have an aunt, and she can tell me all about my mother and father. I will be able to get to know them through her."

"Yes, you will," he agreed, "especially since my mother has already extended an invitation to our wedding to her and her family."

"My aunt has a family?" Carissa said excitedly.

"A husband, two sons, and two daughters."

Carissa squealed with delight.

"They do not live too far, and their village does not thrive well," Ronan said. "I had an idea how you could help them."

"Tell me."

"You have a good-sized mercenary troop, many of whom have grown tired of battle and wish to settle. Why not see who would like to make your aunt's village their home. With their help and protection, the village could thrive. And, of course, they would come under the clan Sinclare protection."

"I know many of them who would like that, though others will wish to return to our camp near Everagis."

"At least they will have a choice," he said. "Something I think they would all prefer."

"This is all so unbelievable," Carissa said, shaking her head.

Ronan reached out and stroked the corner of her eye. "I thought perhaps this news would finally bring tears of joy to your eyes, and yet you still do not cry."

She struggled to find an explanation. "I don't know why I have yet to cry. And I don't know how to explain that it is a sad joy that I feel. Learning that Mordrac killed my father because he wanted my mother saddens me beyond belief, and yet the joy comes from knowing that Mordrac's cruel nature is not part of me. Happiness mixes with sadness, and yet I feel no tears."

Carissa drifted back into his arms. "I was once told that when at last I cried, it would be with tears of joy."

Ronan kissed her softly before she settled against him. "Somehow I will find a way to bring joyful tears to your eyes."

Carissa sighed. "It has been so long since I cried." She shook her head. "The tears I remember were sorrowful ones. I have never cried tears of joy. I don't think I know how."

"I will find a way," he repeated.

She snuggled against him. "You make me happy, that is enough."

Ronan rolled her on her back and leaned over her. "It is not enough for me. I want to give you all I can and more."

"You want to make me cry?"

He gently touched the corners of her eyes. "I will never make you cry in sadness, but I will see you cry in joy."

"That's a tall task you set for yourself, Highlander."

"There you go challenging me again," he said with a smile.

"You do well with challenges."

"I succeed in all of them."

"This may be one time you don't," she said sadly.

He kissed the corners of her eyes. "I promise you that tears of joy will spill from these eyes soon enough."

"A promise." She sighed. "Then it will be so, though soon?"

"Trust me," he said, his smile spreading.

She reached out and pressed her hand to his cheek. "I was taught to trust no one, but you changed that. I can't say when I began to trust you. It just seemed to follow a natural course, and somehow trust developed on its own. It was there staring straight at me, I only needed to recognize it."

"Like love."

"You're right," she said with a nod. "Like love. Suddenly you realize it's there staring you straight in the eyes and tearing at your heart."

"And love has you and won't let you go," he said with a kiss.

Carissa stared at him for a moment.

"You don't agree?" he asked with a raise of his brow.

"No, I mean yes, I mean . . ." Carissa smiled. "I was thinking that you have proved Mordrac wrong. Love not only endures, it conquers hate."

"That loves does," he agreed. "And it's time for us to—"

"Make love again."

"You're not too tired?"

"I am, but I want you more than sleep," she said, and kissed him with the desire of a woman for the man she loved, and it set his soul on fire.

They joined eagerly and impatiently, yet didn't rush. They wanted this joining to last, to linger in every touch, every kiss, every moment of pleasure.

They explored each other with their hands and with kisses and nibbles and laughter and sighs. It was a cherished joining, a beautiful memory that would linger long in their minds.

When finally they found it too hard to deny themselves, they came together in a frenzied rhythm that had them catapulting in a climax that left them both completely breathless as ripples of pleasure burst over their damp, tingling flesh.

And then they finally slept.

Chapter 39

"**A**re you sure of this wedding gift?" Zia asked.

"I couldn't be more confident," Ronan said.

"But mother has offered you the emerald necklace she wore on her wedding day to give to Carissa," Zia said.

"I will not do what Mordrac did to her. Dress her in fancy jewels for all to admire," Ronan said. "I know this gift will bring great pleasure to Carissa."

"All right," Zia agreed with a smile. "You obviously know what pleases your future wife, and I will have it ready."

Ronan leaned down and kissed her cheek.

"Hey, what are you doing with my wife?" Artair teased as he joined them in Zia's healing cottage.

"Thanking her for the perfect wedding gift to give to my wife," Ronan said.

Artair slapped his brother on the back. "A few more hours, and the last of the Sinclare brothers marries."

"I can't wait," Ronan said with a broad smile.

"It will be here too soon," Zia said, hurrying to grab her cloak off the peg. "There is much to do. I will see you later." She gave her husband a quick kiss, then stopped, grinned at him, and gave him a kiss he wouldn't soon forget. She left the cottage with a grin.

Artair turned on his brother. "Damn, why did you have to be here?"

Ronan laughed. "If I have to wait until tonight, so do you."

"Let's go find Cavan and Lachlan and make sure that they're suffering too," Artair suggested, and Ronan agreed.

Carissa hugged Addie as the woman tried to help get her into her wedding dress. "I cannot thank you enough for all you have done for me, but I am particularly grateful for having my aunt and her family here to share this very special day."

"They are very nice people," Addie said, finally getting Carissa's arms into the long sleeves of the dark green velvet gown.

"I am sure Aunt Kate is just like my mother, and Uncle James is delightfully funny and then there is Cowan, so intelligent for ten years old and Wallace, who is an excellent bowman at fifteen, and oh, sixteen-year-old Colleen has her mother's skill with yarn and twelve-year-old Aggie chatters all day! I love them all."

"As I'm sure they love you."

A knock sounded at the door of Ronan's bedchamber, and it was Addie who cried out, "If it is a man, go away."

The door opened, and Kate peered in. "May I enter?"

"Of course," Addie said, waving her into the room. "It was men I looked to chase away. They have no business here now."

Kate agreed, though her smile faded. "You have a gown. I thought since it has only been two months since the wedding was decided that there would not be time to stitch a gown."

"Addie had this fitted for me from one of her older gowns," Carissa said, realizing yet again how much she resembled her aunt and, therefore, her mother. The thought filled her with loving warmth.

Kate stepped forward. "I took the liberty of bringing your mother's wedding dress with me. Shona stitched it herself, she was so talented with needle and thread. You are your mother's size, and I thought you might like to wear it."

Carissa reached out and took the folded white wool she had thought a shawl at first glance. When she lifted it, the garment fell to reveal the most gorgeous gown she had ever seen.

Even Addie gasped. "That is stunning."

Kate lifted one of the long sleeves and gently touched the handsome embroidery along the edge. "Your mother worked on this dress day and night, and when her wedding was done, she washed it with gentle hands, and after it dried by the fire, she wrapped it away with plans to give it to her daughter."

The wool was so soft Carissa could not stop touching it.

"Your mother was wed in the winter, just like you are about to be," Kate said.

"You must wear your mother's dress," Addie said, already pulling the green gown off Carissa.

"You don't mind?" Carissa asked.

Tears clouded Addie's eyes. "I would want the same from my daughter. We will give your mother what she wished."

Carissa hugged the woman again. "Thank you."

"Let's get you done," Addie said. "Kate, you help her dress."

Kate gave Addie a thankful nod for allowing her the privilege and joy of helping her niece on this very special day, while Addie continued to wipe tears from her eyes.

Knock followed knock until Honora, Zia, Alyce, and Kate's daughters filled the room. They laughed and teased, and when they were done dressing Carissa, there was not a dry eye among them, except for Carissa.

The gown her mother had stitched for her own wedding appeared made for Carissa as well, for it fit her to perfection. The thought made her realize that she was truly her mother's daughter. The white wool fell over her body, accenting every curve and mound down to her hips. And then it fell in a swirl of wool to her feet. The square neckline was embroidered with the same gold thread as the sleeves, Kate explaining that her sister had traded a traveling merchant several of her fine wool pieces for the gold thread. She had wanted something extra special for her dress, and she had gotten it, for it was the talk of the village for months following the wedding.

Carissa wore it proudly, as she did the lovely crown of winter greenery Honora had fashioned for her head.

She couldn't have been more joyful and, when the time came for her to descend the steps and join in marriage with Ronan, she did so with a wide smile and a happy heart.

The ceremony was performed by a family friend, Bishop Edmond Aleatus. People had come from far and wide, just as Ronan had said they would, to join in the celebration.

Bethane had arrived a week before the wedding so that she could spend time with Zia and her great-granddaughter, Blythe. Septimus and Dykar and several more of her men were also in attendance.

It was wonderful having so many true friends there to share in their joy.

"Have I told you how beautiful you look?" Ronan asked when they had a moment alone.

"Five or six times," she said with a smile. "But that's all right, for I do not grow tired of hearing it."

"Good," he said, "for I do not grow tired of telling you." And he lowered his lips to steal a kiss.

"Aunt Carissa, Aunt Carissa," Aggie shouted, running up to the couple and grabbing Carissa's hand. "You must come and see the trick Father is about to do. You must."

Carissa shrugged as if to say there's nothing I can do to prevent this and sent Ronan a smile as Aggie carted her away.

"I am glad to see that you finally opened your heart," Bethane said, joining him.

Ronan gave the woman a kiss on the cheek. "I didn't open it, Carissa did."

Bethane laughed. "You opened it, and she stole it."

"That I agree with," Ronan said.

The celebration went long into the night, though the happy couple slipped away well before it ended. They went to the small cottage where they could be alone and where they planned to start their married life together, though plans for building a larger cottage were set for the spring.

Ronan kissed Carissa, his arms wrapped around her waist. "You feel well."

"I keep telling you that I am fine. There is no need to worry," Carissa said. "Besides, I have Zia when the time comes for the babe to be born, late summer or early fall from what she tells me."

Ronan rested his hand to her stomach. "I wonder what it will be."

"Bethane says a girl," Carissa said. "And from what I hear, she is never wrong."

"A daughter?"

"It disappoints you?"

"No," he was quick to say. "It's just that I'll forever worry about her."

"Have no fear, I will teach her to protect herself." Carissa laughed. "Though she will have enough male cousins to do that, as Bethane predicts another boy for Honora and Cavan."

"My brother must be bursting with joy. Three sons he'll have."

"I'll give you as many sons as you want," Carissa said, slipping her arms around his neck.

"Sons or daughters it matters not, for I will love them all as I love you."

They kissed, and he eased away from her.

"I have a wedding gift for you," he said, going to retrieve a basket partially covered with a cloth near the hearth.

"A gift for me?" Carissa said joyfully.

"A very special gift for you and you alone," Ronan said, and holding the basket in front of her, he slipped off the cloth.

Carissa peered in and gasped. She stared for several moments, then her eyes filled with tears, and she looked to Ronan.

"Joyful tears, my love?" he asked, and scooped the tiny sleeping puppy out of the basket and handed him to his wife.

Carissa hesitantly reached for him, then drew her hands away.

"No one will *ever* hurt him or you, I promise you that," Ronan said. "Now take him, he's yours to love."

Tears fell freely from her eyes as she reached out and took the tiny pup into her hands. He barely filled them and, when the little fellow opened his eyes, Carissa brought him to her chest, and he yawned, licked her chin, nestled against her, and went back to sleep.

"I never thought that I could love you more than I did," she said through tears, "but I was wrong. I love you, Highlander, so much more than I ever thought possible."

She kissed him then, the first of many kisses throughout the night and the many years to follow.